MURDER SEES
THE LIGHT

MURDER SEES THE LIGHT

A BENNY COOPERMAN MYSTERY

HOWARD ENGEL

St. Martin's Press
New York

Library of Congress Cataloging in Publication Data

Engel, Howard, 1931–
  Murder sees the light.

  I. Title.
PR9199.3.E49M84   1985   813'.54   85-2560
ISBN 0-312-55324-2

First published in Canada by Penguin Books Ltd.
First U.S. Edition
10 9 8 7 6 5 4 3 2 1

This is a work of fiction. No resemblance is intended to any actual events or to any persons living or dead.

For my brother, David,
who knows about canoes and loons.

MURDER SEES
THE LIGHT

Chapter One

Patten looked at me, then again at the board. He hadn't expected me to move my Queen's Pawn. He'd decided I'd save my endangered Knight. Not a bad play for somebody who claimed to be in the ladies' ready-to-wear business in a small town. Maybe I should have taken a more conservative line, but what the hell, I had to make the guy like me. He had enough flunkies lying around. He didn't need another gofer. My appeal was to his intellectual side, such as it was.

He was wearing those reflecting sunglasses that should be outlawed by the rules of international chess. I couldn't see his mind working behind them, and I had the distraction of the lake, the first island, and the far shore to deal with. David Kipp was out in his custom-made canoe again. Gloomy George was running around the lake in his big outboard like he was King of Algonquin Park. George's motor was too big for him. Patten lit a black cheroot with a Spanish rope lighter, then let his hand hover over the white pieces. By now he could see that I'd opened up my Queen's Bishop. He moved his Bishop as I expected, and we sparred for a few turns. He snapped up a Pawn, and we each took a Knight. I could see sweat rolling down his tanned cheek into the wool of his beard. That was all the reassurance I needed. I put my Queen to work on my tenth move, forced a crisis, and declared mate on my twentieth move. Patten flicked the cheroot to the patio and leaned back from the rattan table.

"What do you call a game like that, fella? That's book-learned chess, that's not rough and tumble. I bet that's got a fancy name, Benny. What do you call it: the Shmata Defence? The Hebrew Gambit? What's its name, fella?" He took a tall glass with condensation blurring the effect of the orange against the white of his shirt or the blue of the lake and sipped aggressively. I didn't tell him it was the Scotch Gambit. It would only open up the territory to wider national slurs. I shrugged as though I'd just made up the game as I went along. Funny, he never got racial when he was winning at something. In the boat, for instance. He was the better fisherman, netting more fish and bigger ones than I hauled in. He could swim farther than I could, and I'll bet he could pump iron with the professionals. He didn't try me on tennis, golf, or tenting on the old campground, but I'd be willing to guess he'd walk over me. Luckily up here at Big Crummock Lake we were at least seventy miles from the nearest golf course, and tennis wasn't one of the approved sports inside the provincial park. In fact, he couldn't show off at sailing, because there were no sailboats. This was a wilderness area, or as close to it as the Ontario government and the lumber companies allowed it to be. Here the shore wasn't cluttered with cottages or trailer parks. That wasn't the style on Big Crummock. Nor did the far shore boast of colourful boathouses like the ones in Muskoka. Wilderness meant no large motorboats, and except for the big Rimmer cruiser and George's speedboat, the typical water vessel was the canoe. They came in various sizes and colours. I don't think pastels are allowed yet, but there are signs of softening on that point.

My big moment with Patten came when I pulled him off the burning front end of his motorboat. He was still holding the starting rope in his hands, and the stern end had completely disappeared. I dumped him into the lake to put out his burning shorts, then hauled him, sputtering, out of the shallow water to the dock. Since then he liked to have me around, even if I did beat him at chess. Hanging around the Woodward place suited me fine. Patten didn't need to know that I was being paid to keep an eye on him. I didn't just happen to be fishing two hundred yards off the end of his dock for the fun of it.

From where I was sitting facing Patten and the lake, the

scene of our first meeting lay just over his shoulder. In fact the charred pieces of the boat could be seen bobbing in the reeds to the left of the dock. The blisters on Patten's face now looked like sunburn. Under the reflecting sunglasses you couldn't see his partially charred eyebrow.

Two weeks ago I'd got a call from Ray Thornton of Reeder, Ansell and Thornton, an old Grantham legal firm on Queen Street across from the post office. Ray had been at Edith Cavell School with me from kindergarten through to grade six. I lost sight of him for a few years, and then he turned up asking me to tail the wife of a client of his. That was just after I set up as a private investigator with a shingle waving over St. Andrew Street. That first report led to other assignments. Somehow, in those early days it always ended up in the divorce courts. Now they've changed the laws, so I take what I can get.

Ray met me for lunch at the United Cigar Store, just up the block and across the road from my office. There was nothing fancy about the United. It was fast and clean and didn't hide its mistakes under a sprig of parsley. I was already into my second bite of a toasted chopped egg sandwich when Ray dropped a clipping from *The Globe and Mail* on the green marble countertop. It was a wire-service story about how the former friends and colleagues of Norbert E. Patten were trying to find him. I'd heard of Patten, and from what I'd heard, I couldn't get excited about the fact that he'd got lost.

"How do you come into it?" I asked Ray.

"I have a client who has sunk a lot of money into Patten's Ultimate Church, and he's very concerned about Patten's to-ings and fro-ings. Especially now that the U.S. Supreme Court is about to render a decision on the tax status of the church. We should hear the judgement before the end of the week after next. So my client doesn't want his boy to slip away from the steely grip of the law, if that's what it comes to."

"That's all Patten's good for. He's got more cute tricks in

him than a magicians' convention."

Patten, besides getting blown out of motorboats and losing his temper after chess, was the bright boy who linked up evangelism with the franchising techniques of modern business. He'd set up a world-wide corporate structure, collected millions, part of it in tax breaks, and become a well-heeled saver of souls with an amalgam of Zen, Spiritualism, and that old-time religion of the American Bible Belt. The Ultimate Church was more than just a cult, it was a super-cult. I shook my head thinking about the mixture of Bible-thumping and the American Way. "Didn't Patten slip out of California a year or so ago?"

"That's right. He left Burbank and surfaced in Chicago, as busy as ever."

"That's my boy."

"But he's not running the tight ship of yesteryear. There have been defections. Early this year his yacht was seized in Spain, and the crew members were arrested by the *guardia civil*. Patten didn't raise a hand to help out."

"And the defectors?"

"Princes of the church every blessed one of them. They couldn't sign affidavits fast enough. The picture I get from them is that Norbert E. Patten is much given to excesses and tantrums and has developed a sincere need to rule the world."

"Everybody should have a hobby, Ray. And the world could use some of his money. Why do you want me to spoil it?"

"I haven't asked you yet. But since you're here, I'll tell you. The defectors have launched a four hundred million dollar class-action suit against the church. My client is in the way of picking up part of that if Patten turns up to face those charges. If the Supreme Court rules against Patten on the tax-evasion business, Patten's going to walk away from the States without going back for his hiking boots." I chewed on my sandwich, listening to the crunch of toast and finely chopped celery, while in my head I was trying to count a chorus line of zeros that were high-stepping to the right of a four.

"When you say that Patten's disappeared, what do you mean? He's not been gathered to his fathers, has he?"

"A week ago he crossed into Canada at Port Huron. He was travelling with five others. A little bird close to the people who make a living knowing these things tells me he's holed up in Algonquin Park."

"What a way to go. How old was he?"

"He *is* forty-three. And he's a long way from becoming the dear departed. What we need first of all is a positive identification. Can you get that for us? Then we'll need to have a resident baby-sitter until he makes a move. Will you be our limpet, Benny? It will mean staking out the place for a week or so. There's a lodge on the same lake where you can stay."

"Well, I don't know."

"Come on, Benny, don't look so glum. You can get a lot of fishing done while you're waiting for him to show his face. It's a great place from what I hear. Christ, Benny, I'm offering you a fat fee for sitting by the water getting a suntan. When's the last time you were paid to be a tourist?"

So, I spent the weekend cleaning up my desk and explaining things to my parents. I threw some clothes into a club bag and headed north to Petawawa Lodge on Big Crummock Lake.

"Another game, fella? Give a man a sporting chance to get even," Patten said. I grunted, and we began setting up the pieces again. This time I'd let him win. A wasp was busy doing himself in in the dregs of my orange juice. They'd tried blowing Patten up, maybe they'd try poison next. Before I got to knit my brows and worry about it, Patten's girlfriend, Lorca, arrived with a fresh glass. She had a smile on her face that led me to believe she knew where the real stuff was hidden. I watched two distorted versions of her long-legged self in Patten's glasses as she walked back up the rustic stone steps to the cabin.

"Lust not after her beauty, Benny, she's mine." Patten knew more about reflecting sunglasses than I gave him credit for.

I was to play black again. I tried to throw him the advantage by castling too early. I popped off a few offensive Pawns, thinking that would get me in enough trouble to keep me concentrated on the game. It didn't work. I thought of the long dusty drive north. I thought of Petawawa Lodge, a ten-minute paddle from where I was sitting, out of sight, but nestling on its own cove on Big Crummock Lake. I thought of Joan Harbiston showing me my cabin and teaching me the mysteries of coal-oil lamps and propane stoves. In spite of her instructions I managed on my first night to wolf down a dinner of half-burned, half-unthawed french fries. I remembered the thrill of walking into my first suspended yard of fly-paper. It was a real treat.

Algonquin Park wasn't new to me. As a kid of twelve I'd been sent on a canoe trip lasting five days beginning at Canoe Lake. Camp Northern Pine taught me to paddle, to swim a mile, and to make hospital corners. Nowadays I preferred urban landscapes where the symbol of untamed nature is the dandelion growing between the cracks in the sidewalk.

For two days I had sat in an aluminum rowboat with my fishing line in the water and my eyes fixed on the activities at the Woodward place, Patten's nest in the woods. Usually there was nothing stirring except for a curl of smoke hanging above the large fieldstone chimney. Whoever it was in there, I thought, hated the damp as much as I did. I'd noted comings and goings from the cabin to the white Mercedes parked in the clearing at the end of a rustic lane which connected with the one-lane lumber trail, the closest thing to a freeway in this part of the world. I'd given names to Lorca and the others as I watched them carrying groceries into the house after foraging missions to Hatchway. Until the boat had exploded, I hadn't had much to put into the report of what I'd been doing with my time. "Subject has not been sighted. Body Beautiful and Mr. Clean drove to town. Shorty went for a boat ride in an aluminum boat like mine. Pair of suspicious loons came within one hundred feet of surveillance craft and submerged. Detected no limpet mines. Baited hook with worm number twenty-three. Lowered same into lake to depth of forty feet. Remained in position for sixteen minutes. Removed fishing line from water. Examined where worm had been nibbled away at both ends. Retired remaining mid-section and fitted worm number twenty-four in place. . . ."

Patten was moving his Queen around like he hadn't an-other able-bodied piece left on the board. He'd allowed a cunning grin to bend the line of mouth visible above his beard. I'd have to try to get him in a poker game later on. That grin of his promised a good evening. I threw him the last of my Knights and prepared to hustle my King from square to square as he tried to pick me off with an alliance between his Queen and the edge of the board. I could imag-ine his eyes narrowing behind his glasses. He had the true killer instinct. I was glad I'd studied up on him before I packed my flannelette pajamas and drove the Olds up here.

Patten. I kept calling him that in my head, and it was going to get me into trouble if I called him that out loud. I had saved, and was now playing chess with, Norrie Edgar. That's what he was calling himself. With the beard and sunglasses he could get away with it. On television it was clean-cut smooth grooming that made his face memorable.

"Mate!" said Patten with a smirk. I looked at the board. He was right, and he swelled with triumph. I made a clicking sound of appreciation in the corner of my mouth. He had the scent of blood now, and began setting up the pieces again. "I'm going to clean my shoes with you, fella." Luckily, Lorca, the girl I'd been calling Body Beautiful until Patten intro-duced us, called down to him.

"Norrie! Ozzie's just driving up." Patten looked with regret at the chessboard, as though it assured him of an endless run of victories, and got up. I followed him from the dock to the house. A black Buick had just driven into the clearing. Slowly the doors opened and two men got out, arching their backs to unlock their spines from the miles. Lorca went over, and they looked happy to see her. The driver, a tall, blond kid in a blue T-shirt, carried a briefcase. The other guy, getting a hug from Lorca, wore new blue jeans, a short-sleeved shirt, and a bald head to rival that of Mr. Clean, Norrie's man of all work. The driver, who I was already starting to call Surf's Up in my head, gave the briefcase to Ozzie, his boss. They both looked like they had tried to dress down for the occasion. Patten in his ratty tan army shorts went over to the car and shook Ozzie with one hand and gave him half a bear-hug with the other. I hung back, feeling outnumbered. They started for the house. Patten turned back to me, lighting up another dark cheroot with his Span-ish lighter, and tilted his head back like he was smoking a three-dollar cigar. I felt like I was the gardener or somebody hired to rake leaves.

"I got business, Benny. Better clear out. Looks like it's clouding up. May not get another chance for a return match today. Anyhow, seize the day, fella. Time's a gift and time's a-wasting." And he was gone. I got into my rowboat and pointed it in the direction of Petawawa Lodge. A couple of loons gave me the raspberry as I passed them, then got out of sight. The sky was getting dark.

Chapter Two

A hot, mid-afternoon heaviness hung above Petawawa Lodge as I came around the point where the lodge's cove began. Ghosts of lightning far away lit up the insides of the clouds like fireflies in a smoky bottle. The dock was deserted unless you count the various boats rubbing their flanks against the rubber bumpers nailed to it. I tied up the rowboat and stowed the oars in the tack shed. The beach was guarded by an inflated innertube and an abandoned pail and shovel in the sand. A scrap of wind began to whip dust on the road and play with a line of towels and bathing suits hung out to dry.

The lodge was made up of two medium-sized buildings and about six individual cabins fanned out under the trees at the edge of the lake. The large log building near Joan Harbison's cabin was the Annex. This served as Joan's office and the general get-together point. The long low building with the shadows of agitated birches blowing over it looked more like a bunkhouse or a primitive motel running parallel to the road. It contained four joined cottages, the Algonquin equivalent of row-housing. To the Annex, the motel, and the cabins, add a leaning double gas pump and an electric bug-zapper by a notice-board and you have Petawawa Lodge.

My cabin was dark when I closed the screen door behind me. I couldn't switch on the light. There wasn't any electricity until Joan started the Delco generator. I pulled a coal-oil lantern from its nail in the beam above my head. I was still trying to light it when the sky opened up like it had something personal against us. The rain drove itself into the dust of the lumber trail. It flattened the petunias around the notice-board and beat upon the screens and windows. Across the lake the rain blew in waves and patterns from the first

island, outlined against the hazy far shore. Nearer home it
bombarded rowboats tied up to cleats on the dock. It was like
a machine gun opening up from above. The tarp covering
the big cruiser at the end of the dock looked like it had given
particular offence; a froth of white water splashed off it in all
directions. The cover looked riddled. My roof took a beating,
but until I got some light I was helpless to see whether a
puddle was collecting on my bed. Through the window,
steamy with humidity, I saw Joan Harbison park her red
Honda, unpack a carton of groceries from the back, and
close the hatch with her shoulder. Her old straw hat dripping,
she carried the box out of sight along the duckboards. She
had a plastic bag of milk for me in there somewhere, but I
could wait until the weather cleared. Meanwhile thunder
rattled the spoons in the porcelain jar on the counter and
lightning showed between the cracks in the two closed shutters.
I got a candle going and tried to concentrate on what my
next step might be while I stared through the patched screen.
In the cabin, the only sign that life was still going on was a fly
stubbornly struggling against the inevitable at the end of a
coil of fly-paper.

Before I'd left Grantham, I'd asked my old friend Ella
Beames at the library to dig out for me all she could find on
Norbert E. Patten. Ella was the farthest thing from a detective's
assistant in the business. She looked like a sweet, middle-
aged woman with bright eyes under freckled lids, with velvet
jowls on either side of a small perfect nose. Ella didn't know
she was on my payroll for the simple reason that I'd never put
her there. Her cover as a librarian in charge of the Special
Collections Department was too perfect to share even with
her. She handed me a fat file and indicated a table.

"Spread it out here, Benny, and tell me if you need more.
We used to have a lot more on your man, but somebody
walked off with every scrap we had about three years ago and
didn't bring it back. We had to build up the file from scratch."

"But you don't let this stuff circulate?"

"Of course not. I mean it was stolen. When I was at a librarians' convention in Toronto I found out that the Patten files had been lifted from libraries right across the country. They even cleaned out the morgues of two newspapers. So, what I'm saying is, we are still sketchy on your Mr. Patten and his Ultimate Church."

"This will get me started, Ella. Thanks."

Norbert Edgar Patten was born in Huntsville, Ontario, forty-three years ago. I checked an atlas and found Huntsville about where I expected, 215 kilometres north of Toronto. His parents ran a bakery on the main street, were nominally Baptists, but admitted to being only "wedding and funeral Baptists." Patten went to local schools, appeared in *The Mikado*, and took summer jobs in nearby Algonquin Park. When he was eighteen he went off to the States. It was a break in the pattern. What could he be doing in Washington, D.C.? I sifted through the rest of the file without seeing what had taken him from Huntsville to the Harland Lee Academy in Maryland for two years. The Vietnam War halted the American adventure for a time. Like a lot of young Americans, he went north to Canada until the heat cooled. But no sooner had the U.S. Army evacuated Saigon than Patten was back in the District of Columbia area. It was on the road to Washington, near Alexandria, where Patten claims to have seen a blinding light. "With the nation's capital shimmering in the distance, like St. Paul of old, I saw it and it changed me as it changed him. . . ." There was a newspaper clipping advertising a rally near the historic Presbyterian Meetinghouse in Alexandria, and a write-up describing its success. Taking full-page ads quickly became Patten's style. Thousands attended a rally near the Lincoln Memorial the summer after the war. He packed a stadium with sailors in Annapolis. Norbert Patten became news. He began to rival the Bible-belt evangelists with his calls for making an end to war.

Soon after the east-coast success, he went off to California to consolidate what he called the Ultimate Church in that hotbed of cults and religions. His first California branch was located in Burbank, with others starting and slowly spreading up and down the San Andreas Fault, and across the Midwest to New York, New England, and finally the birthplace of the movement, Washington.

Patten was the first of the new wave of evangelists to make full use of television. Preachers had been seen before on the tube talking to thousands in a stadium and millions on the air, but Patten had hit on the idea of pitching his sermons, whatever the size of the audience, to one viewer at a time. It didn't seem to matter whether you caught the show in the flesh or at home; Patten made you feel like he was talking to you. He was also the first into the field of prime-time television when nobody in the networks had guessed the audience potential. Or maybe they'd guessed and decided to forget about it. Patten made them take him seriously.

In 1976 he was pictured on *Time*'s cover wearing a white robe of office. He was quoted in the article, when asked about his globe-trotting, as saying that if God ever looks in on us, we'd better look busy. In a piece in *Newsweek*, the same year, he defended the church from being lumped with the California cults that had so often been confused with his flock. He was notorious for catching all derogatory comments in the press and suing writer, editor, publisher, right up the line. He'd retained a fat stable of lawyers who rarely lost a case. For example, one well-known magazine devoted to the lives of men and the bodies of women lost an undisclosed amount in a hard-fought case that was finally, at the last minute, settled out of court. That was in 1977. Patten's victory had given cults a new lease on life, and only the most foolish papers tried to pillory them after that.

From the articles before 1977, I was able to get a fair idea about how the cult operated. Patten was the absolute despot; his rule was law. All submitted to his whim. He was suspected of seeking sexual favours among the faithful, and most certainly relieved the members of their private property. Everything was owned in common by the church, but on paper the church was Patten. At the beginning, Patten urged his flock to imitate the practices of early Christianity: they met in secret, referred to the mysteries of faith in anagrams and symbols; there were no churches as such. But there were collections, and the proceeds maintained Patten in several earthly kingdoms. There was a large estate near Reno, Nevada, formerly owned by another celebrated multi-millionaire, a hideaway on the coast near San Clemente, and later a villa outside Palma de Mallorca.

I couldn't find any evidence among the clippings that Patten's empire was in any way corkscrewing down from its eminence. But there was a shipbuilder in Spain who had repossessed a yacht in Palma, and the U.S. Army, in light of the many ex-GIs who had flocked to the Ultimate Church, was checking whether the events described in *The Blinding Light*, Patten's uplifting best-seller, ever in fact happened. A fifty-year-old hack journalist from Baltimore claimed in one of the clippings to have ghosted the book in 1975 from six hours of tape Patten had dropped off in a Georgetown apartment. Nevertheless, the book remained on *The New York Times* best-seller list for twenty-two weeks. And even in Grantham I found a copy nestling on a shelf next to Kahlil Gibran's *The Prophet*. The bookseller told me it had been translated into seventeen languages and was on sale wherever books of any kind are known. He said it in a funeral director's voice. I couldn't figure out whether he was a consumer of Patten's doctrine or simply impressed by the book's sales.

Well, Patten was a long way from *Time* magazine this afternoon. The rain was falling on the just and the unjust alike. I wondered how the park looked to him after *Newsweek* and CBS. What was it like to come home again when you couldn't whisper who you are. No drums and no trumpets for the local hero, not even in the *Huntsville Weekly Register*.

I heard the bang on the screen door and guessed Joan was coming across the duckboards between our cabins. She came in, bringing the rain and a scent of freshness and earth with her. Her glasses were steamed up, and she took them off along with her big soaking straw hat.

"Gawd, what a downpour! This is what the weatherman called intermittent showers." Thunder shook the roof; a reminder not to take the name of the Lord thy God in vain. "I brought your milk."

"You didn't have to bring it over at the height of the storm. That's above and beyond the call of duty. I've got the kettle on. Tea?"

"Fine. Only, let's get some light on the subject." She took the lantern from the table where I'd left it and primed it and pumped it until it hissed. She added a match and a high intense light brought colour back into the cabin and sent long shadows from the ketchup bottle and the salt and pepper shakers radiating along the caramel-coloured table top.

"That's better," she said, climbing out of her black raincoat and setting it on the horsehair sofa. "The Goddamned beavers have blocked the culvert again. I knew those bedsprings wouldn't keep them out of there. There's a lake across the road a foot deep. And after this rain . . . Oh damn, I don't want to think about it." I made the tea and kept my mouth shut. In my line, that's the way to find things out. When it happens. A set of ironstone mugs for the tea were finally located on the shelf above the sink. I bashed the teabags to cut down on the waiting time and got out the open can of evaporated milk.

"But I just brought you fresh," she said. She had cleaned her glasses on a piece of pink Kleenex and put them on again.

"New habits die hard. Take it easy. I'm just learning the ropes around here. First you show me how to do everything, then you come over to see that I do it your way. There's more than one way to trim a wick." She smiled and I poured her a cup. I took out the fresh milk and punctured the plastic bag. Joan, the diplomat, took a drop of both, then showed how a real frontiersman stows the plastic milk in a plastic pitcher.

"Are all my chickens safe?" she asked.

"I guess. I haven't taken a proper count, but I haven't seen anything unusual. Your coming in with the groceries was the big event of the afternoon." I lit a cigarette and put the wooden match in an ashtray with the name of a defunct brewery on it.

Joan Harbison had a good ordinary face with blue eyes that didn't grab you all at once. It took three days. Under light eyebrows, their effects were subtle, like the way the dimple on her right cheek played tag with a little brown mole. Her hair, when it wasn't soaking wet, was kept in a light and airy brown tangle. Now it hung in dark fangs stuck to her forehead. She didn't use makeup and she didn't have to. On the day I arrived she was changing the air filter in her Honda and confessed that she was stealing time from the generator which really needed attention. Since then, I'd seen her cutting the grass, chopping and stacking cordwood, rebuilding an outboard motor, flinging a pail full of fish heads to the four cats, and wrapping a piece of brown paper around an ovenproof casserole. She was followed everywhere by a twelve-year-old boy who belonged to the American in one of the log cabins.

She sipped her tea. The downpour gave her a few minutes to relax. The Delco, the cats, the boats, and all of us could run around the block until the weather cleared.

"I've got to do something about that beaver," she said, watching my cigarette smoke drift up to the rafters. "He can build a dam faster than I can pull it down. It's a pair, really. For two cents I'd scalp both of them, sell the skins in Toronto, and fix my chainsaw with the proceeds." Outside, the belly of the window screen was luffing in the wind, sometimes flattening itself against the glass with a muffled smack. Joan hunched over her cup. "I'll let the rain settle overnight," she said, "but tomorrow's another day." She heaved an exaggerated sigh and reached for the teapot again, just as she'd reached for the Nescafé I'd made that first afternoon. Beyond the screen door, the fury of the rain was settling down. It was losing its tropical passion; the wind was no longer raking the ground and blowing the puddles from one depression to the next. One of the cats peeked in the door, and I gave it a dirty look: let it walk with its dirty, wet feet over a floor I don't have to sweep. I was taking my domestic responsibilities to heart.

"It's giving up," I said, nodding at the weather. Joan smiled distantly. "Good weather for fishing." She didn't seem to hear.

"When Mike and I moved into the lodge, it was a day like this. We looked like a couple of drowned rats by the time we had the truck unloaded. Everything had been left in terrible shape, and in the rain it looked like we'd made a bad bet. Then I found mice running around in the oven, after I got the generator going. When I saw that, all I wanted to do was pack up and head back to Toronto."

"Is that where you and Mike go in the winter?"

"Of necessity. As it is he can't leave his city job except in August. I'm glad to see him on weekends though. Maybe next year we'll go south." Joan sighed at the sound of that. She was too realistic to allow herself to dream, even on a rainy afternoon. "Fat chance," she added, like a footnote. "To be brutally frank, Benny, the lodge isn't the gold mine we thought we were buying. I made more teaching. We've taken ads in the papers and magazines, put up signs, but our main business still comes from the people who've been coming up here year after year. Oh, there's a little word of mouth but not enough to retire on." We listened to the rain slacken off for a minute.

"It's giving up," I said again. This time you could hear the difference. Individual plonks of rain were hitting the roof. I could see drops form, grow fat, and drop off the leaves outside the window. "This is the best fishing weather, they say."

"Well, make sure you put motorboat fuel in your tank and not straight gas. I wouldn't want to lose another boat like the one I rented to Mr. Edgar over at the Woodward place."

"That was your boat, was it?"

"Oh, he paid me for it. But I just meant be careful."

"What makes a motor explode like that? Do you have to be *that* careful?"

"I get all kinds of people through here, Benny, and most of them know nothing about motors. This is the first time I've heard of one blowing up. It had to be more than the wrong fuel to make it do that."

"You're not saying you don't think it was an accident, are you?"

"I wouldn't go that far. What a funny idea. Why would anybody want to hurt Mr. Edgar? I could understand somebody putting a bomb under George McCord the way he zooms around the lake, but . . ."

"It was just a thought on a rainy afternoon. It's just a game I play. If life's a mystery, who are the suspects?"

"Hey! Your suspects are my paying customers. Of course, you are free to suspect Maggie and George McCord, and I'll throw in the Rimmers. You can have them for nothing."

"I didn't mean to suggest . . . I haven't really met many of them."

"Well, I've been neglecting my duty as owner then. I'll see that you meet all the suspects you want in the Annex tonight."

"Fine. I'll sidle over and you can fill me in when they aren't watching."

Joan left a handful of change on the pine table, put on her boots and the grim expression of someone who has a generator to fix, and disappeared splashing into the subsiding weather. I pulled on a sweater, a waterproof groundsheet that also worked as a poncho, and collected my fishing gear. The red fuel tank was where I'd left it the day before. I used the rowboat in the mornings; couldn't stand the noise of the motor until the afternoon. It didn't take me long to attach the tank to the motor again and untie the soaking painter. I tipped out the puddles in the indentations in the plastic-covered cushions and steeled myself to pull the starting cord.

Chapter Three

". . . Of the nine of them, Manfred Gunning is the only one you can be sure of. At least Gunning will write a minority opinion that will go down in legal history." It was Patten's voice on the cassette recorder I'd planted on the island nearest the Woodward place. Not guessing that I would become a friend of the great man himself after picking him out of the water, I'd set up some fancy borrowed surveillance equipment in two plastic garbage bags under a groundsheet hidden by pine boughs and leaves. It took me five minutes to locate the hiding place myself. Inside the machine, the tiny reels turned slowly. ". . . It's not Gunning I'm worried about," Patten said in a controlled whisper. "It's Harper, and Bartenbach, and the woman, what'shername, McCready."

"Because they're Democrats? Surely . . ."

"I'm not talking politics, Ozzie. Haven't you been listening? Harper and Bartenbach both have a history of upholding decisions made in the lower courts, everything else being equal."

"If the decision goes against you, they'll be opening up a can of worms that every church in the country's going to yell about. There will be shouting from the pulpits in every hamlet in America. Think of it, Norrie."

"What do you imagine I've been thinking about? I've been through all the arguments. Diodati made only a third of the points I raised with him. . . ."

"Now, Norrie . . ."

"You told me he was the best."

"Diodati? He is the best. He's one of the club. You need that. You can't parachute an outsider into Washington. They've got to start from the same mark. Diodati gave it his best shot." Considering the compactness of the microphone and the distance between it and the island, I was getting excellent value from the equipment. It even knew when to turn itself on and off. I'd never want to own stuff like this; I'd use it maybe once in ten years. I moved the tape ahead. There was more crackle now. It was Patten again with Ozzie.

"I want to talk to Van," Patten said.

"Norrie, please, leave him out of it."

"You heard me. Or is he leading this vendetta against me? Maybe it's him I can thank for dragging my name through the courts. My friends scorn me. That's the first step."

"Norrie, the senator's been your most loyal friend since the beginning. Since *before* the beginning. Please don't start up with him again. Why he even let you use this place. Is that unfriendly?"

"He could have been behind that motor exploding like that. He was one of the few who knew where to find me."

"Norrie, you're not talking sense. The senator loves you."

"In the last days men shall be traitors. I don't trust Van or you or Lorca, here. I don't trust anybody. You're all out for yourselves. Don't think I don't know your little games."

"Norrie, you know we all love you."

"I only know one thing: I'm Norbert Patten. That's my beginning and my end, my going out and my coming in. The rest of you have your hands out."

"Be reasonable, Norrie."

"You too, eh, Ozzie?"

"Norrie!"

"Shut up, Lorca. If Ozzie wants out, that's all right. We'll pay him off right now. I've been alone before. Man is born to strive by himself. Everything else is an illusion. Ozzie, it's up to you. If you're with us, good; if not, Lorca'll write your ticket."

"Norrie, I've never been a 'yes-man', and I'm not going to start now."

"The ancients used to kill the messenger, Ozzie. That wasn't such a bad idea."

"But there hasn't been any news. Van's holding the phone

like the rest of us. We all have to sit and wait. By Friday
we'll know."

"Seven days! God built the universe in seven days and took
the last day off. Don't you think we can be undone in seven
days? Here I sit in the middle of nowhere while out there the
whole organization is waiting for a sign. If I live through this,
is it going to be a victory cruise or is it time to leave the
sinking ship? I know they're thinking that. You tell them,
Ozzie, tell P.J., tell them all that whatever happens I'm counting on them."

"They know that. You don't have to . . ."

"Say it, damn it! Get it into the papers. Bring out extra
editions of *Good News*."

"Whatever you say."

"Whatever the Supreme Court says, our ministry must go
on. You got that?"

"Sure, it'll be in *Good News*, and I'll see that the press gets
hold of it. Now, don't worry about Van, Norrie. He's all
right." I heard Ozzie sigh, like he'd started running down.
"My plane leaves at six, Norrie. I have to get back to Toronto."

"Well, cover your trail. I don't want the whole world knowing I'm up here. Having somebody on the lake who's trying to
kill me is enough."

Eavesdropping is a funny business. As a peeper doing divorce
work I spent a lot of time listening in one way or another.
After a while you wish people would snap up their conversation a little. When you're standing in the muck getting dripped
on every time a leaf moves, you'd like to edit out the long
pauses and the false starts to every thought. But I liked that
last bit from Patten. I rewound the tape a few feet and played
it again: "Having somebody on the lake who's trying to kill
me is enough."

My feet were sinking in the ooze, and I didn't want to waste
too much battery power playing back what I'd recorded. I
had another machine back at the cabin. Whenever Joan's
generator was working I could hear the rest of this summit

meeting. I replaced the used tape with a new one, removed the earphone, and set the thing recording again inside the camouflaged setting. With shoes squeaking in the muck, I took to the boat again. I'd pulled it up on some flat rocks and fixed the painter to some bushes. Once aboard, I took her out to my usual fishing ground, two hundred yards off Patten's dock, and dropped anchor. I'd stopped counting worms. I drowned a few, keeping my eyes on the cabin. Nothing moved for half an hour except sweat into the creases around my neck. The Buick had gone, but the Mercedes was beginning to fry in its usual place as the sun broke through the clouds.

Van was the senator, Senator Woodward, who was with Patten before the beginning. I salted that away. I would have to phone Ray Thornton in the morning about Patten. He wanted reports every other day. He already knew about my daring rescue and my positive identification. Now I was a limpet, a baby-sitter.

I was wondering whether I knew Patten well enough to come out and ask him during our next game of chess what his plans were for after the Supreme Court decision, when my fishing rod jumped out of my lap and jammed against the gunwale of the boat. I could hear the reel spinning. I grabbed the cork handle before it disappeared over the side. I could see water skipping off the line as it went taut. God damn it, I thought, what a hell of a time to catch a fish! The reel was spinning so fast, the handle of the reel was a white blur. I knew enough not to try to check the line as it ran out, as the fork in the reel ran back and forth across the diminishing yardage. I tried putting my thumb lightly against the line and gave myself a rope burn. The core of the reel was coming up fast, and I had no other play. The short rod I was using didn't have much bend in it, and it took all my strength to hold on to it.

Then I felt the pressure easing on the line. He'd run as far as he was going to, or else he'd turned and was going to ram me. God, I hoped he wasn't *that* big. Instead of thinking, I began to reel in the slack. I was expecting him to take another run any second, and I was ready for him. I'd picked up an end of the boat's painter and had it ready to use inside the reel instead of my thumb next time he took off. I could feel that he was still there someplace. I hoped that he wasn't running under the boat. He could have me tied up like a birthday present if I let him.

When I had about three-quarters of my line back on the reel he started to take it away again. It was a see-saw operation. In the movies the fish ends up in the net; I didn't even have a net. The fishing line was as tight as a power line and met the water at a sharp tangent. Then I remembered, or my thumb did, that there was a ratchet on the side of the reel which added a drag to the line. I liked the drone it added to the banging about of my feet against the hot bottom of the boat. He didn't run as far with it this time, and I was working the reel again. It was funny, this fishing business. Some of the things I was doing I'd never done before, but my hands seemed to know what they were doing. There wasn't any thinking to be done, just keep things calm and simple. The fish was there all right. I could feel him through the rod and line. It was a different feeling from the drag of a snagged line. There was something electric or living about it. Suddenly as I started reeling in again, it wasn't drowning worms any more.

When I finally got my first look at him, I wanted to call the whole thing off. He was long and as big as a supermarket pyramid of canned salmon. My rod wasn't long enough to keep him from sounding under the boat, but that wasn't one of the cards in his deck. His shadow came closer and closer to the surface. I didn't know what to do next. I needed a landing net. I had to make do with my shirt. As I lifted his slate-grey nose out of the water, I grabbed him with the shirt in my other hand. There was a little splashing, but when it was finished, we were both in the boat.

I lay back trying to catch my breath for a minute, while

the fish — it looked like a lake trout to me, but I'm not asking you to take my word for it — flopped about. I bashed its head with the small bait pail and it stopped moving. It was mottled and speckled with bright colours showing through a darker greenish brown. I put a line through the gills and tied it securely to the boat seat before throwing it back into the lake.

I headed north along the shore for about half a mile, then turned the motor so I'd be able to see as much of the long lake as possible, out past both islands. A couple of loons started a serenade but cut it short, as though their hearts weren't in it or the acid rain was getting them down. From the middle of the lake I turned the sharp end of the boat towards the shore and watched the lodge get slowly bigger.

Nobody was on the dock when I brought in my catch. There was an electric hum of heat in the air, and most signs of the recent storm had vanished. I hauled my fish in and dallied on the dock, but the whole population of the lodge was off boondoggling or pressing flowers or something. I put the fish in the propane refrigerator. As I sat at the pine table eating soda crackers, I thought that somebody up at Petawawa Lodge knew quite a lot about my chess partner and right now might be planning further means for reducing the total number of cult leaders in North America.

Chapter Four

The main building of the lodge was called the Annex, although it wasn't near anything except the edge of Big Crummock Lake. It was a one-storey rectangular log house with a big fieldstone fireplace at one end and an office and tack shop at the other. The unpainted log walls were decorated with chinking plaster and bear skins. There were a number of comfortable, over-stuffed sofas and chairs arranged around the fireplace, where a hardwood fire was falling away into white ash. To the right of the fireplace and dwarfed by it stood an old upright piano with the hammers and strings showing through the gap where the front panel had been.

When I'd arrived I asked Joan about the name, the Annex, and she explained by pointing to the south end of the property where I could see a smoke-blackened remnant of stone and masonry rising through the bracken. "That was the sawmill," she said, "built in the 1880s, as far as I can find out, and burned to the ground about fifteen years ago. There's rusty machinery under the brush. Kids are always bringing me pieces of it or skinning their knees on it. The Annex was the office. I guess it seems funny still calling this the Annex, doesn't it?"

Lloyd Pearcy was bending over an old wind-up Victrola phonograph near the ping-pong table. His wide-open eyes were concentrated on the deep, rolling music that came out of the tattered cloth of the speaker. Lloyd had been there the night I arrived from Grantham and was still there the night after that. I'd seen him on the dock getting in and out of his boat, but in the evening he was seldom far from the Victrola. Back in my Grantham office it had seemed reasonable that up in Algonquin Park I should appear to be a fisherman. So I bought a medium-sized pickerel, had it cleaned, and brought it north with my fancy eavesdropping equipment. Lloyd had caught me filleting the pickerel and right away knew what kind of fisherman I was. He told me he'd worked for the parks commission in Sudbury for twenty-five years and was a regular up at the lodge. Right now he was trying to write down the words to the song on the turntable. I think it was Paul Robeson. He kept taking the tone-arm off the old 78 and putting it back again.

Lindy Lou, Lindy Lou!
O Lawd, I'd lay right down and die . . .

There was a card game going on by the fireplace. I knew some of the faces from the last couple of days, but there were faces new to me too. Both kinds looked up at me as I steered in their direction.

Mah liddle Lindy Lou-oo-oo.

An urn of coffee was perched on a corner of the ping-pong table. I drew a cup, added milk and my usual two heaping teaspoonfuls of sugar. From here I tried to sort out the faces. George McCord was in the card game. He was the chief source of noise on the lake, running his powerful speedboat up and down Big Crummock like he was on an assignment for the Mounties and the park rangers rolled together. His sweating head rested its chin on his chest while he examined his cards. From under meeting eyebrows he watched the other players while doing arithmetic on the inside of his cheek with the tip of his tongue. Lloyd's wife, Cissy, was sitting next to George and frowning at the cards she held, like they were making them smaller this year. The player who looked like she had all the cards was Maggie McCord. She was as smug as a Persian cat on a pillow.

"Three, no trump," she said, almost licking her lips.

"Oh, Maggie, have a heart!" That was Cissy, who palmed her cards and then had to fan them out again. The fourth card player was David Kipp. It was one of his tow-headed kids who was always following Joan around. Kipp was staying at the lodge with both of his sons. His wife, Michelle, was in hospital in Vermont. The kids had that kind of blondness that takes to a tan. Kipp was fair too, but his short legs and long arms took the shine off it. Looking at the kids you could imagine Michelle with the kind of fragile blondness that makes you think of dandelion fuzz.

Maggie handled her cards with small, delicate hands. Small hands and feet aside, everything else about Maggie McCord was huge. Joan, the source of most of my information, had told me she was the widow of a park ranger, who'd left her with property on the lake next door to the lodge. She looked like she was somewhere in her seventies. Bridge wasn't my game, but I watched them through the bidding just to be polite. Maggie's skilled hands managed her cards and her chain-smoking with a rare elegance under the naked electric lights of the Annex.

Honey, did you heah dat mockin' bird sing las' night?

I found a quiet corner by a bookshelf that contained copies of *National Geographic* going back to before Columbus. Behind one of them I recognized the elder of Kipp's two boys. He told me his name was Roger, and he was thirteen. Before I asked him he told me that his mother was laid up in Bennington with hepatitis she had caught eating at a vegetarian restaurant. I thought this might lead to further conversation, but the lure of the girls of the atolls consumed the boy's attention.

Lloyd continued to write down the words of his song. Maggie McCord added another trick to the pile in front of her. Her son was glaring at her with a grab bag of emotions displayed on his face like Spencer Tracy wondering whether he has Mr. Hyde tucked up for the night.

On my first night at the lodge, I'd seen a furtive couple who sat knee to knee as far away from everybody as possible. I called him Silverthorne, just to put a name on him, and his lady, Griselda. There was something patrician about him, something awkward and withdrawn about her. During the day, I didn't see either one of them, but in the evenings they came to sit near the people, like wild animals at the edge of the forest clearing. This time they were sitting next to the log wall, with an inverted bearskin hanging overhead, the savage mouth leering at the occasional words that passed between them. They both looked like they were slightly in pain. Even behind the protective cover of mosquitoes, black flies, and miles of dirt road, they weren't having a hell of a time of it. He was the sole occupant of number six in the motel unit. His girlfriend was just the kid next door. Not even that; a dull couple of newlyweds lived between them. Their name was Hellman, and they took picnics and went off by car to other parts of the park. Tonight they were probably curled up in front of a fire on Lake Opeongo eating soft ice cream from the outfitter's store. I was just beginning to get depressed thinking how many city people were up here, when we all turned towards the sound of a car coming into the clearing. The noise drowned out the Delco generator. I could hear voices after the doors were opened and closed.

"It's the Rimmers!" Lloyd announced, turning off "Mah Lindy Lou." "Former owners," Lloyd said to me in a stage whisper, "with a place across the lake." I put down my coffee as the voices grew closer and finally burst through the double doors.

"I'll be damned if I'll pay a nickel for that tire. I tell you that right now. I won't have any wedges or plugs or patches, I promise you that."

"Dalt!"

"Peg, I'm telling you straight out I'm not spending good money to have a flat tire with less than two hundred miles on it. No, sir. Good evening everybody. Is Joan here? We've got some things from town."

"Hello, Maggie," said Peg, doing the rounds of the people she appeared to know. "Say, it must have rained bad up here.

The culvert's flooded again. Joan should keep it clear."

"Never mind about that now, we'll have that cement washed off the dock where I left it." Dalt Rimmer didn't try to make sense. He knew what he meant and that was good enough for him. For a man of less than five feet four, he made a lot of noise. He strutted into the Annex like a little bantam rooster followed by his adoring hen.

"Dalt, it was covered with a tarp. You put it there yourself."

"Tarp is it? We'll be lucky to see tarp or cement again. Did you not see the water in the parking lot, woman? They've had a dousing here, and we've had the same thing over the water. Where is Joan, Lloyd? We've got to be getting across." He had a lined face that turned small worries into big ones. He pulled his nor'wester hat from his head and slapped it against his leg and then over the back of a chair, like it was still his own. At this moment, wearing her yellow boots and carrying a Coleman lantern, Joan came in with two men no taller than she was. The two men slipped along the wall and melted away into the shadows.

"I thought that was you, Dalt. Hi, Peg. Did you see our new lake?"

"We had a flat on Highway 37, Joan, and the tire was brand new."

"You'll lose that bit of road if it's not attended to, girl."

"I know. That's what I've been talking to Aeneas about. Damned beavers!"

"I've seen a twenty-foot section of good road washed away like that. And this is only sand and gravel. You'd better hop to it. You need that husband of yours up here at a time like this, doesn't she, Peg?"

"Joan does just fine, just fine. And don't scare her. Aeneas won't see her stranded."

"She'll get more than a scare if it washes out, lass. We can always go home overland by our own road. I'm just talking for her own good."

"You usually are, Dalt." That was a voice from the card

game — Mrs. McCord, without even looking up. The two men who'd come in with Joan were pouring themselves coffee silently.

"There's a new country heard from," said Dalt, and sniffed. "Let's get the things out of the car now so we can get on with loading the boat. It'll be late enough by the time we get to the point."

"You won't stop for tea, Dalt? Peg?"

"Well . . ."

"Lass, you know we'd best be about our business. Thanks all the same, Joan. Another time. Aeneas," he called to the men at the coffee urn, "will you lend a hand?" Dalt Rimmer fitted his rain hat over his sparse nest of fading red hair. Peg followed him through the door with the dark man in faded jeans at her heels. The big car was parked on the soft grass margin in front of the Annex. When the doors opened, the Cadillac lit up like a Chinese lantern, and Dalt and Aeneas got busy shifting cardboard cartons around. They each carried one into Joan's cabin, squishing their way through the damp mud and gravel. Peg thanked Aeneas, and Dalt told him that the two of them could manage the rest of the work. He drove the car down to the dock, where Dalt stripped the tarp from the cruiser, while Peg began loading smaller, more compact boxes.

"Hell," Joan said, looking at the ruts the Cadillac had left in her sodden lawn. I grinned and shrugged, and Joan introduced me to Aeneas, who tried to slip quietly back into the Annex.

"You are the steady fisherman," Aeneas observed. "I've seen you in the tin fish near the senator's." I didn't know what he meant, and I'd certainly not seen him, so I just nodded and asked him a fishing question. "The water is shallow between the islands. The lake trout stay in the shallow water with the island between them and the sun. You have found a good place to fish. But there are other places. Fish the shadows."

Back inside, the card game continued. Maggie McCord had another stack of tricks in front of her, and Cissy looked like she was breathing "Oh dear" to herself. I hovered nearby, partly watching the game, partly watching the fire and just about everything else in the room. Aeneas had gone back to sit out of the light with the fellow he'd come in with. I was about to go over and find out if they'd met the tenant of the Woodward place, when Joan grabbed my arm and dragged me over to the card players.

"I don't want to break up the party, but I don't think you have met our new guest, Mr. Cooperman. Benny, I think you know Cissy Pearcy. This is Maggie McCord and her son, George. George was playing dummy and looked like the casting suited him. "Benny's becoming an enthusiastic fisherman, isn't he, David?" Kipp nodded good-humouredly. We'd talked bait on the dock.

"Unfortunately, it's easier to catch enthusiasm than lake trout," I said after acknowledging the how-do-you-dos.

"You're from Toronto, Mr. Cooperman?" asked Mrs. McCord.

"Grantham. Please call me Benny."

"That's across the lake, near the Falls, isn't it?"

"Yes, it's three exits off the Queen Elizabeth Way, exactly eleven miles from the Falls."

"Well, I hope they teach you to play bridge in Grantham. We could use an infusion of new blood."

"That's transfusion, isn't it?" asked Cissy.

"Whichever, I'll try to be a donor when needed."

Sometimes I sound so phoney to myself I want to bring up. Next time I'll tell them it's a pity I didn't bring my polo pony. George was the only one who caught the hollowness of what I'd said, giving me a dismissing look and rubbing his fleshy nose with the inside of his thumb.

"Joan," he said, "when are you going to start stocking some beer? I swear I'm dying of thirst, and I'm too lazy to walk the quarter-mile back to my place."

"I can't sell it, George. You know that as well as I do. I haven't got a licence yet. We're working on it."

"Haw! That didn't stop old Wayne Trask, did it, Ma?"

"You hush up, George, and watch your cards." George curled his lip like Raymond Massey and picked his cards up slowly from the table. Joan moved away from the game, and I followed her.

"Joan, I think I've swallowed everybody's name now except for Aeneas's friend and the couple by the wall talking to the bearskin." Joan tilted her head in Silverthorne's direction, caught my eye, then my nod.

"That's Des Westmorland and Delia Alexander. He's from Ottawa, she's from Hull. They're a nice quiet couple, just met by chance. I understand he recently lost his wife. Now, Benny, don't try to turn them into suspects. Can you see either of them blowing up the neighbours?" I wasn't buying surface appearances tonight or any other night. But Joan didn't have to see my shopping list. She kept talking. ". . . And over there talking to Aeneas is his brother, Hector. He's a teacher in Hatchway. They're a part of the history of this place. They were here first. Aeneas sort of came with the lodge. He worked for the Rimmers when they owned it and for Wayne Trask after that. Trask was a nasty piece of goods; fought with everybody when he was sober. Aeneas's ancestor is the Amable DuFond they named the river after. It's hard to get Aeneas talking, but he has so many wonderful stories about the old logging days." We sailed over to the abandoned old-fashioned record player where Aeneas and Hector were standing with their hands wrapped around their coffee mugs like it was mid-winter. Joan introduced me to Hector and his brother, then left us to share the awkward pause that followed by ourselves. We all watched her put more birch logs on the fire and then replace the wire screen.

"I thought that there weren't any private lodges inside Algonquin Park anymore." Hector shared a smile with his brother, who hitched his gum to the other side of his mouth.

This seemed as useful a way to get a conversation going as any, but for a moment it looked as though I'd made a blunder and they weren't going to let me in on it. Then Hector decided to include me.

"Here you'll find just about every sort of thing. There's campers like Aeneas and there's dispossessed former landowners like Lloyd and private places like Dalt Rimmer has on the point across the lake. We even have absentee landlords like all the best societies. I mean the Woodward place. Woodward hasn't been seen in the park since before the Vietnam War. He's an American senator."

"But the place is rented?" I thought I wouldn't chase away unexpected leads.

"Yes, there are lots of rented places. There are two on the other side of the second island and an empty place up near where the lake curves into a little hook."

"There is a man there," said Aeneas. "I saw him today."

"Well, there you are: the lake is full again this year."

"But you haven't answered the question. I thought that the park was provincial land and that—"

"The park was created ninety years ago," said Hector, trying hard not to look like he was giving his set speech on the subject. "In that time the policy has changed every few years. At one time you could build a cabin. Now you can't. They tried to get rid of the cabins that had been built. They wanted it, you know, a wilderness area. They want it all wilderness by the turn of the century. They keep getting reports made every dozen years, and the objectives change. That's how Lloyd lost his place, but Dalt Rimmer didn't. Dalt's timing was better, I guess. He wasn't in with the lumber companies, and he isn't a big supporter of the powers that be." Hector smiled, a little embarrassed at catching himself on a soapbox. "The history of the park makes fascinating reading. Every time the policy changes down in Toronto, there are big changes up here. Aeneas is lucky he's squatting for the summer. That counts as camping and the govern-

ment can't really discourage that." Aeneas hadn't said anything, but he nodded and watched the effect his brother's
words had on me.

Then his eye was on George, stretching to accommodate
an enormous yawn. He'd left his chair at the card table and
had just returned from outside. I could detect the outline of
a flat bottle of whiskey in his shirt. His face was red with it.
When he was like this, I automatically began to measure his
reach and to keep well outside it when I could. He grabbed
Joan from behind, and I started to feel like a Boy Scout.
Luckily she could handle his bear-hug without making him
angry. She peeled his big hand off her shoulder and unwound
the unwanted arm, handing it back to him like she'd found a
mislaid item belonging to George on her porch.

"Ah, Joan, don't be cross with me. I was just being friendly.
Hell, I ain't no trouble."

"That's right, George, you're a dream. Where were you
when I needed my firewood cut?"

"I forgot about the firewood, Joan, I just forgot. I'll help
you with the beaver. I will."

"All right, George, but Aeneas promised to do it in the
morning. There's still the wood. You know lots of ways to be
helpful." At the mention of Aeneas's name, George began to
turn about looking for him. He hitched up his trousers and
headed in our direction. I decided that I needed more coffee
and left just ahead of George's strong breath. When I looked
back, Hector was talking to David Kipp and George was
standing closer to Aeneas than necessary. He was looking for
a fight, but I couldn't imagine him finding it talking to
Aeneas, who held his ground and listened, with his head
tilted gravely. Lloyd was still at the Victrola.

I'd lay right down and die . . .

Now Aeneas was talking and George's big paw was on
Aeneas's arm. Hector was watching too, but before anything
happened, Aeneas pulled away, saying just loudly enough for

me to hear, "I do not like the man, but I will see him. What you do is wrong."

"I'll get you if you do!" Aeneas had a good moment then. He looked at George, from his messy engineer's cap to the tangle of his shoelaces, and said:

"I don't think so, George. You will not hurt me."

The card game had now completely broken up. David Kipp went to the coffee urn, Cissy rejoined her husband, and Maggie McCord lifted her ample body out of her chair and moved it to the piano bench.

Maggie McCord must have been a very handsome woman in her day, but that was a long time ago. She glided about with that slowness of movement which to younger people looks like stateliness, but which is probably a question of joints. She was wearing a flowing, gauzy dress that flattered her figure by not adhering to it too specifically. It reminded me of the failing fire with oranges, reds, and yellows mixed in with darker hues. As she sat at the piano, looking down at the keys, her cascade of chins shivered. She brought the room to attention with a loud two-handed chord. The first was followed by a second with each note answering some message in the first. She made the old piano boom like a church organ. It sounded like an old hymn tune. The other guests put down their magazines and books as though Maggie McCord's playing was itself a fearful summons. She played the verse through once, then started in again with everybody but me singing as if his life depended on it.

From Greenland's icy mountains . . .

It made me feel peculiar. This wasn't the north woods. This wasn't keeping an eye on Norbert Patten. In fact, it sounded like the competition. Maybe if we sang loudly enough we could shake him up at the Woodward place. Then something funny started to happen. They were well into the hymn, and somehow it was reaching me. All those years at Grantham Collegiate hadn't abandoned me. From some hidden depths inside, I could feel the words of the next verse bubbling up to the surface and coming out in an unsteady but loud baritone.

> *What though the spicy breezes*
> *Blow soft o'er Ceylon's isle;*
> *Though every prospect pleases,*
> *And only man is vile . . .*

Mrs. McCord looked up from her many-ringed fingers to carry me forward into the next verse with an encouraging nod. Cissy Pearcy, at my elbow, shot me a conspiratorial smile. I felt I was there under false colours, but I didn't know how to stop and the words kept coming to my lips just as I needed them. It was strange and a little frightening, as though the dark side of my brain had been salting these old words away without breathing a word. Now the game was up.

> *In vain with lavish kindness*
> *The gifts of God are strown;*
> *The heathen in his blindness*
> *Bows down to wood and stone.*

Nobody was going to take me for a heathen, not that night. They weren't even going to take me for Jewish. What was a nice Jewish boy like me doing singing hymns? Was I just trying to fit in or what? Was it for this that my father had sent me to learn to read Hebrew? In school you have to make compromises, you either stand in the hall looking at sepia engravings of Queen Victoria or you join in with the singing. I had always hated the hall, and I liked singing. I didn't see that I'd necessarily sold my birthright.

When Maggie got to the end of the first hymn, she launched into another, and here too I was able to join in. Join in? Hell, I led the band.

> *Brighten the corner where you are,*
> *Brighten the corner where you are;*
> *Someone far from harbour*

You may guide across the bar,
Brighten the corner where you are.

That one I owed to Miss McDougall in grade five. Ray Thornton would remember her. She used to lead a forty-minute hymn-sing every morning, and we all joined in, Jew and Gentile alike, because we knew that oral arithmetic followed inevitably. I was glad I thought of Ray. It was Ray Thornton who'd sent me up here in the first place.

When the last great chords died out, we were standing there elbow to elbow, listening to the sound come back at us from the lake. And there, unmistakable, in the middle of all the other voices, I was singing my fool head off and enjoying every minute of it.

"Well, now; well now, Mr. Cooperman, you have a rare voice, indeed," said Mrs. McCord when she surrendered her place at the piano to David Kipp. "Have you studied?"

"I'm afraid I'm just another shower baritone."

"You're too modest, Mr. Cooperman," said Cissy Pearcy, handing me a mug of coffee I hadn't asked for. "It's a very true, pure sound, isn't it, Maggie?"

"You're turning the poor man beet red, Cissy. We both are. Come sit down by me, Mr. Cooperman, and enjoy the last of the fire. We all enjoy a little sing-song of an evening. It's become quite the institution. Lloyd Pearcy doesn't often join in. He thinks it's sentimental. But we all like it. Good exercise for the lungs. We don't have to talk about the spirit, do we?"

I sat down, and the coven hung about on both sides. It was my night to be a novelty. Tomorrow I'd be old hat, like the grinning bearskins hanging on the wall. Chris, the younger Kipp boy announced to the room that he and his father had sighted an Olive-sided Flycatcher. But they didn't score any points for that. Music was still in the room, but now it sounded secular and rather French. You couldn't sing along with David. But you could talk through it.

"David's so competitive. He's always trying to show me up. I always tell him that I can play loudly, and that's my only virtue at the keyboard."

"That's Debussy, I think," said Cissy, half turning it into a question. It was the way she had with most things. "Do you play, Mr. Cooperman?" I shook my head trying to show my profound regret.

"I like this bit," said Maggie McCord, hooking the air with a finger, and we all listened. Maggie's smile lasted into the next phrase and faded only when a loon far out in the lake added his own inane counter-tenor.

The rest of the evening consisted of more of the same, although we had done with the singing. George had disappeared after his argument with Aeneas; the Pearcys sat close to the fire; Roger and Chris, the Kipp kids, read *National Geographic*; their father held on to the piano bench, playing introspectively with his head hunched over the keys. The shifty couple, Des Westmorland and Delia Alexander, watched the rest of us with their backs to the log wall. Hector said good night at about ten-thirty and we listened to his car drive off in the direction of Hatchway. Aeneas was studying a map of the park which told the whole story, township by township. Without saying anything much he showed me where we were and then pointed to several spots not too far away. "Good lake trout," he said. "Over here, splake. Up here in the west — walleye and pike." I'd never heard of splake, but I thanked him for the tips.

At eleven o'clock it seemed that the generator suddenly got louder and then began to die away to nothing. At the same time the electric light slowly faded to black. Having stumbled home on the first night at the lodge, this time I had come prepared with a flashlight.

A small knot of us had moved outside the darkened Annex, where we were about to pronounce our good nights, when the trim figure of a strange brunette walked up the slope from the dock with a blanket over her arm and carrying a paddle. I could make out the shape of a canoe drawn up on the shore and rolled bottom up. The woman smiled as she passed us but made no attempt to join in.

"That's a nice bit of crumpet for somebody," said Maggie.

"For somebody with his pockets full," said Lloyd. "Did you see the car she drives?" He shook his fingers like he'd burned them. A well-simonized Lamborghini could be dimly seen sinking up to its expensive hubcaps in the parking lot muck. Next to my rusting Olds, the yellow sports car looked pretty good.

"Her name's Aline Barbour. Arrived the same day Benny did," added Maggie. "If you ask me, she's just broken it off with her boyfriend. I can sense these things."

We watched the car retreating back until it was swallowed up in the shadows shortly before we heard the sound of her cabin door. "Not much of a mixer, is she?"

"Has she been here before?" I asked.

"One . . ." began Aeneas, but he stopped short.

"Not to my knowledge. Oh, you mean my knowing her name. Benny, there isn't much that goes on around here that I don't know about. I know, just for example, that you saved Mr. Edgar's life yesterday."

"He what?" asked Cissy, and Maggie gave a brief account of my heroism. From the look of the assembled faces it came as news. But you can never be sure about a thing like that.

"Poor Benny," said Cissy.

"To say nothing of the lucky Mr. Edgar. Well, now, good night." The group began to break up. "Good night, Cissy. Good night, Aeneas. Good night." Maggie headed north towards the lumber road that ran through the lodge grounds; the rest of us moved in the other direction.

"Good night, Maggie."

"Good night, Mrs. McCord."

"Good night. God bless. Call me Maggie, remember. Everybody does. Come over for tea tomorrow if you like. Good night."

Chapter Five

Early the following morning, when the chattering of the birds had made it impossible to sleep, I boiled four brown eggs, chopped them in a bowl, added mayonnaise, and made a couple of sandwiches. These did nothing to supplant the United Cigar Store in Grantham as my idea of dependable eating, but they didn't turn out badly considering the primitive conditions. Through the window the lake looked calm, the white birches framing my view of the dock made the whole panorama look like an ad for hooks, lines, and sinkers. I heard kids squealing down by the dock. This was accompanied by splashing and laughter. From my front door I heard Joan start up the Delco. She didn't usually start it this early, so I took advantage of having the power to put on the cassette I'd brought back from the island. While I listened, I wrapped the sandwiches in the plastic the bread came in.

". . . Norrie, you can't afford . . ."

"This is somebody I practically grew up with. Haven't I ever mentioned Aeneas DuFond?"

"I'm talking security, Norrie."

"Take it easy, Ozzie. He doesn't know who I am. I'll bet he doesn't see a dozen papers a year. I knew him before I met Van. Stop sweating, Ozzie. He's an Indian guide. He never leaves the park. Thinks Hatchway's the Big City."

"It's enough that that haberdasher comes here . . ."

"Benny? Have a heart, I'm learning to beat the pants off him."

"I could watch that yo-yo fishin' all day." That was a new voice. I pegged it as the body I'd been calling Mr. Clean. He looked like a bodyguard and now he talked like one, ending in a moronic laugh. But I might be considered prejudiced.

"Shut up, Wilf, we're busy." So, Mr. Clean is Wilf. Glad to know you. "Funny thing about Aeneas, though," Patten continued, "he looked me up for a purpose. He showed me this." I could hear Lorca taking in her breath as something hard hit the wood of a table.

"Son of a bitch!" Another voice. The one I'd been calling Shorty, I thought.

"Crudely put, Spence, but I agree with you there, fella."

"You haven't got time to get mixed up with some Indian guide."

"Don't crowd me, Ozzie. All souls are equally precious."

"Where do you think he got it, Norrie?" Lorca asked. From the sound of her voice, it must have been something to look at. I tried to imagine diamonds, sapphires, emeralds.

"You see, DuFond remembers when Van was trying to get me interested in minerals. You know he was a practicing geologist before he became the junior senator from Vermont. He took both of us into the bush and tapped away at rocks with his hammer."

"But he isn't going to go to the papers?"

"Relax, Ozzie. Aeneas isn't going, and neither is the dimwit fisherman who sells the boys his fresh catch."

"Oh, my God! Another breach! Norrie, your security is shot front and back. If it's known you're not at San Clemente . . . These guys should be shut up. There's too much riding on this. What if they blab?"

"You worry too much. Now, you'd better get going. Don't forget to speak to Van. Sift him. Test him for leaks. I want to know he's still with us."

"I talked to P.J. before I left. He knows what we want from Van."

"And have Ethan take this thing in and get it assayed."

"Damn it all, Norrie!"

"A promise is a promise." I didn't know who P.J. was, but I was ready to bet next year's tan that Ethan was Ozzie's driver, Surf's Up. P.J. sounded American, part of the U.S. operation, somewhere between Van and Patten.

Then they got into a squabble about whether Lorca had been drinking or not. She made a valiant defence and was getting a sermon on the evils of drink when the power faded away stopping the machine. As Patten began to lose his grip on the whole empire, he stuck it to the few of the faithful who were ready to follow their leader into exile.

With the sandwiches tucked into a knapsack, I went out into the sunlight. The screen door slapped the frame behind me just as the heat gave me a rabbit punch in the solar plexus. The tin fish, as Aeneas DuFond called my aluminum rowboat, was too hot to touch. I had to be careful how I deployed my carcass. I postponed the moment by going back for the equipment.

Aline Barbour, the owner of the Lamborghini, was lying spread out on an inflatable air mattress at the end of the dock. She was wearing a pink bikini with black piping. There was a lot of tanned skin to be looked at, and Aline Barbour shielded her eyes from the sun and watched me look.

"You're up early," she said in a drawl. I lowered my eyes. I was no good at these staring contests even with the sun on my side. "They told me your name was Cooperman."

"Still is. I'm going fishing." That sounded a little pale coming from a man with one foot in a boat and a fishing rod under his arm. She smiled and tilted her big sunglasses up to her forehead. Her eyes were brown and slightly wild.

"I'm Aline Barbour. I'm sorry, I keep forgetting that everybody doesn't know who I am. I spend most of my time in the theatre. I'm a designer and fairly well known. I forget that the theatre isn't the world." She took the cap off a tube of white cream and began rubbing it on her shoulders. She did it in a languid way that I don't always associate with eight o'clock in the morning. "See you later," she said, flicking her mane of hair like a model in a shampoo commercial, and went back to her rubbing. I pulled myself off the dock and into the scalding rowboat.

I took a run down the lake past the Woodward place. The car was still there. At least they hadn't bolted overnight. I picked a worm at random and slipped it along my hook. Over the side with it. Through the water it looked almost white as it slipped out of sight.

I sat like that for half an hour. Nothing moved. My head was getting hot. I should have worn a hat. That made a pretty picture as I closed my eyes against the magenta light creeping through my eyelids. My normal hat would suit the north woods like a bikini at the opera. Couldn't get that bikini out of my head. Was it the pink or the black piping? I took off my shirt, removed the undershirt and dipped it into the lake. After wringing it out, I fitted it to my frying brow. For a minute or so, refreshing rivulets of lake water ran down my shoulders and disappeared into the folds where my belly rested on my belt. Up here in the park, I should take advantage of the opportunity and try to get rid of the flab I'd acquired in the city over the winter. I could hike over to the woodpile and watch Joan chop wood, then hike back for some lunch.

From where I sat in the boat, I could see a fair piece of the lake. The lodge was hidden in its sheltering bay, and the top of the lake was behind the island north of me. The lake was surrounded by rolling hills which came down gently to the shore. Only on the west side was there an abrupt change from land to lake, and here you would have to stretch things to call it a cliff. It was a big lake to get around in in a rowboat, but not much of a challenge for the Rimmers' big cruiser.

From somewhere out of sight, probably one of the bays that marked the west shore, I heard a motor start after three pulls at the cord. It was a big motor, and it sounded out of place at that hour. Before I had really decided from behind which headland the boat would appear, I saw it coming fast around the nearest point and heading straight for me. It looked like a police launch in the movies scaled down a trifle.

I kept my eye glued to the huge headlight or searchlight mounted in front and watched the bounce of a light craft skipping over the water being chased by a motor that was going faster than it was. It was George, all right. He was too big for the boat too—a massive chest mounted over a large belly, both visible through the water-spotted windshield as the boat cut its motor and came alongside.

"Good morning," I shouted over the noise of the suddenly choppy water. "Nice day."

"If it don't snow. You here again. What's so special about this part of the lake?" He pulled tobacco and papers from his breast pocket and made a cigarette mostly with one hand. When he lit the end, I was happy to see, it flared and reduced its length by half.

"Aeneas told me about this place. He said fish the shadows. At this time of day, that's the west of the first island. Since you ask," I added to see if it got to him. It didn't.

"You should try the far shore in the morning. Unless you're out for splake."

I still didn't know what splake was, but I could see that George didn't consider splake-fishing a grown man's sport. He spat loose tobacco into the water and gunned his motor loudly enough to scare all nearby lake trout out of Big Crummock Lake altogether. He only needed a short burst to land him at the Woodward dock, where he tied up and headed towards the house with a string of fish that looked like they were worth mounting and bronzing or whatever you do to fish you don't want to eat or throw back. He was out of sight for about five minutes, then he returned to the dock and his boat. Running by me, he made sure I got all the benefit of his wake. My little tin fish was nearly scuttled by the turbulence. George looked back and laughed. A simple sort was George, a man of uncomplicated pleasures. He raced his engine so that he disappeared from view in less than two minutes, the boat getting smaller and smaller until it was a dot heading up towards the top end of the lake.

I shipped my fishing rod, put the oars in the water, and rowed myself over to the island. With the boat pulled up on an elbow of sand, I hopped out (soaking my foot) and crawled through the bush to the other end of the island, where I could see the Woodward place from a new angle. I couldn't see it as close as from the boat, but at least I could look at it steadily without being called out for staring.

There was some activity near the car. I'd brought binoculars from the boat and focused on the three-spoked wheel on the hood of the Mercedes. To the right of the car Lorca was talking with Wilf and Spence. The men were wearing shorts and T-shirts, Lorca had a navy blue man's shirt tied in a knot under her bust. Her long tanned legs were set off by white tennis shorts. For a few minutes it looked like some of them were going to drive to Hatchway leaving Lorca, but in the end they all got into the car, which turned around and headed down the lane that rose to meet the lumber trail. In five minutes they'd be driving through Petawawa Lodge. Patten was alone in the cabin. Time for a chess game, I thought.

First, I changed the tape on the machine in the plastic garbage bag, escaping the earwigs that now called it home, and had the first of my sandwiches. With nothing to drink, it went down like cardboard. I tried to sort out what I knew about Patten and, on the basis of that, guess what he was going to do next.

He wasn't up here to get a tan or to try out his fishing gear. With the future of the Ultimate Church in the hands of the U.S. Supreme Court, he was waiting out the decision in the nearest neutral corner. If the eight old men and a woman found in his favour, that the church was all he said it was, then he would return to his mammoth rallies and his TV *Hours of Destiny* until Internal Revenue found another chink in his holy armour. If the decision went against him, that was the end of the line, in the States at least. There would be no sense in returning to face the music. There was no money to pay back so much. It would take him years of pulling himself from one courtroom to another. And in the end he'd have nothing to show for it except that his lawyers would be as angry with him as the tax people. He was smart to have left town before the verdict was announced. But it was unreasonable, in spite of the fact that he was born in these parts, to conclude that this was where he meant to spend his declining years. He was too accustomed to the European hot spots. He was in the park for two reasons. He needed a place to sweat out the decision, and he probably needed to get new papers. It was still possible to get a Canadian passport illegally, and that was probably what he was doing. Passports, like everything else that goes through the mail, take time. I could figure on him being at the Woodward place until the Supreme Court decision and after that, if it went against him, only long enough for the delivery of a passport made out to a brand-new name. Of course, all of this would be yesterday's paper if somebody on Big Crummock Lake got any better at assassination. The job he did on the motorboat needed just a little more luck to put Patten where he wanted him. But practice makes perfectionists.

While I was daydreaming, I saw the subject of my days and nights launch a red canoe from the short dock across the lake. He stowed a paddle and got in, sitting a little off centre and slightly towards the rear. He was coming in this direction.

I tidied away my equipment, throwing in the binoculars, and covered the garbage bag with the groundsheet and the leaves, twigs, and branches that I'd enlisted in the service, and when I could hardly find the place myself, I returned to my boat. My legs were cramped from spying—nature's way of telling me what a dirty business I was in. Once aboard and cast off from the island, I let myself drift while I rubbed away the stiffness.

"Hello there, fella!" His paddle wasn't breaking the water. Although I was expecting him, I didn't hear him.

"You should have a horn on that thing to warn people you're coming. I'm glad I don't have a weak heart."

"It's a trick I learned from the Indians up here when I was a kid. You're not fishing."

"I just pulled my line in to give it a rest. I've got enough fish back in my cabin to feed an army anyway."

"I've been looking at that wreckage. The boat?"

"I know what you mean."

"Well, I found a wire coming out of the motor and attached to the fuel leads."

"I know. I saw that too. That's why I've been hanging around. There's somebody on this lake doesn't like you, Mr. Edgar. If you looked at the fuel lines you'd find that the crimping around the hose has been loosened. When you primed the motor, you leaked fuel all along the fuel leads."

"So when I pulled the motor cord . . ."

"You set off a spark outside the motor. That ignited the gas, and it's a miracle the whole tank didn't go up."

"Not much fuel left in it. That's what saved me. That and you."

"Somebody tried to kill you, Mr. Edgar, and they'll probably try it again. I hope you're planning not to stay around much longer."

"I'm waiting for some news, fella, then I might finish my holiday someplace else. Ever been to Spain?"

"No, I've never been farther away than Miami. No, I went to Las Vegas once. Lost my shirt. No wonder I stay close to home."

"I sometimes think I'd like to live on a yacht in the Mediterranean and call in at all the ports. Ports are where the action is in those places. You really *know* a city when you arrive by water. When you land at an airport, you don't know where the hell you are: those airport strips all look the same." Patten had a wide, flat face above the beard. He had a way of saying something, then smiling to show his good will, when he wanted to. The smile re-asked his questions for him. It was a generous toothpaste smile, and he used it a lot on me, especially when I was winning at chess. I didn't see him wasting samples on Lorca or Spence or the others.

"What line are you in, Mr. Edgar?" I thought I'd see how well worked-out his story was. It couldn't hurt. I'd told him I was in ladies' ready-to-wear. He looked at me, let me have a blast of the smile, then told me he was a writer on religious themes.

"Sort of journalist, right?"

"Yes and no. I've written several books on religion."

"Well, they should sell well. They're the only kind of books you see in some places—greeting cards and religion. But that's not quite my line of country," I said.

"It's everybody's line of country. 'As cold waters to a thirsty soul, so is good news from a far country.' " He really was a preacher. Funny, I had discounted that part, at least in private. I thought the TV image was just that—the TV image. After all you don't expect comedians to always be cracking wise in private. I tried to nod deeply letting Patten's homily take hold.

"I guess I'm just one of those miserable sinners you write about."

"Remember, sin destroys all hope of heaven. It's an abomination."

"Sure it is, but the good Lord'd be out of work if we were all like you. Take me, for instance. I'm an ordinary guy, sort of average. Average height, average weight, average interests. If I'm average, how come I can be such a sinner? If I'm average in everything else, I must be average at sinning too. So maybe things won't be so hard on me in the next world."

"Since God expelled the Evil One from heaven, He has a law that sin can never enter there. 'He that committeth sin is of the devil.' " He gave the address of the quotation in case I wanted to look it up the next time I was staying at a Holiday Inn.

"If that's right, where does Jesus figure in this thing? I thought He got a kick out of reforming sinners. Isn't the deathbed confession of a real bastard worth more than a life of kneeling and praying?" Patten shook his head, fished out a slightly bent cheroot and put it between his lips.

"You don't begin to understand." He felt in each pocket in turn and, not finding anything, went around a second time. He finally cupped his hand over the match I struck on the aluminum gunwale. "This is complicated stuff, fella."

"I can't say I've given it much thought."

"Then, like the man says, you must be ready to take the consequences. Damnation, eternal damnation!"

"Wait a minute. I thought you believed that Christ died for sinners? Well, here I am. What's the catch? Either He did or He didn't. If He didn't, then nothing's changed. God's the eternal bookkeeper with a double-entry system telling who's heaven-bound and who's going to hell. If Christ is the Redeemer, as you say He is, then what's the last hour for being redeemed? A last-minute conversion would suit most people."

"You're stone blind."

"The way I see it is, like here we are, both of us puffing on a smoke and not making total war on anybody. I can't see how that can be wrong."

"You have eyes but will not see."

"I mean what's the trick in saving a teetotal church steward for heaven when you can get a mass murderer? If you're saying that God loves to forgive sinners, then I think that's just fine with us sinners. Where would we both be without the other?"

The conversation was restoring my circulation. My knees felt like mine again. The boats had drifted towards each other, and then Patten held his canoe fast to the rowboat with his paddle.

"With a name like Cooperman, I thought you'd be Jewish." Patten smiled an apology in case his observation gave offence.

"That's right, I am. But in a small town like Grantham, where I come from, you grow up Calvinist no matter what you hyphen it to. In fact the synagogue is at the corner of

Church and Calvin. You can't get more protestant than that."

"Where'd you learn theology?"

"Hotel rooms. Where'd you learn yours?"

"Cooperman, you're a lost sinner. I weep for you and I'll pray for you."

"Can't hurt, I guess." I couldn't think of any rule against it. I felt my ancient heels dig into the bottom of my boat. Enough was enough. I was glad when he brought out a metal chessboard with magnetic pieces adhering to it.

"Now, Sinner, I'm going to beat your pants off." He set up the men and he got to play white. But it didn't help him; after four moves he quit when he saw that his fifth move would involve either check or the loss of his Queen.

"You stay up all night practising that, Benny? Damn it, I resent your book-learned antics. Think you're better than the rest of us?" He went on in that vein. He always did when he lost. But he came out of it after he'd chewed his lip a bit.

We'd been drifting away from the island. We could see the Rimmers' point and a cleared camping spot on another promontory. "This is all second growth in here," he said. "Time was this place was blue with white pine. In the old days half the masts in the British Navy were driven down the Petawawa. I used to listen to old Albert McCord tell his stories about life in the cambooses."

"What?"

"Cambooses—bunkhouse shanties for lumberjacks. The men lived on saltpork, beans, and bread washed down with green tea. Can't say I'd care for it, fella, but there's a fascination it has for me."

"I guess if you didn't get out when you did in twenty years you'd be sitting on the hotel porch in Hatchway with the other old-timers."

"Benny, you've nailed it. That's the name of my nightmare."

Patten continued to tell me things I didn't know about the park. He told me that behind the lakes the land was honeycombed with old lumber trails, some of them well over a hundred years old. He told me of another old-timer named Berners who had a shack on a lake connected to this who'd been a lumberman and a prospector.

"He got his face burned in the air force during the war. Now he lives like a hermit. Like Job, he eats his morsel alone. I'd like to see him while I'm up here. Sort of a distant cousin of mine. He showed me how to survive in the bush if I have to." He looked like he was getting lost in his past for a minute, staring up towards the end of the lake. Finally he slipped his paddle back into the water. "Drop around for a chess game later," he said and I promised. Silently he moved away from the rowboat. He slipped around the far side of the island from his place. I watched him begin to paddle up towards the end of the lake, then bent my own shoulders to the oars. A fish popped out of the water about ten feet from my bow. Was it a lake trout or a splake? I couldn't say.

Chapter Six

It was a funny feeling getting into the car and heading back towards the park gate. I'd grown accustomed to moving no faster than my arms could row, now I was moving at the amazing velocity of fifteen miles an hour over the ruts and bumps of the lumber trail. When I came around one bend, I ran straight into the flood that everybody'd been talking about. The water splashed over my hubcaps and I got the feeling very strongly that it would be a mistake to stop the car and have a look around. There was an old movie about moving nitroglycerine by truck over a road in South America. I felt I was behind the wheel of that truck. With some skidding, I managed to get clear of the water and the muck under it. From there on, it was a straight country run, more or less, to the Kingscote Lake Road and the park boundary. Technically it was supposed to be a two-lane road, but practically speaking only a fool would insist on his half of the road and ignore what was happening across in the other lane. Here ordinary cars took the measure of one another before they tried passing, and trucks stopped to let their drivers discuss the matter from all angles over a rolled cigarette in the shade by the side of the road.

The road past Elephant Lake ran along the shore for a mile. It was a biggish lake with cottages and boathouses dotting the shore and motorboats pulling waterskiers along the line of the farther side. The road was yellow with the fine sand of the area. On a raft about a hundred feet from a green boathouse with white trim, a skinny kid in a blue Speedo went off the high board. She came up a few seconds later hoisting herself back on the raft and tugging at her bathing suit.

When Benny Cooperman from Grantham, Ontario, tells you that the village of Hatchway is small, he means *small*: a handful of stores and a couple of gas stations. It's the sort of place you usually see going past you at fifty miles an hour. I stopped the car in front of the gas pumps at a garage and told the attendant who was trying to decide what to do with a strange-looking credit card to fill the tank and check the oil. Meanwhile, I put a call in to Ray Thornton in Grantham from a phone booth.

"Benny! You still in love with life north of the forty-fifth parallel?"

"It'll be fine when the ice melts and kills off the ice worms and black flies. Listen, Ray, about that party. I think he's waiting for a new passport to come from Ottawa in a false name."

"Those loopholes were plugged years ago. What are you talking about?"

"I'll get you a passport in any name you like. You just have to need one bad enough to take the risks."

"Okay. You'd better stay up there and keep an eye on him. If he leaves, stay with him and don't let him get out of the country without letting me know."

"This is running into money."

"The least of your worries. Just stay with him."

"Okay. I just hope you're near your phone if he makes a dash for the airport."

"Whatever happens, don't lose him. You got that?"

"Remember that when you get my invoice."

"I'm keeping a record. Don't be so nervous, you lucky bastard. Here I am cooped up in the steaming cement jungle and you're up there up to your knees in cool, cool water. Wanna change places? Honest, Benny, the humidity on St. Andrew Street today . . . I'm thinking of calling 'Early Closing.' "

"You're breaking my heart. But next time, I'll take the

right clothes with me. I stand out up here like a stockbroker in a soup kitchen."

"It's so hot right now, Benny, my glasses are steaming."

"Okay. I'll stick it out for a few more days and keep in touch."

"Don't get sunstroke."

"Easy for you to say."

"See if you can get close to Patten."

"I just left him." Ray drew a breath and let it out slowly along the wire.

"Sleep tight, Benny."

"Yeah, it's the only way."

When I came out of the phone booth, the garage attendant still hadn't done anything useful to my gas tank. It took another five minutes. He moved like he'd never seen a car before. While I was waiting, I inspected his stock of bumper stickers, pennants, and various patented bug killers. The place was wired for electricity, and two or three dirty bulbs were burning over the grease pit, but kerosene lanterns were hanging from beams nearby, just in case. For a while I looked at a collection of pieces of metal used to change tires. It looked like with luck he could rotate all my tires in about a week and a half. The principle of the lever was the newest technology in this neck of the woods.

The Hatchway general store had a big sign out front with the word "Onions" in large letters. When you got closer, the words "general merchandise" came into view. It was a large, rambling place with sections added at odd angles as though by whim. Since it sat on a large lot next to the wooden bridge with nothing leaning against it on three sides, it could afford to be eccentric. Inside, I took off my sunglasses and tried to locate myself. To the left it was hardware: sump pumps, wire fencing, paint, roofing supplies, hinges, hasps, bolts, stove pipes, all looking bigger and more serious than in the city. This gave way to kitchenware, with objects I thought had been discontinued in my grandmother's day. I'd walked through most of the store, with its heavy winter jackets standing out in dark reds, blues, and greens, past the meat counter, to the fresh vegetables. I picked up some limp carrots then went on to the canned vegetables. At the check-out counter the girl packed my beans, Campbell's soups, and sardines in a cardboard carton. I was going to buy some canned salmon too, but I remembered what was filling the refrigerator back at the cabin. Just leaving the store, I recognized the tanned legs of Lorca of the Body Beautiful walking past me with a shopping basket. Through the store window I followed her down the street to the Blue Moon Café. Neither the Mercedes nor the Buick were visible. I dumped the groceries in my car, then doubled back to the restaurant.

The Blue Moon was done up with red and white gingham curtains surrounding the windows on one side, and dark, stained gumwood booths down the other. Orders were taken by a girl in a matching gingham apron and negotiated through a hatchway in the wall at the back which connected with the kitchen. Lorca was sitting with her eyes on the front door, so she started her smile before I was more than half-way to her. "Are you alone?" I asked.

"Sure. Help yourself. The boys are off getting the heavy stuff. Have you got a cigarette?" I sat down and passed her my Player's. She fingered the cigarette deliberately like the next steps were the blindfold and the firing squad. She lit up, threw her head back, and blew a smoke ring at the slowly moving wooden ceiling fan.

"Thanks," she said. "Norrie doesn't like it, so I have to watch myself. You won't give me away, will you?"

"For smoking? Don't be silly. Norrie frowns on drinking too, I hear."

"Yeah. That's another of his little games. 'Look not upon the wine when it is red . . .' "

" '. . . for in the end it stingeth like an adder.' Something like that."

"Are you some sort of preacher, too, Mr. Cooperman?"

"Nope. Call me Benny. I just happen to remember the quotation."

"You're funny." She'd ordered coffee, and it arrived at that moment. I ordered the same. She added a pill from a small round pillbox to the coffee and it foamed quietly.

"Lorca, who do you—Lorca," I said, interrupting myself. "What kind of name is that?"

"He was a Spanish writer. My parents' idea. I've never even read anything by him. Mom and Dad were political and arty. I got as far away from that as I could. I grew up in a house where everybody sat on the floor, listened to Bach, and drank tea without milk or sugar. Dad didn't own more than one suit, the one he lectured in. My sister, Marin, says that they were hippies, but it must have been before the hippies came along. Hippies don't wear button-down collars. I never saw a real bed until I left home."

"Okay, sorry, Lorca. I didn't mean to pry into your life story. Have you any idea how long you'll be staying in the park?"

"The quicker we get out of here the better. The woodsy life, trees, you know; we weren't made for one another. I like nature and all that, but I like it better in a book, away from the bugs." She looked across at me trying to improve her case with the intensity of her eyes on mine. "I love Norrie, you understand, but I also have these few weaknesses of the flesh that he doesn't adore. Like smoking. He lives for those cheroots of his, but that's 'cause he's special. All the rest of us have to quit, or pretend to, 'cause we're not Norrie. Back in the States it's easier to look after my weaknesses without Norrie finding out. He's not petty, you know. He just takes these little things seriously."

"Doesn't it seem a little unfair?"

"Oh, you get used to it. That's just his way. He's not like anybody else. He's Norrie."

My coffee had arrived. Now I took a sip. She watched me

and I watched her back. She should have got the boys to take her for one of their joyrides. "Maybe you should get out a little. Do you see anybody at the cabin?"

"Get out more? Are you kidding? Norrie keeps us so bottled up I feel like mineral water. The only guest we've had is an Indian guide."

"Aeneas DuFond?"

"Sure. He came to see Norrie the other day. Oh, it was a treat just to see another face. Now, he's my kind of Indian. He and Norrie go back a long way together. He . . ." She tightened up on the stream of information. I must have started sounding like I was asking questions. I took another tack.

"Do you like Europe?" I asked. That sounded general enough to get restarted on. "Spain, now! What a country!"

"You can have it. In spades you can have it."

"But a port like Palma. The Mediterranean. That's a great little town."

"I was stuck there on a boat for a month. He said I'd love it, and it turns out to be a fucking island. Jesus! I was that far from leaving him that time." She didn't bother to gesture. She was so run down in her self-esteem she didn't think I was watching or listening. Or so I was thinking, when her head tilted. She'd seen somebody come into the café. She took another cigarette from my pack. "For later," she said, getting up. I turned to see Spence at the door. The car was parked out front with the other eager faces looking through the café curtains.

"See you," she said, gathering up her treasures.

"See you," I said, following her with my eyes out the door.

The road back to the lodge went faster. I didn't turn right around; I went back to the general store to buy a hat and a few more things I'd forgotten about. I should have invested in boots. I could have used boots. All in all I was feeling good about the day so far. By the time I got to the raft in Elephant Lake, the sun had shifted and the girl in the blue bathing suit had abandoned it. I saw her on the dock, spread out like a trapper's pelts working on her tan. Just like Aline Barbour.

Before I got to the culvert, I came across Joan's Honda with the hatch door open. I pulled up behind her and turned off the ignition. As I expected, there she was, out in the middle of the flood, her rubber boots awash, pulling at a half-submerged bedspring. I took off my shoes and socks and rolled up my pants. I should have taken them off altogether, because they got completely soaked and muddy during the next couple of minutes. Wading out to help a lady in distress hadn't been ruled out by Ray Thornton, so I thought, why not? At least I would have a fine view of all traffic in and out of the lodge while I was there.

"You're going to ruin those trousers, Benny."

"I'll be all right. Have you found the trouble?"

"Damned beavers, that's all. Just like I told you, they can build up their dam as fast as I can pull it apart." Joan was wearing a faded grey T-shirt tucked into muck-spotted white shorts. Her tanned legs were also muddy. This was my first beaver dam. I'd never even seen a beaver, except on the back of a nickel. I didn't know anything about them except that they built dams, represented industry around the world, and bit their balls off when they became frightened. I didn't have much to go on, but I hoped that my brawn would be of use to Joan.

Joan smelled. The hole she was digging up smelled. In a very few minutes I smelled like they did. Nobody ever mentions the stench of all this unspoiled nature in the travel books. I worked around in the muck to where she was standing at the edge of the submerged road. It was under about a foot of brown water. From the movement of the water near her, I could see that the culvert itself was very close to the bedspring. It had been used to try to keep the beast from building right against the mouth of the culvert.

"There are two other springs down there," she said, " but they are loaded down with waterlogged wood and mud. If you can help me move them, Benny, we can set up the three of them again. That will slow the beavers down until the water subsides, I hope."

I moved farther off the shoulder of the road up to my knees and tried to feel underwater to get hold of the frame of the spring. I could feel the current pulling at me. I saw the way it pulled the dirty water I'd churned up down out of sight in a business-like way. I nearly lost my balance a few times and felt better when I had the spring in my grip so that it could make me a more substantial piece of flotsam. Together Joan and I were able to move it up to the road level. It came with beaver-chewed pointed branches and the usual muck smelling of decay and stagnation.

"The other one's over here," Joan said, her chin nearly at water level and the front of her T-shirt skimming the tide. Underwater, her hands were feeling for the remaining bed-spring. I could see she had something and watched as her back straightened. What she brought up from the bottom wasn't a bedspring. The thing that broke the surface had an elbow and fingers on it. It had been in the water for a short enough time that there was no doubting what it was. She looked down at the open fingers. It looked like a distorted picture of King Arthur collecting his sword from the Lady of the Lake. Only this arm belonged to no lady, and it wasn't clad in white samite. Joan looked at it, looked for a moment as though she was going to shake hands with it — it was a right hand — and then she looked at me. The noise in the air, much more highly pitched than a cicada, was Joan Harbison's scream.

Chapter Seven

Corporal Harry Glover was a tall silent man who was, like most good police officers, better at listening than at talking. He'd taken over the Annex and had placed his regulation Ontario Provincial Police boots under an antique pine table. He'd left his hat in his cruiser, but his gun was on his belt and his notebook was in hand when I went to talk to him. Joan had just come out after a lengthy session and indicated without saying anything that it was my turn at bat.

Glover looked up as I pulled up a kitchen chair. His face was long and streaked with lines, odd in someone who couldn't be much more than thirty-three or so. It was as though all the lines were attached to strings which were all being pulled down at the same angle. His teeth were uneven and his grin was friendly but off balance, favouring the left side of his long, foxy nose. The collar of his shirt was open and the tie pulled to one side. His boots smelled of the scene of the crime, but that was nothing new, we all did.

"What's a private investigator doing at Petawawa Lodge, Mr. Cooperman?" He handed me back my wallet as he drawled out his question.

"Same as David Kipp or Lloyd Pearcy. Catching fish. Not catching fish. Getting a suntan."

"I'll remember that. Thank you for the information. Now back to my question. You haven't been here before, Mr. Cooperman, the way Kipp and Pearcy have. No, this is your first year, your first week at the lodge, and look what's happened."

"You're working on a pretty broad assumption, Corporal. You've no evidence to suggest that there's anything sinister in my being here."

"That's right, but I like to see the way it rubs you. Right now I don't care a pinch what brings you here, but I will later on, and when I do, I want answers not citified malarkey."

"Fair enough. I told you down the road what happened. I told you I'd only seen the dead man once. And I still haven't any idea how he got wedged in against the culvert."

"Dead man's Aeneas DuFond," Glover said, like he was writing the name at the top of the page. It wasn't news; it hadn't been difficult to square away the face in the water with the man who'd told me to fish the shadows the night before. "What do you know about the dead man?"

"I gather he worked at the lodge and has for the last couple of owners. He worked as fishing guide and kept the boats in shape. That's hearsay. I don't know any of that myself."

"What else do you know about DuFond?"

"That's about it, except that there was a man named Trask who didn't get on with him."

"You suggesting something by that?"

"I don't know what you mean."

"I brought out Trask's body last April. He fell off a ladder and bashed his head on the dock he was fixing. He landed in the water and drowned. Nothing funny about that."

"I didn't say there was." I looked at him, and he looked me straight in the eye for a full minute and then said:

"I guess you didn't. What do you think happened out there today, Mr. Cooperman?" I decided to put a little city savvy on this before I handed it over.

"I guess maybe he could have lost his footing and been dragged under. Maybe he was trying to clear the culvert same as we were. Maybe . . ."

"That's a peck of *maybes*. For a start, Aeneas wouldn't have tried to fix the culvert in his clothes. Second, there's a bash on the back of his head that says he didn't get wet as his own idea. I'm no doctor, but until the medical report says different, I'm looking for a murderer. So that's why I'm curious about what a body like you'd be doing up here. Is there something going on, Mr. Cooperman, that I'm going to find out about?"

"Look, Corporal, I've been here for four days. I've collected a burn across my shoulders, a peeling nose, and dishpan hands. I caught a lake trout a yard long yesterday, and nobody was on the dock to see it when I brought it in. We all got troubles. I haven't the glimmering of an idea about why anybody'd want to kill DuFond."

"Well, if that's your story, you're going to be stuck with it. I've got to ask everybody. You're not a special case."

"I know. I read that book too. I saw Aeneas last night right here in the Annex. He left the same time the rest of us did. Except for his brother, Hector; he left half an hour before. We all said good night at about five after eleven. If you want to know what I was doing between then and finding the body, I'm going to be hard-pressed to give you an alibi for the hours from eleven to eight in the morning. I saw Aline Barbour on the dock at eight, then I went fishing and didn't see anybody but George McCord who asked me if I was getting much. That must have been close to noon. Then I drove into Hatchway, did some shopping at Onions', had coffee with Mr. Edgar's friend Lorca at the Blue Moon. Sorry, I don't know her last name. Then I started back in this direction and ran into Joan trying to free the culvert from the beavers." Glover made notes in his book and nodded to the tune of each fact that could be checked for sure.

"Well, until you want me again, I'll be getting back to cleaning my fish."

"Hold your horses. Don't get your shirt in a tangle. I didn't say I was done with you yet. And when the detective inspector gets here from Toronto, he may want more than the time of day from you."

"You recognized Aeneas right away back there. Did you know him well?"

"In this job you have to know everybody. He was on the ball team at Hatchway. I recognized him when I saw him in his pick-up truck. Know his brother better. Hec's not as shy and quiet as Aeneas. Aeneas was a loner."

"You have some more questions?"

"What? Oh, yessiree, I do. Did you go back in the bush either before or after you found the body?"

"No, I just sat down hard."

"What about Mrs. Harbison?"

"We sat there for a few minutes, then I drove to Whitney looking for you. She didn't go back into the bush either. At least she didn't while I was with her." He stretched his mouth into a practice scowl. When he didn't put another question to me right away, I tried one of my own on him. "If Aeneas was as quiet and shy as you say, how could he have collected a bunch of enemies?" He let his face fall slack. He didn't know the answer to that either. We just sat there for another minute.

"I want you well out of my way, Mr. Cooperman. You understand? I know that the inspector will want the same thing."

"I always try to co-operate with the authorities."

"Bull roar! You keep your ass clear of this business. This here isn't the corner of Yonge and Bloor. We don't need private cops messing about, getting themselves lost in the bush, or stuck in the swamp, or drowning themselves. You got all that?"

"Toronto's where you'll find Yonge and Bloor. Grantham's across the lake, and closer in size to Huntsville than to Toronto."

"Same difference. Anyway, I've got to talk to the rest of the people up here, so you'd better clear off. I'll let you know if I want you." I got up with a squeak of the chair and headed for the door.

"You talking to everybody?" I asked.

"Shit, I said clear off!" I cleared off.

Back in my own cabin, I pulled the fish out of the refrigerator and stared at it. It stared back at me with large lidless eyes daring me to guess what the first step in cleaning it might be. I hauled it out the back screen door and flopped it on the scaling bench I'd seen the others use. Two grey cats appeared from under Joan's log house. A scaling knife was attached to the bench with a lank yard of butcher's twine. I took a few passes at the fish, and silver flecks began to fill the air. I worked it steady and carefully up one side and then down the other, flipping the dead weight so that I could work around the fins.

Dead weight. I was back in the water by the culvert. Joan's scream was like something electric, with an amplified bite to it. I blinked to get the picture out of my head again. Fish eyes looked up at me. Better fish eyes. Much better.

Cissy Pearcy cleared her throat. She was a welcome sight. She crossed the frontier drawn by the cats and blinked up at me, shading her eyes with her skinny red hand. Her summer dress had had most of the blue washed out of it by the sun. She had the sort of face that looked as though it had never made up its mind on any subject. Every expression was somehow contradicted by another, running a fraction of a second later. Every smile had a shadow of fear under it, and every jerky motion forward was immediately snatched back. She looked at the fish and then blinked again up at me.

"Hello, there," I said. "The cats have come looking for their supper."

"Lloyd's still out there on the lake, and the policeman wants to talk to him. I don't know what . . ."

"Don't worry. Glover has lots of people to go through. He'll have all the company he needs for another couple of hours."

"Yes, but . . ."

"Don't worry, Mrs. Pearcy. Lloyd'll be back before it gets dark. Long before."

"I know. It's just that, well, he doesn't know what's happened."

"He'll find out all too soon. Let him enjoy himself. Where exactly did he go? Up to the top of the lake?"

"At breakfast he said he might go up back of Little Crummock. He's never been there, and Aeneas would never take him in that way."

"Why's that?" She let a shadow pass over the tentative smile. She frowned, like I was Glover now and she wasn't remembering fast enough.

"Well, I rightly don't know. He just didn't like going in there, that's all. He took Lloyd into Four Corner Lake the day before yesterday, and that's twice as far. My, that's a fine fish you have there Mr. Cooperman!" I gave her my shy but proud smile.

"What was Aeneas like?" I asked. She made a gesture which lengthened her upper lip for a moment, then she began fiddling with the belt of her dress.

"Well, Mr. Cooperman, I'll speak no ill of the dead."

"I'm just curious about what sort of man he was. I'm not taking notes like our friend in there. For the next few days he's going to be on everybody's mind one way or another, and I never really got to talk to him. I feel a little cheated."

"Aeneas was a shy man. Quiet, you know. He'd be sitting there smoking his pipe with Lloyd and me one minute, and the next minute you'd look up and he was gone. I guess it's being Indian. He'd come into the cabin sometimes and bring berries or bait for Lloyd and me and never say a word about it. He never had much to say for himself, but he was a hard worker. I remember one time when Dalt Rimmer owned the lodge, he, Albert McCord, and Aeneas cleared about an acre of heavy bush to make this clearing bigger. They were at it all day and I couldn't tell you which one worked the hardest. Say what you like about Indians, Aeneas DuFond was a hard worker."

"I never said a word against Indians."

"Well, some people around here don't have much use for them."

"Such as?"

"George McCord for one. He isn't half the man his father

was. His mother's a better man than he is. George is just plain mean and envious. It's his nature, I guess. But he's not the only one with prejudice."

"With prejudice? Race prejudice, you mean?"

"There's feeling in some people, that's all I'll say."

"But you're not suggesting that he was killed because he was an Indian, are you?" She thought a bit before she answered.

"Mr. Cooperman, this used to be very rugged country up here. When Lloyd and me started coming north the road was a dirt track most of the way, not just the last fifteen miles. In those days the Indians were part of it all and everybody accepted them. But times have changed and it's the ways of the south that are creeping in along with all the citified gadgets. The new people don't take to outdoor toilets, so we have to dig up the ground and bury septic tanks; they don't like coal-oil lamps, so we have the noise of the generator frightening a body every few hours; they don't like black flies, so they spray the bush. Oh, don't get me started, Mr. Cooperman. You found my Achilles' heel. What I mean is, some people don't like Indians any more than they like the black flies or bad roads."

"Speaking of your Achilles' heel, how did Aeneas and Hector come by those names?"

"Well, it was their mother's doing. She was a remarkable woman. She didn't have much education herself, but she knew all about the Trojan War. She was bound both her sons were going to be teachers. Well, that just wasn't practical in those days before the highways brought up more people from the south. But Aeneas was the elder and he worked so that Hector could spend time in Normal School. That's the way it is up here, Mr. Cooperman, people cover for one another. Hector must be the best-educated Indian for a hundred miles around. And his brother was one of the best guides. The family goes back to the very early days, long before this was a provincial park."

"Joan told me something of that."

"My, Mr. Cooperman, I do admire that fish you have there. When you can buy a fish that fine, I don't see why some people spend all day trying to catch one. Why, that's every bit as good as they catch right here in the lake. Every bit." I was just about to tell her that I caught it when we heard the Delco turn over. Events had bounced Joan out of her routine. "She's keeping busy, you know. She's had such a fright. I don't blame her. I'd sometimes like to talk to that husband of hers. He should be with her at a time like this. The poor child." I didn't know how to get the conversation back to my catch, and in another minute, Cissy Pearcy wandered off like she was hunting cobwebs in the bushes. As I cut the fish up the middle, the cats (there were three of them now) moved closer.

I'd never cleaned a fish before; there are surprising things inside that don't go along with the picture of crisp golden fillets frying in a pan. My heart wasn't in it I guess. I threw the head to the impatient cats. They didn't know about Aeneas. They weren't finding themselves sickened by his death all over again. I cleaned up the mess on the bench with the blade of my knife, letting the guts fall into the pail provided. The cats grabbed the head and tossed it back and forth. I took the more or less filleted remains back into the cabin with me, left one piece on the counter, and put the rest in a dish back in the fridge. Fish for supper. I didn't like the sound of that. Most of the fish I eat comes in cans. Fish for supper is a problem that goes with being alive. Poor Aeneas was beyond problems of breakfast, lunch, and dinner. I put the fillet in the pan. I put the pan on the burner. I turned the stove on and then I turned it off again.

Chapter Eight

Maggie McCord had made herself very comfortable in her little house overlooking the lake. Down at the water a small dock sheltered a beamy rowboat with a small battery-powered motor for trolling as well as George's compact coast-guard cutter. A rack between two trees held three canoes that looked like they were ready to be donated to a museum. The paddles were cradled in a hand-carved holder that had obviously been whittled with love from cedar. A large screened-in porch surrendered glimpses of the lake and island that looked like ads for coloured film. Bluejays were feeding out of a flat can on a rail at porch level and cedar waxwings were eating out of another.

Inside, the main room looked like a Victorian sitting room with antimacassars on the arms and backs of the chairs and the couch. In fact, every flat surface had been covered with a doily or scarf. The biggest of the latter showed a stag at bay with a hound already biting into its shoulder as hunters with spears closed in for the kill. The biggest piece of furniture was a large harmonium. This supported a skinny pyramid metronome on top. A hymnal lay open on the music rack, and I felt a little twinge as I remembered my performance the night before.

"Well, now, Mr. Cooperman, I'm glad you were able to come. That chair's the most comfortable. Men like a chair with backbone. It's we women who are given up to soft ways and luxury. Although, between the two of us, and since it's an old woman I am, I'll say I like a hard chair. A hard chair, like a hard pew, is good for the character, don't you think?" She didn't wait for me to answer, but swung out of the room into the kitchen and continued her polite chatter from there.

I could hear cups and saucers colliding with one another. I got up from my place — I felt like I was taking advantage — and roamed the room looking at knick-knacks on what-nots and taking in the pictures, mostly watercolours and oils of scenes around the lake. They were all signed "R.B." I recognized my island stake-out. A couple of enlarged snapshots, probably from the thirties, showed a man with a pipe and soup-strainer moustache casting into the lake, chopping wood, and holding a coffee pot over a campfire. He looked strong and at home in the woods. The broad braces holding up his heavy trousers were reassuring. I could almost smell the bay rum.

"My late husband, Mr. Cooperman." I turned and she was standing behind me, cutting off most of the light of day, holding a tea tray. "Albert was a good man. He knew this bush like a deer or a bear. He could walk in with a hatchet and a clasp-knife and live off the land for a week or for a month. Never needed a compass or matches. He never could understand how other people were always getting themselves lost up here." She put the tray down on a coffee table made from an old blanket box and straightened herself formally to pour the tea. Her many rings caught the slanting light from the lake and her chins quivered in tandem with the heavy flesh of her arms. She was wrapped in another of her flowing gowns that looked as out of place on the lake as a chipmunk in a boardroom. She was wearing make-up too, laid on a bit thick but not obscuring her best features. She'd been a handsome woman in her day and I wouldn't have minded knowing her in her prime.

"One lump or two, Mr. Cooperman?"

"Please, it's Benny. Everybody calls me that. Three, if you don't mind. I have a sweet tooth."

"When you say three, are you admitting to the full size of this tooth? I have one myself, and I'm glad to see that you are similarly enlightened. Will you have four?"

"With great pleasure, Maggie, with great pleasure." I felt

relaxed for the first time at a tea party. I saw Maggie put four lumps in her cup and stir with one of the little spoons with figures of men on the stems. She must have seen me staring.

"Apostle spoons, Benny. I have a large collection from my mother's family. If you look close, you'll see they're all different." I grinned over my cup and took a slice of chocolate cake from a crystal cake dish. We stopped talking while we both ate, washing the cake down from time to time with a swallow of tea. When she swallowed, Maggie's chins bobbed like the Pacific at the change of the tide. There was something Scottish about the way she said *look* and my name, but for the most part her speech was standard flat Canadian, with maybe a trace of heather around some of her vowels.

"You seem to have recovered from the shock of your unfortunate discovery this morning, Benny." She wanted to talk about the murder. Fine.

"I won't go out without my flashlight tonight."

"Well, I just hope that Harry Glover didn't frighten you. He has that effect on people who don't remember when he used to poach game in the park along with the other boys his age. He tried to—what's the expression?—*grill* me about poor Aeneas this afternoon. It seems an unthrifty extravagance when his superior will have to do it all over again. Or will they have lost interest by that time? Have another piece, Benny, I can see you looking at it." I did. She refilled my cup and I settled back. Maggie McCord knew how to live, and I admired her for it.

"Why would they lose interest?"

"It seems they'll have to admit it was a bizarre accident. Dear me, poor Aeneas never caused such a fuss when he was alive."

"What sort of man was he?" She tasted the question, moved it around in her mouth a little to get the proper flavour of it, then settled back farther in her seat.

"Aeneas DuFond? Albert said there wasn't another guide like him in the park. I don't wish to introduce clichés about

Indians, Benny, but Aeneas was born to it as surely as Hector, his younger brother, wasn't. Hector learned about the bush the way you or I might. But Aeneas just knew. Strange, isn't it. And when you try to explain it in words, it sounds very backward, even racist. I think he was a good man. I'll swear he didn't have an enemy in the world. It's a great shame, really. But I think it's absurd, Harry Glover jumping in and calling it murder. Murder? It's ridiculous." She was prodding her open right hand with her left fist. Small hands, alive with flashing rings.

"What do you think happened?"

"Oh, it was some strange kind of accident. Something quite simple if you could have seen it, but because he can't explain it, we'll probably never know." I nodded at the possibility. "It's like that painter who was drowned in Canoe Lake during the Great War. People are forever thinking up plots that will explain how an expert woodsman and canoeist can be discovered drowned in water he knew as well as I know the recipe to that chocolate cake. I can't remember his name. But it's the same thing with Aeneas." She paused, waiting for my nod of agreement. I didn't agree necessarily, but I nodded to be polite.

"Cissy Pearcy says that Aeneas wouldn't take Lloyd into the bush back of Little Crummock Lake. Why would that be?"

"Superstitious. He'd never go in that way. He didn't hold with that country back in there. Didn't like it, kept away from it. That's the way he was with people, too. If he didn't like you, he kept his distance."

"Who didn't he like that much?"

"Well, for a start he didn't think much of Harry Glover. How's that for an ironic garland?"

"The police aren't everybody's favourite people."

"Something more than that. Something they should know about. And he didn't get on with Mike Harbison, you know, Joan's husband. Mike didn't like the way Aeneas played up to

Joan while he was away in the city. They had a big fight the time Aeneas built that cedar-strip canoe for Joan. He wouldn't take any payment. He just left it for her on the dock and never said a word."

"Sounds like what you're saying is that Joan's husband had a gripe against Aeneas. How did it affect Aeneas? Did he stop coming around?"

"Oh, Aeneas was like the weather. You couldn't out-guess him. He never gossiped, but he knew everything that was going on like he was the keeper of the forest. When a family named . . . no, the name doesn't matter . . . started pumping their septic waste into the lake, I always suspected that it was Aeneas who found out about it and got the authorities to put a stop to it. He was simple that way. Something wrong? Get it fixed. Put a stop to it."

"What about George? How did he get along with George?"

"I don't know that I like that question, Benny. What's a mother to say about a quarrelsome son? George goes his own way. He's not a diplomat. Aeneas rubbed George the wrong way."

"For a man without enemies, Aeneas put a few backs up."

"He did and he didn't. He was a quiet man. Private, you know?"

"And he's always been a guide here at the lodge?"

"Aeneas was here before I arrived, and that's going back. He helped Dalt and Peg fix up this old lumber camp and build more cabins. After they sold it to Wayne Trask he tried to help him out too, but Wayne was stone-headed most of the time and drunk the rest of the time. That man doted on noise. I never met anybody who had a good word to say for him."

"Then the Harbisons bought the lodge from Trask's estate?"

"That brings you up to date. More tea?" I nodded, this time because my mouth was full of cake. Together we'd made a fair dent in it, about as wide as the Niagara gorge. I reached into my pocket and brought a pack of Player's into view.

Then sensing that the time wasn't ripe, I started putting them back again. Maggie set her chins wagging, miming her insistence that I make myself at home, and produced an ashtray to prove her goodwill. I lit up and settled back watching Maggie McCord. Maggie held her pinky out straight as she poured. Very lady-like, I thought, the way her mother had taught her.

"You seem to know a lot about the people up here."

"Well, Benny, there are no books. If you don't read people, there's nothing to read at all. My late husband wasn't a reader, and living with him for so many years I got out of the habit. I used to love reading romances when I was a girl. Of course, I always made myself the heroine. But up here I've learned to read hands and faces the way a gypsy reads tea leaves." I looked into my cup to see what my leaves were whispering about me and my business. I stopped myself from pocketing my hands. "I guess," she went on, "I've always had a gift for reading character. My father noticed it and told me it would serve me well throughout my life. And it has. Albert McCord was a good man, even though he wasn't an educated one. Nobody could have provided for me better. I gladly changed my Highland home for the peace and tranquility of this northern clime. Excuse me. It's a touch of the poet in me."

"Not a bit. I'm on a sugar high myself. That's good cake."

"It's my mother's recipe, and hers before her."

"You said that you came from the Highlands?"

"Yes, and now I'm going to end my days here in the Highlands of Haliburton. My late father was Daniel Cruickshank, a doctor with a practice in Dundee. Have you ever been to Scotland, Benny?"

"No, but I was in a play at school about the escape of Bonny Prince Charlie. I liked the sound of the place names: Rannoch Moor, the Atholl hills; the soft sound of the language: '. . . and those in hiding, no used to sore lying, I'll be thinking . . .' " I looked down into my tea, turning a little warm on the back of my neck. I hadn't recited a line from that play in more than ten years. I tried to concentrate on the initial "T" on the silver service. Then I added, a little lamely: "I always thought it would be a nice place to visit."

"Indeed it would. Albert said that we'd return for a visit, but we never did, we never did." We listened for a moment to the sound of regret running its finger over the dust on the window sill, then I changed the subject.

"I was admiring the pictures. Real oils."

"Painter was a smelly silent old hermit who owned a shack back in the bush. He was a trapper, outside the park, of course, but he pretended to be a prospector. Old Dick Berners said he was looking for gold."

"You used the past tense. He's not there any more?"

"Oh no. He died. Cancer. He went back to his shack after checking himself out of the hospital. He went in there to die. Wouldn't be talked out of it."

"I'll have to break the news to my chess partner in the next cove. At the Woodward place. Mr. Edgar says he knew Berners when he was a kid."

"Oh, he knew him all right. Until the senator took a shine to him, then Dick Berners was just a quaint part of the scenery and not Uncle Dick anymore. Just a funny old prospector. Gold! Imagine prospecting for gold up here."

I heard a screen door slap open and then shut against the spring catch.

"George? Is that you, George?" Maggie had a high, flutey voice for George. I heard heavy footsteps coming into the front room. Looking up I saw yellow Kodiak boots with laces like spaghetti, dirty drill trousers stuffed into them, and a faded green flannel shirt hanging out over an ample beer belly. The face over a thick neck looked a little small. He was like a kid's idea of a fully grown adult: huge feet, tiny head. It was a trick of perspective, I guess. I was sitting down. But I wasn't as far down as all that. George's head was small. He had a red nose the shape of my thumb, deeply lined on either side, and heavy meeting dark brows with frightened little eyes under them. Perched on top of his head was a striped engineer's cap. On George, it looked wilted. He didn't have the features of a big, shaggy dog, but he moved like one.

"Ma, I'm just over to see Harry. He's talking to Cissy Pearcy and he wants to see me next. Oh, sorry. I didn't see you had company."

"George, come in here. You won't keep Harry Glover waiting long. I want you to say hello to Benny Cooperman. He's got a voice like your father's. He's staying at the lodge." They both overlooked our introduction in the Annex the night before. George grabbed the back of a chair like he had no pants on and nodded his how-do-you-do. A smile showed that he'd thrown away most of his molars. It was a flicker of recognition but some miles short of an offer of friendship. I put down the hand that had been about to reach for either his outstretched hand or more cake. He didn't offer a hand, and I thought I'd had enough cake.

"George, say hello to the man." George was a man in his forties, it looked like, but around his mother he acted all of fourteen. He blushed, and his mother settled back satisfied: she'd drawn blood.

"Ma, I gotta talk to you." I shook the crumbs off my lap and got up.

"You're not leaving, Benny?" Maggie's voice sounded surprised, but her hands were already folding her table napkin.

"Yes, I'd better get back to my place. With this Aeneas business, there's lots of things I haven't attended to. Nice to have met you George. Thanks for the tea." I began backing off towards where I remembered the door sound having come.

"Well, now you've found your way, don't be a stranger."

"G'bye," said George.

"Probably see you over at the Annex later for coffee." I found the door and made it slam behind me. I thought of making loud noises on the steps and soft ones coming back to listen close to the door, but I gave up the idea. In a screened-in cottage, you could never tell when you were in sight and when you were invisible. George's reluctance to talk to Glover sounded genuine enough. I didn't much like talking to him myself. Everbody has guilty secrets.

I put a black frying pan on the propane stove and added the last of my butter. I thought about sniffing it, but decided not to. My mother always says that if you have to smell something, you might as well get rid of it. Ma was never stuck in a place miles from a fresh pound of butter. I'd heard that breadcrumbs were a good thing to fry fish in, but I hadn't brought any. So I bashed up some soda biscuits and rolled the fish in them, then, before they all fell off, I dumped the lot into the pan. While I was at it, I put a couple of eggs in a saucepan on the other burner. I could use them for sandwiches, I thought. The eggs floated to the top of the water. I couldn't remember whether that meant that they were fresh or old. Old was my guess, but I put a lid over them so no one would notice. The fish was beginning to look better. The butter was browning it, and the noise sounded very convincing. It even smelled good. I set a place for myself at the table and poured a glass of milk from the ugly plastic pitcher. I considered eating the fish from the frying pan, but I lifted it out onto an ironstone plate. To hell with washing up. Let the maid look after it.

The trout went down very well, if it did taste a little too much like fish. I added a little pepper and salt at the table and was sorry there wasn't a sprig of parsley handy for garnish. Just under the edge of my plate I propped open *The Princess Elizabeth Gift Book*, the only book in my cabin, and dined royally. When I was through, I dumped the plate and the pans into the sink and went out to the pump for a pail of water.

Harry Glover was sitting with his tie pulled loose on the dock having a smoke, watching the shadows darken along the shoreline. I left the pail under the nozzle and walked down to the water with my hands in my pockets, feeling the inshore breeze coming off the lake.

"Nice night," I tried for an opening.

"Uh huh." This was a very conservative play. *Pawn to King Four . . . Pawn to King Four.*

"Still holding the fort all by yourself? No reinforcements in sight?"

"Whitney's not going to send for Criminal Investigation Branch help from Toronto until they've seen the medical report. Too far to come if it's an accident." *Knight to King's Bishop Three, twice.*

"But you don't think it was an accident?" He ignored that.

"Then the coroner will get into the act. God, the coroner has a lot of clout. Under the Coroner's Act, he can seize anything. He could take possession of the whole goddamn park if he wanted to."

"You've decided it was murder. Why?"

"You've never been a corporal. You've never been a cop in a three-holer town like Whitney." I must have missed a few moves, because it looked like he'd castled early on his King's side.

"You can grow old behind a desk in Grantham or Toronto just as fast."

"But hell, Cooperman, time limps like a one-legged centipede in Whitney."

We both scanned the water. The islands were standing out against the farther shore. As the light changed they blended in and disappeared like a startled loon. "A case like this could get me out of the rut for a few days. You know, I've never been to Toronto. I wouldn't mind doing a little CIB work instead of writing up a report on another accidental drowning. I could use some attention, just to remind the force I'm alive."

"So that's why you're going by the book." Another dose of silence.

"Sit down, Cooperman. You make me nervous standing

there. Take a load off your dogs." I pulled up one of the white slatted deck chairs. "Smoke?" I took his package of filtered cigarettes and fished in my pocket for matches. A line of light was moving into the dark reflection of hills on the far side of the lake, a bright knife blade the colour of the sky.

"That'll be Lloyd Pearcy, I guess," Glover said. I nodded, and we both watched the shape of a boat materialize, getting slowly bigger and bigger. For a long time you couldn't hear anything. "He knew Aeneas pretty good," he said slowly. "I guess I better tell him." He threw his half-smoked cigarette into the water. His face looked older than it had this afternoon. I could see the lines it was settling towards—Harry Glover at fifty, with a little grey hair sticking out of the unbuttoned top of his shirt. "I remember one time climbing the stairs to a walk-up apartment over a store in Haliburton. This was some ten years ago. We got there fifteen minutes after some reporter from the paper arrived asking for a picture of the deceased before the family knew that the head of the house had become deceased. A three-car pile-up on Highway 35. It took most of the night to get them settled. Yes, sir: 'We need a picture of your daddy for the paper.' " You could hear the outboard getting closer now. Lloyd's shape was visible in the stern, almost a silhouette. "Lloyd Pearcy and Aeneas did a lot of fishing together. Yes, sir. A lot of fishing, a lot of years."

Chapter Nine

That night in the Annex, away from the smell of scorched hard-boiled eggs, I got to see most of the regulars. There's nothing like a little gore to make people huddle together and congratulate one another for still being counted among the living. The Kipp kids, Roger and Chris, were perched by the fire, supervising the four birch logs in the grate with pokers, waiting for some promised marshmallows. Their father sat in a far corner. He looked hunched, almost truncated, sitting in a high-backed rocker, reading a detective novel.

So far neither the Pearcys nor Maggie and George had appeared, but an ample place had been left for Maggie on the couch by the card table. Des Westmorland was sitting on the piano bench next to the fireplace with Delia, his friend from the end motel unit, next to him. The fire made both their faces look ruddy and took a decade off his age. Delia had brought knitting with her, but hadn't done anything about it. I was watching all this from the coffee urn. The silence in the room was almost noisy. I could hear coffee gurgling inside the urn. I tried to stop it, but I only succeeded in rocking the ping-pong table. The coffee in the glass gauge exaggerated the whole incident. Was this better than sitting alone in my cabin, I wondered. A log crackled and fell sending a shower of sparks up the chimney. David Kipp turned the page of his Simenon. Des Westmorland caught my eye. He introduced himself and Delia. He called her "his friend." It was nice to have it official.

"What do you know about this business about the guide, Mr. Cooperman?" He sounded like I might have some obscure information that was being kept from me. "What was his name?"

"DuFond. Aeneas DuFond. I don't know much. He was a good guide, but a little suspicious and shy. A loner. A quiet man with a touch of superstition who knew his way around in the woods."

"I don't know how anyone can think that we had anything to do with it. Corporal Glover kept Delia with him for nearly half an hour. I mean, really. We didn't come up here to get involved in a backwoods feud." He looked at Delia, who was trying to smile through makeup put on in the dark, or so it looked.

"I ony have two weeks off, Mr. Cooperman. From my job, I mean. I hope Corporal Glover won't keep us here. I don't think he can, legally, without laying a charge I mean. But if one is asked to *assist*, that puts the moral pressure back on one, doesn't it?" Delia Alexander had been a very attractive woman, now that I saw her up close. Good bones don't lie, but I got the idea from the way she was always fussing with her hem even when she was wearing jeans, that she'd blossomed long after the rest of her generation.

"You're in the cabin next to Mrs. Harbison, is that right?" Des was working at getting less intimate. "Terrible thing about that fellow. Time was when you used to need a special government form for reporting the death of an Indian," he said. I tried to show my fascination, but I wasn't at my most convincing. My coffee tasted burnt.

Back at the fire, the Kipp boys were busy with marshmallows in a silent, businesslike way. This wasn't their idea of a picnic either. Joan Harbison stood nearby, a new arrival, suddenly there, keeping her eye on young Chris, whose marshmallow was ablaze. The couple on the piano bench began to console one another, and it built up a wall between us, so I took off towards Joan.

"Harry Glover told me that Hector and Aeneas were seen arguing outside the hotel in Hatchway Wednesday night," Joan said.

"Does that mean he's decided to pin it on the brother?"

"I don't know anything," she said, and looked like I'd taken a swipe at her with a two-by-four.

"They were friendly enough in here last night," I said, putting my hand on her shoulder to make things better. She squeezed out a pained smile and moved off to pour herself coffee.

Maggie and George were suddenly in the room, she in one of her voluminous caftans, and George in yellow boots and his usual sartorial indifference. He laid a four-cell flashlight near the coffee urn and drew a cup for himself and one for his mother. His nod in my direction was not convincingly friendly.

Maggie and George McCord used the lodge, or at least the Annex, as though they were paying guests instead of next-door neighbours. So did the Rimmers, but at least they were former owners. I wondered whether Joan's hospitality ever extended as far as the Woodward place and its tenant.

In a few minutes everybody was seated around the fire with Maggie acting as keystone in the arch. Soon the Pearcys came out of the night, with a squeak of the double screen doors. Tonight we were all moths drawn to the fire. It was good to be warm, with company, and alive.

"Well, we're a bloodthirsty lot," announced Maggie after looking around. "Your faces are a study. Mine too, I'm sure. A lynch-mob without a rope, that's the lot of us tonight. I don't think I could bid straight, Cissy, so there will be no cards tonight." Lloyd laughed a little too loudly, and stifled it when he found himself alone. There was the kind of silence in the room that stepped on talk. Nobody else said anything, so Maggie started in again, keeping the show together, keeping up her spirits, whistling in the dark. "I know what," she said, "Let's tell murder stories. The messier the better. It will clear the air. It will work like a dose of salts. Come along. The policeman's gone back to Whitney. I'll start the ball rolling myself. Let me see. Did you know that when they hanged the notorious Captain Kidd, the rope broke and they had to do it again?"

"Really, Maggie, I think you could lift our spirits without dangling our feet," Joan said, and everybody laughed.

"They say that the man who invented the guillotine was beheaded on it," said Cissy Pearcy in a confidential voice that allowed only two or three words to burst out at a time.

"Justice for all," Lloyd chimed in.

"It's easy to make jokes," said Westmorland. "I'm sure he deserved what he got."

"What Dr. Guillotin got," said Maggie, "was an immortal name and a pension from the French Assembly. The man died in his bed long after the Revolution."

"So much for poetic justice," I said, with a look at Westmorland.

"Well," said Cissy with some effort, "it may not have been *him*, but somebody who invented something was killed on it. I'm sure I read it."

"You're quite right, Cissy. You're thinking of Lord Morton. The enterprising Earl of Morton introduced into Scotland a guillotine-like machine he'd seen in Halifax, Yorkshire, for the execution of felons. Long before Dr. Guillotin. They called it the Scottish Maiden, and the poor earl was one of its victims." Cissy smiled at Maggie for this help and then at everybody else in the room.

"Where on earth did you learn that?" Joan asked from where she was leaning against the fireplace.

"Ask any Scottish schoolchild. We were all solemnly taken to see it in the Edinburgh Museum of Antiquities."

"There's a sort of guillotine in the police museum in Toronto. I've seen it there," said Delia Alexander. "Horrible thing. A man named—what was it?—Malbeck, John Malbeck, made it to commit suicide on. About a dozen years ago. It was in the papers. Terrible, really. He worked for Revenue Canada."

"A fitting end," said Maggie, and George began to laugh at the thought of it.

"What would make a man do a crazy thing like that?" asked David Kipp, moving closer to the group. We all looked to Delia for the answer.

"It appears he was some kind of mystic, belonged to a devil-worshipping sect. He was insane, of course, and if I remember he was disappointed in love." George sniggered.

"In Germany," David Kipp said, "there is a Crime Museum at Rothenburg. That's where they keep the Iron Maiden. Michelle and I saw it when we were in Germany."

"I thought that 'Iron Maiden' was just a political term of abuse," said Des Westmorland. Our conversation, in spite of its grizzly subject matter, was integrating Des and his friend into the group, as my old counsellor at Camp Northern Pine might have said. "Was there really such a thing?"

"In the olden days it was a wooden shame-coat that women who committed certain crimes were forced to wear," said Kipp.

"With steel spikes on the door," whispered Cissy, making Her s's hiss like coiled snakes.

"Well, I don't know about that," shrugged Kipp. For a moment it looked like Maggie was going to regain the spotlight, but Kipp had tasted the power of regurgitated travel yarns. "There is another crime museum in Paris. It's the official collection of the Paris Police Department. I've seen that, too. It has all the usual Black Museum sorts of things, along with a history of law enforcement from the earliest times. There are documents dealing with the Revolution, and mannikins wearing the old-fashioned police uniforms as they developed through the years. I spent most of an afternoon there. Fascinating."

"Get back to the 'usual Black Museum sorts of things,' " said one of Kipp's boys. It was a mistake, because his father at once ordered Roger and Chris out of the Annex to bed. That seemed to lighten spirits a little.

"Too bad he can't hear this," David said. "That part of the collection is full of shabby-looking knives, daggers, and guns. I suppose if you're looking for something specific it might be interesting, but to me a bread knife looks like a bread knife whatever its sordid history."

"That sounds very brave. I wonder whether you'd spend the night there."

"I don't believe in ghosts, if that's what you mean, Maggie."

"Oh, these new rationalists! I'm sure that the angels weep for you."

"If any place has ghosts," said Joan Harbison, "it's this place. The police left the body of Dick Berners, the old prospector, in this room overnight. And three months later Wayne Trask was laid out here waiting for them to arrive from Whitney."

"Albert told me that two lumbermen were killed in an accident on a log boom out on the lake. They brought the frozen bodies in here and stood them up against the wall like sticks of timber."

"Honestly, Maggie. You're a storehouse of the strangest information."

"Well, I have a head full of odd things, I'll not deny it. I have to fill my head, you see, I have no books."

"What was this fellow Trask like?" I asked Maggie. "From what I hear he wasn't a very savoury character."

"Unsavoury. Yes, that's the word for him all right. For a while the police thought he'd been murdered; there were many hereabouts who'd have liked to have seen him dead. But they gave up that line."

"He did have lots of enemies," Cissy said. "He was a madman. He used to chase women in here. One time he held a shotgun to his own wife's head, and she ran out through the bush naked as a jay-bird and flagged down the first car that came by."

"He spent time in the loony-bin one year," Lloyd added, looking at me for some reason.

"They ran him out of Cornwall, Ontario, for fooling around with a doctor's wife," said Maggie.

"He went after one of my girls one time," Lloyd said. "He was a crazy man for the drink, you know. Once he got to drinking there was no holding him."

"He was the former owner of the lodge? Is that right?" That was Des Westmorland again. He was taking in more than I imagined. His lady beamed shy approval of his taking an interest. Cissy, suddenly animated, nodded.

"Flora, his wife, was the only one who did any work on this place. Wayne Trask didn't lift a finger. And when she left, the place just ran downhill. After Trask died, they practically gave the place away it was so rundown."

"Flora was a great one for crocheting," Lloyd added. "She sold tea-cosies, scarves, and sweaters to the people staying at the lodge. That's how she put by the money to leave Wayne. She left for a visit to see her mother and never came back. Practically with just the clothes she was standing in. How do you like that?" We all made noises by way of answering, and he began to chuckle to himself, very much aware that he had his audience hooked.

"Trask, you know, old Wayne was a character though. He came up to Sudbury one time and I gave him some work. He was coming off a tear and was short of money. He'd come in to see me and we'd have a drink, and he'd stay and have a few. Then I kept him on the job after there was nothing for him to do—just out of sympathy like. And then one of the last times I saw him, my young lad was with me up here at the lodge, you know. The lad had a Coke and Trask said, 'That'll be thirty-five cents, please.' I thought he was making a joke."

"After all the meals he'd had at our house," Cissy put in.

"Was Trask a prospector?" David asked, a little confused.

"You've been hearing about Dick Berners. He was the prospector," Joan Harbison said. As though she was feeling a sudden draught, she picked up a heavy piece of birch and threw it on the fire, sending up another shower of sparks.

Everybody was quiet for a minute.

"Old Dick was a joke all over," said George sitting at his mother's side. "He went prospecting all right, but any fool knows there's nothing to prospect for up here. And even if he found a ton of gold, he couldn't mine it because it's illegal to do any mining here in Algonquin Park."

"Albert and I used to have many a laugh at poor Dick's expense. He was so sure there was gold up here, they say he wrote the Department of Mines. All he ever found was a chunk of quartz, no different from the one Joan's got the door propped open with. Claimed that he should know about gold because he was a mining engineer one time. Albert knew all the men who used to work for the Dunlap Lumber Company in the old days and he found out that Dick was just as much of a joke back then as he was in our time. He'd go into the bush, stay there a few weeks, then come out again. He always said he was getting closer and closer. He finally retired somewhere around Huntsville or Haliburton. He'd done pretty well with his trapping, you see; that was his main occupation. He lived comfortably until he got sick. That's when he came back." Maggie was looking me in the eye. I was beginning to fidget in my seat.

"Old Dick came back up here to die," Lloyd said. "No two ways about that. He had cancer and he came back up here, went in to his old camp, and died."

"Oh, he was a character," George said. "You could smell him coming through the bush. And always covered with soot from his campfire. You wouldn't want to get closer to him than the end of the cottage units across the field. He was *that* high." He started to laugh through his teeth, as the picture of old Dick became clearer.

"Oh, let's hush up about poor Dick Berners," Maggie said, holding her puffy hand to her cheek like Queen Victoria. "I'm sorry I encouraged this. He was a good man, better than any of you will ever know." She didn't enlarge on that. It was the sort of statement that you have to leave alone. It tended to kill conversation. Joan took a look at her watch and left the Annex.

"Nobody mentioned the incident that happened half a mile north of here at the Woodward place. That fellow had a close call and it was no accident." I said this and looked around to find guilt written on one of the assembled faces, but all I saw was either blank ignorance or very good play-acting.

"He must have had God on his side to have escaped," Maggie said, making a private joke.

"Poor Aeneas wasn't so lucky," Cissy said, half whispering to herself. It was the first time the name in the back of all of our minds had been mentioned. Poor Aeneas.

"You wanted him to take you fishing in the lake northeast of here, didn't you, Lloyd?" Lloyd grinned uneasily.

"Little Crummock, you mean?"

"Yeah. Why wouldn't Aeneas take you in there?"

"Damned shame about Aeneas," said David.

"I hear he would never go into Little Crummock, Lloyd." My voice sounded a little more than casual. I tried holding my breath.

"He'd go anywhere else," said Lloyd.

"But not into Little Crummock." I stayed with him.

"Superstitious."

"In what way?" I asked, and Lloyd slowly leaned across to me.

"He said he wouldn't walk into country where he's heard thunder during a thunderstorm without seeing any lightning. That's what he told me."

For a moment all you could hear was the steady throb of the electric generator. Nobody said anything, and then the lights began to fade as the generator died. The silence that took hold in the dark seemed a million miles deep.

Outside, a few minutes later, the stars were out, more than I'd ever seen before. I looked north for the dipper and found four rather misshapen ones. Cissy and Lloyd bent their necks with me for a few minutes, carrying the indoor silence outside.

"That Maggie's a caution," said Lloyd.

"She means no harm," Cissy explained. I looked at both of them, puzzled.

"She is colourful," I admitted.

"Yes, I love her stories. She just lets them carry her away too far, that's all."

"I don't understand. She has a good imagination."

"She has that! In spades. But you see, Benny, she makes things up. You have to take what she says with a grain of salt."

"A grain?" said Cissy. "You mean a cupful! You can't believe a word she says, she makes everything up."

"She wasn't born in Scotland. That's one thing for a start. Oh, I allow she was over there one time."

"But those stories?"

"Something she heard or read about years ago. I think sometimes that she really believes her stories."

"Is the truth about her so awful?"

"Not awful, just humdrum, like the rest of us. She has a way of talking, though, that hints at a past. I think it's because she looks like a woman with a past. She just plays it up."

"She comes from Cornwall, Ontario. How's that for a past?"

"I'll have to sleep on that," I said.

Chapter Ten

"What are you daydreaming about?" Patten looked cross. I'd beaten him in the first game and I was throwing this one his way with a silly Queen's Knight's Pawn opening that wasn't going to do me any good. Patten was wearing a buff-coloured safari jacket over his usual torn khaki shorts. Without his sunglasses, he looked less menacing. His eyes were narrow and appeared to be lidless, as though the brows themselves were enough protection for those deep blue, cautious eyes. Up close, the end of his nose was red and shiny, with tight skin pulled over a bum-shaped bulb. This and the thin lips seemed to have been added to his broad face by accident, clearly having been intended for a long lean face. But that was the chemistry that worked so well on television: his features had the look of a man who'd not had a square meal in months but were set in a face that was well fed and content. The beard confused things, of course, but nobody'd ever seen him with a beard on television.

"I'm wondering what plans you have for my unfortunate Bishop."

"I have no plans, fella, only designs." He didn't rub his hands together, but he might as well have. I hadn't meant to pass the game to him in a brown paper bag.

"Did the Provincial Police come up here?" I asked touching the wrong piece and then pushing it into the glare of Patten's Queen.

"Oh, they arrived. But we're just poor American tourists who see, hear, and speak no evil. That corporal bought that. We're just minding our business. Too bad about that guide. The Lord giveth and the Lord . . . Check-bloody-mate, fella!" He had me all right; a little sooner than I expected. I examined the positions while Patten did everything but an imitation of a victorious fighting cock. At last I shook my head slowly so that the inevitability of it all showed. Clean living and the good life won again.

"One more?" he asked, already rearranging the men.

"Nothing doing. When I'm licked, I stay licked."

We'd been playing inside the house this time. It was still early. I'd done an hour's pretend fishing near the island. I hadn't tied a hook on my factory-tested line. I was busy thinking about a couple of incidents that happened before I went to bed the night before. And while Patten was busy in the narrow kitchen of the cabin making a fruit drink for both of us, I had a chance to think about them again.

After the Annex lights went off, the night before, the party dispersed. Everybody went back to their cabins, or at least to the cabins of their choice.

I took a walk down to the water and watched the lights blinking through the trees at the Rimmers' across the lake, and listened to the conversation of the idle rowboats tied up to the cleats. I sat down in one of the deck chairs, lit a cigarette, and tried to make my mind a blank.

I was nearly dozing off, when I heard the sound of paddle strokes coming quietly over the water. Under the stars, the lake was dead, a dance floor lit by a mirrored globe. The canoe came closer, out of the shadows near the shore. It was Aline Barbour. She beached the canoe, stowed her paddle, dragged the boat a short distance up the beach so that the bow was on grass, and turned the craft bottom up. There was a tidiness about her movements that was almost like dancing. Or maybe I just like to watch other people do the manual labour. Anyway, she wasn't hard to watch.

"Nice evening for a paddle," I said, not raising my voice more than was necessary to cover the distance. She turned around quickly like I'd caught her signing my name to a cheque. She located me after a second on the dock.

"Oh, it's you. You startled me." She was wearing slim jeans

and a dark denim jacket over a tight turtleneck pullover. Her running shoes made squishing noises as she joined me. "You shouldn't sneak up on people like that." I mimed innocence and pulled up another chair. She settled into it and accepted my pack of Player's with a smile. "All by yourself?" I nodded the story of my life, and she changed the subject. "It's a little cool out there tonight." She lit the cigarette with her own butane lighter. Her face looked bright surrounded by her dark hair, but her cheekbones were flattened until the flame disappeared. For a moment, as she crossed her legs, I thought of her rubbing suntan cream on her shoulders that morning. Funny how clothes change things. She was still a very sexy lady, but somehow different.

While I was taking her apart and putting her back together, she was giving me the same business. "You've got a burn on your nose," she said. I ran my finger over the roughness and peeling.

"Is this your first time up here?"

"Yes. Wonderful, isn't it?" I agreed, and we sat and smoked and listened to the whippoorwill auditioning from a distance. "Those stars," she said, and I looked up towards the Milky Way. "Each one of them is a sun with whirling planets. Do you think they know as little about us as we know about them? Are there networks of information that we know nothing about? What do you think, Mr. Cooperman?"

"I'm no expert on space travel or flying saucers. Do you put stock in them?"

"Oh, there are presences. I call them presences. I think I'm Manichean. I believe in the presence of evil. Good is only a temporary absence of evil. There's no end to it, really. It just goes on and on like those suns up there." Again we both sat rubbernecking the universe. At last she stubbed out her cigarette on the dock and said good night. I liked the sound of her voice, even if I didn't follow everything she said. Then I remembered that Aeneas had started to say something about knowing her. What was it he said? I looked off into the trees after she'd gone and tried again to make my mind a blank.

Patten was making a noise in the kitchen. When I collected myself back to where I was, I could hear him, but only gradually did I recognize that he was singing. It was an old hymn that I remembered from high school:

> *Our Shield and Defender,*
> *The Ancient of days,*
> *Pavilioned in splendour,*
> *And girded with praise*

Patten couldn't carry a tune in a wheelbarrow, but he seemed to be enjoying himself in there. He was making a Hollywood production number of his juice-making.

I drifted back to the night before on the dock at the lodge. It was some time after Aline had left. Had I drifted off? I remember hearing voices. They were familiar because I'd been hearing them in my head before I opened my eyes. There was a nagging insistence to them, like the banging of a window blind when the wind comes up in the night. At first I couldn't make out what was being said. What sense can you make from the Morse code of a badly anchored blind?

"You're just being silly David. Someone will hear us."

"I don't care who hears. I've got to talk to you."

"I'm sure it's nothing that won't wait until morning. Look, you're very sweet, and I don't want to hear you say anything you'll regret."

"Joan, please listen to me."

"Not if it's the same tune you were humming before. I don't think you're thinking straight."

"I'm not thinking at all, Joan. Listen to me!"

"No! Let go of me. David! Christ, David, someone will hear!" I couldn't see anything from where I was sitting except the odd falling star slipping out of place and dropping towards the rim of the lake. I knew that if I turned, cleared my throat, and got up, I'd be making a mistake, so I kept my eyes on the Big Dipper. Gradually the human noises were replaced by those of bull frogs and crickets which didn't seem to give a damn if anybody heard or not. I gave them another fifteen minutes and then went in to bed. I had another cigarette lying on the bed. I didn't bother to light a candle.

"Ouch! Damn it!" It was Patten and I again returned to the present. The exclamation was followed by the sound of a bag of groceries dropping to the floor. Then something broke, a glass, probably. I rushed into the kitchen to see Patten sucking his fingers. There was blood on his cheek.

"What happened?" I took the hand and ran it under the cold tap. Thank goodness for the senator's modern conveniences. It didn't look serious; a few jagged cuts on his fingertips. I repeated the question; he nodded towards the split paper bag with oranges rolling all over the floor.

"I don't see anything. Was it something in the bag?" As I said it, I could see blood on the brown paper. Patten held his hand under the tap and I bent to see what was inside the broken bag. I'd like to say I did this fearlessly, but the truth is I probed inside with a long-handled wooden spoon with fragments of dried spaghetti clinging to it. Oranges, lemons, a couple of limes, and the screw-top from a large bottle of ginger ale or soda water. There was no bottle. Then I saw that the bottle cap was the problem. The metal flanges that held the screw-top secure on the bottle had been bent out, away from the round top, turning the innocent cap into a mean-looking jagged cutting wheel. Anybody probing the bottom of the bag would end up with his fingers gashed. I spooned the bottle cap closer and sniffed it. I couldn't detect anything sinister like burnt almonds. But to be on the safe side: "Come on," I said. "Wash out your mouth and try to vomit."

"What? I cut myself. It was a shock, that's all."

"Do what I say or you could be dead in ten minutes." It's surprising what saying a thing like that does. I heard retching within seconds. "Drink some water. Do the same thing again and wash your cheek carefully." I began to recall the clever murderous implements in Rex Stout and Ellery Queen. I guess I panicked. "Come on!" I pulled him by the wrist into the parking lot in front of the cabin, first making sure to wrap the strange weapon in a dishtowel. Spence was sitting talking to Wilf, both stretched out on lawnchairs with a cribbage board between them.

"What's up?"

"Mr. Patten's had an accident. Get him to the nearest hospital on the double. Bancroft's closest. There's not a second to lose. I think he's been poisoned."

The cards and board went to the ground and Spence had the Mercedes turned around in seconds. It took three-quarters of an hour to get to Bancroft. They dropped me in Hatchway from where I telephoned through to the hospital. I told the senior voice at the other end what I suspected and what I'd done by way of first aid. I told him about the bottle cap and warned him to be careful.

When Dr. Gemmell hung up in Bancroft, I felt abandoned by the action in Hatchway. There was no way back to the lodge. I didn't have taxi fare either on to Bancroft or back to the park. I told myself that getting overly excited only increased the feeling of abandonment, so I tried to make myself calm for Patten's sake. Christ! Then I remembered: I'd called him Patten. It was game over for me even if he didn't die.

Chapter Eleven

I knew that Ray Thornton wouldn't be in his office on a Saturday, so I called the number just to be right about something. It rang five times before I hung up. If he'd been there I could have told him all about the excitement of the last hour. I could have told the recording device on his phone if he had one, but Ray must be the last guy in the world to hold out against the electronic age. That reminded me of another hold out. I phoned my mother in Grantham.

"Hello?"

"Ma, it's me, Benny."

"You're back? You just left town. You can't be home already."

"No, I'm still up here. Looks like I'll be here for another week."

"I see. So, you're having a good time up there, Benny?"

"My nose is peeling. I miss your cooking."

"Canned salmon you can get in any store, Benny. I'll melt in this heat. Benny, you remember the last time you were up in the woods? Camp Northern Pine?"

"A little."

"You remember the load of rocks you brought home?"

"Ma, I was ten years old. What do you want from a ten-year-old? Handmade moccasins? Besides, they weren't rocks, they were quartz. That's next door to gold."

"It could be next door to Baron Rothschild. Next door is next door. I nearly had a fit wondering what you'd done with your clothes I stitched the labels in. Benny what could have—"

"Ma, that's twenty-five years ago. You've got a memory like an elephant and this is long distance. How are you?"

"I'm fine, your father's fine. 'Fine' is the word around here this week. I get my hair done and your father says it's fine. I made borscht to serve cold with sour cream right out of the carton from Mr. Atos at the delicatessen, and your father says that's fine. I'm sure if I told him the doctor told me I had something inside me, that would be fine by him too."

"You always exaggerate. You miss me?"

"Who's got time? 'Miss me?' You'll be home before you've gone. But you know, thinking of that summer camp; it takes me back."

"Never mind. I haven't got time. I just called to let you know that I'm okay."

"I'll tell your father. You never know. He might ask. I'll tell him you're fine."

"Goodbye."

I walked through to the edge of town, past the feed store, the drive-in hardware outlet, and the marina that serviced most of the boat engines in the area. Beyond all this I followed the road to the wooden sawmill. Here a chain lifted logs out of the lake and hauled them inside. The saw blade whined like a mosquito's dive-bombing warning. Through an opening, I could see a man at a machine like a tractor shuffling the rough-cut lumber like playing cards. I watched them squaring timber in another machine and running logs through a battery of vertical saw blades that turned them into two-inch planks.

A little further along the lake front, two teen-age boys were fixing a dock, nailing planks across the horizontal rails and cutting them off even. The echo of the hammering suggested that another dock was being fixed just out of sight behind a boathouse. There was something very satisfying about watching them work and I watched them for half an hour.

When I got back to town, I caught Ray at his house and taking calls. I gave him the play-by-play account of what I'd been doing with his money and he kept grunting "Yeah" every few minutes to show that he was still on the line.

"Ray, I've got a couple of favours to ask you." He grunted assent within reason. Ray would give me his partner's right arm, but he'd keep reminding me what it cost him. He always put me in the part of someone asking for the moon, and he grudgingly would hand it over. I gave him the plate numbers of the cars in the lodge parking lot and asked if he could get someone to run a check on them.

"Is that all? Are you finished?"

"I want you to find out for me what you can about a woman named Aline Barbour. She's a theatrical designer. She's registered at the lodge and has been keeping an eye on Patten whenever I go off duty." I could hear Ray's breathing getting irregular on his end of the wire. "Do you have two people on this assignment, Ray?"

"First of all, you don't go off duty, and if I'd wanted a relay team I would have gone to a real detective."

"Hell, you could have gone to the Secret Service."

"Benny, how badly off is our friend?" I told him I thought he'd live. I mentioned my first aid and the health of my reflexes under stress. I could hear him shifting ears on the phone so I tried to regain his attention.

"Look, Ray, somebody in Algonquin Park isn't playing games. He doesn't want Patten to leave here, whatever the U.S. Supreme Court rules. He's had two narrow squeaks. He isn't going to survive a third. The odds are against it. How does your client stand if Patten gets killed? Think about it. As it is he's lucky to be alive. Lucky I've read so many mystery stories. Nobody outside a book plays games with bottle caps dipped in poison."

"Well, Benny, you hang in there." Sure. It was time for him to water the lawn or trim the hedge. I held on to his sleeve over the wire for another question.

"Ray, your pulse rate went up when I mentioned Aline Barbour. You don't want to keep stuff like that bottled up inside; it'll give you gas. What do you know about her?"

"Yes, well, yes, I happen to know who she is. But I don't

know what she's doing at Petawawa Lodge. That's not part of the script. I'll have to get back to you on that. Okay?" I nodded assent and he barked at me to buy some decent hiking shoes.

I walked to the café for a cup of coffee.

"You staying up at some lodge around here?" the waitress asked. I was so surprised to be asked a direct question, I let a little coffee go down the wrong way, and the two of us got better acquainted while I nearly choked.

"Uh, huh," I said when I could.

"Land, you oughtn't to talk with your mouth full. Which one? I hear that Neary's is half empty this year and that Coleson's didn't even open up. It's too expensive you know, what with the price of gas. I hear them complaining about it all the time in here. It'll cost you twelve dollars in gas to get to Neary's and back. Tim has to charge fifteen now, if you want his taxi. Used to be five dollars."

"Everything's going up. I'm at Petawawa Lodge."

"Oh yes. Young couple running it now. Used to be Wayne Trask."

"Yes, I know."

"His Flora came through town one night, and you wouldn't believe it, but the woman didn't have a stitch—"

"I heard about that. They say he was a terrible one for the bottle."

"Dead drunk the night of the fire, you know."

"You make it sound like yesterday."

"Now, what about yesterday? Poor Aeneas. That was a shame about him, a nice man like that, never a bad word to say about anybody."

"He lived in Hatchway, didn't he?" A question was beginning to form: was there a link between Aeneas and Patten, apart from old times?

"Aeneas rented the second-floor front room from Mrs. Kramer across from the liquor store. Aeneas scarcely used it in the summer. Preferred camping out. Paid only fifteen dollars a week, and it's a big room. Used to be the master bedroom before her husband died. Maud said she should be able to get twenty-five now without even painting."

"Across from the liquor store?"

"It's the place with the bird bath and the wind chime. It was built for Horace Waggoner, you know, of the Waggoner Mill, but he sold out in the thirties to Ed Kramer who was with the Hydro . . ."

I didn't stay to hear more than another twenty minutes of oral history. I paid up and walked down towards the liquor store. The house across the street was a buff-coloured frame house with a sagging veranda across the front and most of one side. The front door had stained glass in the fanlight over it, giving a cranberry look to a hall chandelier that hung just inside. The wind chime was rusty and soundless, the bird bath rusty and dry. I turned the old-fashioned bell in the middle of the door, and presently saw a woman coming through the lace curtains covering the two oval glass panels in the door.

"Yes?" It was a short, grey-haired, rather transparent woman who answered the door. There wasn't very much to her, apart from the freckles of age on her face and wrists, a hair-net, and steady eyes.

"Are you Mrs. Kramer?"

"That's right. Are you another policeman?"

"I hope I'm the last of them."

"Well, I declare I hope you're right. If I've swept those stairs once, I've swept them a hundred times. You aren't going to ask more questions?"

"Not many, I promise."

"I've heard promises before. I'm an old woman. A woman grows old on promises." She led me through the hall and up the banistered stairs to the front room. "I'll leave you alone in there to look around. Most of the things belong to the house. The carvings and pictures are his." I opened up the door to Aeneas DuFond's room and went in. There were two large windows on the street side, a high ceiling with a plaster moulding all the way around. There was a centred plaster medallion from which dangled an old twisted electric cord ending in a light fixture of monumental ugliness: a cross between a seashell and a hoop skirt. The walls were covered with a patterned paper running through the various coffee tones and set off by watermarks which looked serious. The bed was narrow, but neat marks on the worn carpet showed the bigger bed that the Kramers used to occupy, or maybe the Waggoners. There weren't very many personal things: a yellow hard hat in the cupboard, yellow working boots like George's, overalls, plaid shirts in flannel, plastic slickers, rubber boots, hip-waders, and, at the back, a pair of snow-shoes. The chest of drawers revealed underwear and shirts in various stages of wear. He darned his own socks; I found evidence.

The paintings on either side of the big dark dresser were amateurish and crude. I wasn't surprised to see Dick Berners's name signed in the bottom right-hand corners. Dick had a belly full of expression, but the trail out was badly marked. He was on a par with the restaurant decorators in Grantham who sign their murals with their names and their telephone numbers. The drawers yielded no letters, laundry tickets, racing forms, or code messages. The OPP were pretty thorough, even up here. The best I could do was a wad of chewing gum. It had been well and truly chewed then wrapped in its own well-known Spearmint wrapper. I couldn't make much of it, so I went back to the paintings. One was a view of a lumbermill from a lake. I recognized the smaller building next to the mill as the Annex at the lodge. The hills behind were about the right shape, but I doubt whether they'd ever achieved the degree of mauve shown above the rooftops.

The second picture was more ambitious. It was an interior scene with people in it. There were three of them, two men and a woman, standing in the middle of an octagon drawn on the floor in orange. Behind them a snake dangled like a

fire hose on a cross. The figures were wearing black capes;
the woman was clearly naked under hers. Three candles were
shown burning at the angles of a triangle drawn on one of the
eight sides of the octagon. A pot or cauldron was steaming
inside the figure near the older of the two men. What looked
like a double-edged dagger rested with a drinking horn on
top of a stone that looked like a millstone, but I could see that
it too had been etched or painted with a triangle and a goat's
head. It was a very ambitious scene for old Dick. It had an
intensity about it that none of his other pictures had. A
witches' sabbath, or diabolic ritual, whatever it was, made a
big impression. There was little attempt to show what the
setting was. I recognized the vague shapes of tables and chairs
and even some sort of machinery, but nothing further in the
magic line.

"Oh," a voice said behind me, "I thought you'd be one of
the policemen I knew." I turned around to see the fairly
familiar face of a man about my height. It was Hector DuFond
in a pair of faded jeans and a T-shirt with a collar. "Wait a
minute, I *do* know you. You were staying at the Harbison's.
What the hell is going on?" He looked a little hunched up,
like he was protecting himself with lowered shoulders. "I'm
Hector DuFond."

"That's right, I met you at the lodge. My name's Cooperman. Ben Cooperman." We shook hands formally.

"Mrs. Kramer said you were up here, but I was expecting
someone I'd already talked to. Harry Glover told me I could
come up and make an inventory of Aeneas's stuff. The
coroner's still not released anything to the family." He was
pale and tense. "Are you some kind of cop specialist?"

"I answer to that," I said with becoming modesty. Hector's
eyes scanned my face, trying to make me out. I flashed my
open wallet at him, displaying a selection of credit cards and
a reduced version of my PI licence.

"But you were up at the lodge before it happened?"

"Just coincidence. Don't worry about it." He looked like it

was going to take a while before he'd be able to master that. I thought I'd better sound professional and not just idly curious. "This picture," I asked, turning back to the wall and letting Hector gain a bridgehead in the room. "What do you know about it?"

"Aeneas got it from a fellow called Berners, a trapper and—"

"I know about Dick. Tell me more about the picture."

"Well, now, I don't know. It's just one of Dick's fancies, I guess. I don't think I ever looked at it and saw it, if you know what I mean. Let's see. Looks like some mystical rite going on. That's inside the mill at Big Crummock. I recognize the machinery. Old Wayne never did get rid of it; he just lived around it."

"So, it was painted before the big fire?"

"He gave it to Aeneas when he retired back to Huntsville. He gave me one of a sunset painted from the Rimmers' point at the same time. But I don't know how he dreamed up the goings on in this picture. He wasn't one to go to the movies."

"Then it might be a picture of something he actually saw at the mill?"

"Yes, I guess it might be." Hector reached into a back pocket and brought out a flattened pack of cigarettes. He waved the pack at me, and I took one. When we had both lighted up off my match, I told him that I was sorry about what happened to his brother, and that everybody I'd talked to had a great deal of respect and affection for him. He nodded slow agreement while he smoked.

"I can't get used to the idea that he's really gone this time. He used to be gone on trips through the country around here most of the summer. I rarely saw him from June to late September."

"When did you see him last?"

"The same old question." He laughed through a pasted-on smile and looked at the end of the cigarette. "I told Glover and the others, six or seven times. And you were there yourself, for God's sake. He had a camp at the Pearcys' old place, I mean where their cabin used to be years ago. The dock's still there, but in 1954 the provincial government started trying to phase out lessees in the park. The Pearcys held on for a good few years, but they had to get out. It was a tidy little cabin too. I'm losing track. Aeneas had pitched a tent on the high ground between the old footings of the Pearcy place. He was worried that the blocked culvert was backing up water so that it was beginning to threaten his camp. I hadn't seen Aeneas since the beginning of the spring term."

"I heard somewhere that you met in town outside the hotel and that you'd had words."

"You mean Wednesday night? Yeah, we had words, as you say it. He told me that one of the guests up at Petawawa Lodge, Lloyd Pearcy, in fact, had tried to hire him to take him into Little Crummock Lake. That was always a sore point between us, because my brother was superstitious about that country, wouldn't ever go there."

"Was he like that about other places?"

"No, just that lake and around it. I never heard of him going near there."

"Was the superstition one known to you? Is it part of a tradition or something like that?"

"Well, the story he told about hearing thunder—"

"Yes, I know that part. Do you know anyone else who had similar fears?"

"No. And Aeneas wasn't ever able to talk about it much. He wasn't one for talking much at the best of times."

"Is that what the argument was about?"

"Well, I guess, if you want to call it that. Harry Glover calls it an argument, because it makes him feel important. He has me written down as his leading suspect. Well, that would make my brother laugh, that would. He just doesn't have a glimmer about what happened, that's all."

"Get back to the argument."

"Well, yes. It was about his guiding Lloyd Pearcy into

Little Crummock, like I said. I told him he was being stupid and backward and giving the impression that we were all superstitious and backward. He didn't argue back. That was his big weapon—silence. He won more points by saying nothing than anybody I ever knew."

"You had this argument before?"

"Every year or two he'd beg off going up there, and I'd give him hell. Aeneas was a poor man. He couldn't afford to turn down a guiding job, and I told him. I tried to explain to him the way it is with thunder and lightning, how the one is the sound of the other, and how you can't have one without the other. I told him about the speeds of light and sound. But it didn't do any good."

"How did you part?"

"As usual. He was quiet, reflective, a little drunk, maybe, a little truculent, but nothing wild."

"Was it an 'I'll show you' kind of mood?"

"Maybe. He often went off to prove he was right about something, then dumped the proof on my floor. I remember one time I said there were no pike in a certain river. Next week I found one wrapped in a green garbage bag on my floor. Never said anything about it. He just went and caught one."

"Have you ever been to Little Crummock Lake?"

"I don't get the time. I'm marking papers most of the year."

"Yes, but not right now. What about lately?"

"No, I'd get lost. I'm not much of an outdoorsman."

"Maggie McCord says that you know your way around."

"Maggie's romantic about Indians. She thinks we are all out of Fenimore Cooper." We both smiled, while I tried to remember whether Cooper wrote *The Last of the Mohicans* or *The Song of Hiawatha*.

"But you can paddle a canoe?" I asked. He nodded. "You would be unlikely to get lost or be eaten by bears in the park?"

"No more than my grade-eight kids," he admitted. That seemed to be the end of the conversation, but on my way to the door another question hit me.

"When you saw Aeneas on Thursday night, either at his camp or at the Annex, did he say anything to you that referred back to your argument and his superstition?"

"He didn't say anything. But he had his special look on his face."

"What sort of look?"

"Whenever he'd won a point or beaten the odds. Call it a look of pride, or inner calm. I don't know how to describe it."

I said I thought he'd done a good job of it; we shook hands again. He told me about the funeral arrangements and I repeated my condolences, and found my way down the linoleum-covered stairs into the cranberry-lit hall, where Mrs. Kramer was waiting to show me off the property.

Chapter Twelve

I returned to the lodge in the cab of a lumber truck. The driver was a cousin of a friend of Bonnie's sister. Bonnie was the waitress at the Blue Moon Café. The driver and I spent the first half of the trip bouncing along in complete silence. The view from the cab of a lumber truck makes you feel both giddy and king-of-the-highway. The last part of the trip was as full of gossip as the café. I was reeling with news about the intermarrying heads of the lumber companies and fairly drunk on talk of provincial patronage and evil doings. I slipped into my cabin without seeing anybody but one of the Kipp kids wrapped in a towel.

I picked up my car keys from my other pants and walked through the dust of the parking lot to turn my motor over. That swim I'd promised myself came to mind as I sat behind the wheel. It was hotter than the sweat room in a men's club.

Starting back to the cabin still shaking from the truck ride I came abreast of the motel building, and could hear raised voices. I stopped in my tracks like a milk train. The noise was coming from Westmorland's unit. The voices erupted out of the screen door before I could even turn and hide. It was George McCord reeling out backwards down the steps with Des Westmorland almost on top of him.

". . . and bloody well stay out! You come here again and I'll twist your other arm. Now clear out! Clear out!" George picked himself up out of the dirt and tried to untwist himself from the clothesline full of bathing suits and towels that he had fallen into.

"You won't take on so high and mighty when it's known. You hear? When people find out, you just remember throwing me out of your place. I just come to talk."

"Next time I'll throw you out the *front* door!" Des went back into his unit, and while the screen was open I could see the pale face of Delia Alexander through it. George McCord pulled a bathing suit off his shoulder, hurled it to the ground and shambled off.

Thinking about what that all added up to was interrupted by a racket from the direction of the generator. I wanted to get back to polish off the last of my Cokes, but curiosity again got the better of me.

It sounded like an old-fashioned siren on a fire engine at first, but I then placed it as a circular saw, as it changed pitch. The Delco shed and the woodshed backed on the extremity of the clearing occupied by the lodge. The low ground, where the cars were parked, lifted slightly as you got near the sheds. From here too you could look into the back of the motel units. Only there was nothing to see except rickety back steps and patched screen doors. From the Delco I could see a cloud of sawdust, like an aura, around the open front of the woodshed. I walked around into the yellow fog and noise and could see two figures decked with sawdust on their heads and eyebrows. They were feeding cordwood into the spinning saw. Most of it was birch, but there was a mixture of other hardwoods too. I shouted something but it disappeared in the racket. Joan Harbison appeared from nowhere and killed the switch. That was a shock to all of us. The restored silence sat there like a snared animal, while both of the yellow figures by the saw blinked. One of them — I saw that it was Lloyd — removed a pair of earmuffs and wiped his face with a cloth cap after slapping it on his leg. He looked from Joan to me without reading any answers to his questions in either of our faces.

"Lloyd, give her a rest for a bit. She heats up if you run her steady," Joan said. The other man lowered a yellow kerchief from his nose and removed his earplugs. It was the neighbour from across the lake. He added the last sawn log to the accumulated pile.

"Come away out of the dust, Benny," Lloyd said, and he tipped up a couple of uncut, drumlike tree sections to sit on.

"Lloyd, you were after Aeneas to take you in to Little Crummock Lake. Did you ever find out how to get there?"

"There's no secret getting in there. I just wanted Aeneas's company. We fished every other lake up here just about. Oh, say, you wouldn't be acquainted with Dalt Rimmer, would you?" He indicated the other man who was already glaring in my direction and giving me a look at one of the more neglected mouths in the north woods. Most of his teeth were stumps of blue, stained with tea or tobacco. I reminded Lloyd that we'd met at the Annex Thursday night.

"Up to Little Crummock, is it?"

"Looking for lake trout and speckled," I said.

"That's a rough way in," said Dalt Rimmer. "You'd best take the York River and go up from Four Corner Lake. They call it Buck on the map. Fish is good in there." I smiled my answer and turned back to Lloyd.

"Joan says that other people have been in to Little Crummock. I may look like a tenderfoot, but I think I can follow a trail or carry a pack if necessary." Now it was Lloyd's turn to smile.

"Little Crummock's about thirty feet higher than this lake. The river that joins them—"

"The Durwent River," added Dalt Rimmer with a gleam in his eye.

"Yes, on the early maps it is, but around here you won't hear it called anything but the Tom River, named after Tom Mowat, who was foreman at the lumber camp up on Deer Lake."

"That's Bice Lake on the map," said Rimmer.

"How far up the river can you go by boat?"

"You can go around the first two bends in a motorboat if you stay in the middle of the channel. You may go half a mile farther in a canoe, but it becomes too shallow and full of boulders after that."

"The portage trail goes up the right-hand side about a mile up from the lake."

"What are you saying, Dalt? Dick Berners told me himself that the trail winds up past the dam from the left. The early map, Benny, shows it as Crummock Water, because of the long length of it with a twist at the north end." I must have looked confused. "A crummock is a shepherd's staff, his crook, you see. There's a river feeds into it from Pine Lake."

"And that's called Percy on the map," added Dalt Rimmer to make everything perfectly clear.

"Why not just draw him a map, Lloyd? That would be simpler," Joan asked from the sidelines. "All the fish will have died of old age if he has to wait for you two to agree about anything." Dalt looked lean and awkward on his stump, as though his joints were leftovers from a bigger man.

"Is there a lean-to, or cabin, or shelter of some kind?"

"There's Dick's place. I guess it's still standing. Nobody's been in there since they carried poor Dick out dead. Glover and them brought him out."

"Now if you want another way to get in there, you can take the lumber trail past Kettle Point . . ."

"That's the point past Giffords' Point," Lloyd added by way of clarification.

"You can also go up the Durwent, or Tom River . . ."

"That's Mississippi on the map, right?" I asked.

Chapter Thirteen

It took me about three-quarters of an hour to boil a bunch of eggs until they were as hard as I like them and then make them into part of a cook-out supper wrapped in bread-plastic. I thought of taking the fish fillets on the trip but voted the idea down. One look at them in the refrigerator led me to believe they'd been multiplying while I was gone. Oh, for a little leftover turkey!

Before I left Lloyd, he'd sketched a map of how to get into Little Crummock and where at least two people thought Dick Berners's cabin might be.

There was a new car in the parking lot between the Lamborghini and an OPP cruiser. From the lake I could hear more voices, but these were laughing and squealing with pleasure. Most of the lodge's population was gathered on the dock: Cissy and the kids belonging to a new couple had just come in from swimming. Aline was working on her tan, and Westmorland and Delia were approaching the shore in a rowboat. They'd had all my cooking time to settle down. I saw no sign of George. Or David Kipp. A stranger with a comfortable paunch and a can of beer in his hand and Joan Harbison's arm around his shoulders was sitting in a deck chair. He had a chubby face that still managed to look athletic, although I couldn't see any sign of motion. He was wearing tan shorts and an inverted gob hat pulled low on his brow. Joan stayed close and was apparently telling him the news of the week. Roger Kipp stood to one side watching them. He didn't know how to deal with the fickleness of women. His brother, Chris, was trying to interest him in taking pictures. I walked down to join the people. Joan made the introductions. Mike Harbison took off his sailor hat to reveal curly grey locks that looked like they had been arranged not by the artistry of nature but rather by the cunning of some Toronto hairdresser. He was wearing a Lacoste T-shirt with a little crocodile nibbling his left nipple.

"I've just been catching up on the terrible news," he said shaking his ringlets. "It could do the lodge a lot of harm."

"I see the police have come back. Is it Glover or somebody else?"

"There are five of them. They've got string wrapped around trees, sort of roping off the area around the culvert and the old Pearcy site. That's where Aeneas had his tent. There's a detective inspector and a sergeant. The others are trying to find Aeneas's pick-up truck. Glover's not been back, but I'm not surprised."

"Why's that?"

"Well, simply put, Aeneas had a girl, but Harry Glover put a stop to it."

"Why was that?"

"Aeneas was an Indian, and the girl, well, she wasn't."

"And Glover of the OPP broke it up?" Mike nodded, and I could see he didn't want me to press him any harder.

Dripping kids were running the length of the dock, making Aline sit up quickly. Roger Kipp had taken his brother's camera and was trying to get everybody bunched together for a picture. He waved his hands like a traffic cop, and we all said "cheese," and he pushed a button to make us immortal. Westmorland and his girl, just coming up to the group, were also in the picture. The group expanded after the picture, like we'd all been holding our breath. Roger and Chris were talking to Des Westmorland. Delia stood by.

"Come on, Roger," he said. "You and your brother get in the picture." Roger was pulling back and shaking his head. "Come on. Show some spirit. We'll get one of you and your brother. Come along now. Nice big smiles, before the party breaks up." Roger reluctantly turned the camera over to Des who began examining it from all sides. The two boys jammed into the group between the Pearcys and Harbisons. I could hear Chris muttering, "He's got his stupid finger over the shutter." I found my party smile where it was vacationing and paraded it out again. Meanwhile Des had discovered what all the mechanical outcroppings on the camera were for and was squinting seriously through the viewfinder.

"Make sure it's my good side, Mr. Westmorland," said Joan.

"What kind of cheese will it be this time?" asked Aline.

"Push together more, please, you in front. Look pleasant, everybody." With his eye still on the viewfinder, Westmorland began moving backward. Before anybody could say anything, he had backed off the edge of the dock, like a comic in a movie. The camera went back over his head as he suddenly found himself overbalanced and falling.

"Look out!"

"Mr. Westmorland! Look out!"

"Desmond!" We all got a little wet with the splash. As soon as he picked himself up in the four feet of water, with his glasses dangling from one ear and we were sure that he was all right, we broke up laughing. Mike was first. It exploded in loud bursts. Roger and Chris forgot for the moment that it was their camera and split themselves at the sight of the man standing bewildered and surprised up to his belly in Big Crummock Lake.

"Oh, dear," he said. "I'll never live this down." He began to join in on the fun. Lloyd Pearcy went to the edge and offered him his hand, but Westmorland shook his head, and walked ashore first and joined us on the dock looking very red in the face.

"Would you do that again, so we can get a picture of it?"

"You've fed my best smile to the minnows," said Aline. He took the ribbing as well as he could, but finally retreated to get changed. He took the boys with him, probably making his peace with the owner of the camera.

"I don't know what we can do to top that bit of excitement," said Mike Harbison, taking a sip from the beer can and wiping his chin with the tanned flat of his hand. "I could invite everybody for hotdogs tonight around the barbecue. How's that?" The new kids liked that, and began dancing up and down, then ran off to report the news to their parents. Joan rolled with the punches, I thought.

"I do enjoy an old-fashioned hotdog roast," confided Cissy, looking up at me for confirmation.

"Yeah, they're a lot of fun. We used to hold them at camp when I was younger. A little sing-song, a story, some marsh-mallows. Nothing like it. Unfortunately, I won't be here this evening."

"Not be here?" She was blinking in disbelief, like I'd said that God was a toaster.

"I'm just getting ready to head off on a fishing expedition. I want to get some big ones in Little Crummock Lake."

"Oh, I see. But it's too late to start today. Why don't you make an early start tomorrow? We'd so like to have you. Especially if there's going to be singing."

"Thanks, but I think there's light enough to see me most of the way. I've got a good map. Doesn't look too difficult. Not for an old camper like me."

"I see. Well"—she was adjusting to a smaller universe—"you'll be missed." She was playing balletic games with her small red hands over the back of her chair. "Did you hear, Lloyd? Benny's not going to be here for the roast. He's going in to Little Crummock to camp out."

"Too late to start today, Benny. I'll help you pack so you can get an early start in the morning."

"That's what I told him."

"It's rough going."

"I'll only be gone overnight. Besides I've got your map."

"Well, I guess you know your own mind. The worst of the sun is over. Have you got a sleeping bag?"

"I was just going to take a blanket roll."

"Don't say another word. Joan has plenty of sleeping bags.

Have you gassed up?"

"I've got most of a tank. It'll see me up and back." Cissy passed the word to Joan, and soon everybody was planning my trip for me. For a minute I thought I was going to get a replay of the conversation with Dalt Rimmer and Lloyd. Joan left the dock to find me a pack sack. Cissy went to wrap a piece of cake. Mike Harbison was beginning to tell me how to make bannock over a fire, when I caught Lloyd off at the end of the dock scanning the clouds for signs of bad weather. I'd just about decided not to go when things started arriving back at the waterfront: a canteen of water, a first-aid kit, a knapsack big enough for a marshal of France to set up a recruiting office in, and a heavy-duty sleeping bag wrapped in a ground sheet. There was no way out.

I watched the way Joan packed. She was efficiently made and didn't waste a gesture. Meanwhile, Cissy packed the way she talked, full of sudden pauses and second guesses. I didn't lift a finger; I wasn't allowed to.

"Do you like sardines, Benny?" Joan slipped in two cans. Mike came back into the picture carrying a box from Switzer's Delicatessen in Toronto. He took three frankfurters from it and wrapped them in foil. Franks from Switzer's and I wouldn't be there to help eat the rest of them. I wondered if there wasn't a way out of this yet. I walked out to the end of the dock to talk weather with Lloyd.

"You should be all right," he said, taking his beady eyes off the horizon. His pointed beak of a nose was calling home all the subtle signs of the day to come.

"Think so?"

"Yeah, you'll be all right." Lloyd looked down at my feet. "You know where you're standing?" I looked down to find a clue.

"Nope."

"That's where old Trask hit his miserable head. Right on the end of the board you're standing on. Bashed it in after falling from a ladder where I am."

"You saw it happen?"

"No, but everybody knows what happened. Probably didn't even feel himself rolling into the lake."

I was standing on a very ordinary piece of dock made from two-by-six planks.

"It's the one that sticks out that did for him," Lloyd added, as though knowing which plank made all the difference. It was like old people recounting their last meeting with a deceased dear one who'd "had a warning." To be fair, the plank Lloyd's toe pointed to did jut out from the others because it held a cleat for tying up boats to; it looked like a place where Trask could have put a bad dent in his skull.

"He was working on the dock, somebody told me," I said.

"Yeah. That's right. Dalt Rimmer finished it up before Joan and Mike took over. Old Wayne built her just two boards along from the one he hit. The rest's Dalt's. I can always tell Dalt's work. He'll never use three nails where one will do. Wayne, now, he never drove two nails the same way, always going around half-cut, if you know what I mean. If his right thumb wasn't black it was his left. That was a man for accidents, all right." Here Lloyd shook his head, as though Trask were standing in front of him swearing from a newly banged finger and reaching for a swallow of comfort.

"Well, if I'm going, I'd better be going," I said. I could feel Lloyd's eyes on me as I made my way past those left at the shore end of the dock to the cabin for my lunch and supper. I added a few biscuits and oranges to the eggs and other things, then returned to the pile of supplies. A few minutes later they were all gathered on the end of the dock and I was returning their waves as I started to steer a course up the lake past the first and second islands to the river entrance. I heard Lloyd shouting and jumping around on the shore, so I turned to look back. He was holding my fishing rod and box of sinkers. I went back to collect them. I didn't say anything. There were fewer wavers when I set out on my great adventure the second time.

Chapter Fourteen

I found the river mouth, and then the faded orange portage sign face down in the bushes, where it wasn't much help to anybody. Dealing with nature directly, without names, eliminated a lot of confusion. I'll recommend it to Dalt Rimmer when I see him again. I pulled the boat ashore in a bit of scrub that passed for a clearing and set the motor under it. The sun was still high enough so that I could hope to get to the smaller lake well before dark. I hefted the pack by leaning it against a tree. When I had it on, I wasn't sure which of us was leading. The way ahead led through the bush on a path that had been well trodden at one time, but which was beginning to allow new growth through the packed earth. Off to the right from time to time I could hear the sound of falling water, occasionally glimpse it. If I hadn't been loaded down with my pack and fishing things, I would have made a side trip to see what was what. I kept to the straight and narrow until I thought my knees would give up and quit. I remembered the map Lloyd had drawn for me, now riding near the top of the pack, but now out of reach: three and five-eighths miles. That's a long hike when measured in city blocks.

Apart from the sound of the water from time to time, and the warning from some startled bird, the place was quiet. You could have heard a drunk hiccup at three hundred yards. Light filtered through the leaves like weak coffee. The way the underbrush came up to meet the low-hanging branches of the maples, birches, and other trees made the path into a shaggy tunnel. For the most part the way was dry, but there were spongy places that did in my shoes, which, like me, weren't intended for this kind of life. Settling on a stump, I

took a rest at what seemed the half-way point. After a welcome cigarette, I was on the march again, whittling down
the distance. But there always were more hills and turnings
ahead.

At last I saw a clearing forming in the distance, and when I
got there I could glimpse water spread out ahead through the
trees. It was a twisting quarter of a mile downhill. I was wet
with sweat and out of breath. I'd have thought that the
downward trail would have been easy, but it wasn't. The
front of my shins were yelling at me every step to the lake. I
had another smoke overlooking Little Crummock: another
long narrow lake with what looked like a twist at the far end.
I took Lloyd's map out of my pack. There was a path along
the south shore that was supposed to lead to Berners's cabin.

With my breath fairly caught, I hoisted my rig and set off
down the south shore. This path was in the same poor shape
the other one was in; I wandered away from it twice ending
up in one of the better places in the world to discard old razor
blades in. In fact this whole north country was good for that;
some places were harder to find, that's all. Then I thought
about the stuff in the newspapers about pollution in the
rivers and mercury in the fish, and I decided that old razor
blades take different shapes in different settings. I heard
Lloyd talking one night about the lumbering that is still
going on in the park, and wasn't that a shame. Then David
Kipp told him that cutting helped maintain the place as a
usable wilderness area. You don't know who to believe on a
thing like that. Anyway, I found my way back to the path
and kept on it for another hour and a half. I was feeling
pretty proud of myself for having managed to get so far
without asking directions from a policeman. My feet had got
the hang of avoiding roots and animals burrows. It was like
they had taken over the matter of avoiding a twisted ankle in
order to free my mind for more important things.

The only more important thing I could think of was why
was I going into Berners's cabin in the first place. For all I

knew, Patten could be dead or driving for the border right now. What did I expect to find at Dick's place? Did I think it linked up to the murder? I asked myself these questions but got no satisfactory answers. So I kept walking. By now I was beginning to suspect that I was on a treadmill, and that the scenery drifting by on both sides was a loop that I'd seen before. When you come from the city, you can only take outdoors in small doses. If I saw another blank stare on the frozen face of another deer or another cute chipmunk perched on top of another bracket fungus, I'd throw up. There was the unmistakable hand of Walt Disney in all this. A game bird of some kind I'd seen in *Bambi* ran along the path for a few yards followed by an active brood of eight offspring. All it lacked was a musical score and a philosophical old owl.

Then I saw it. Dick Berners's cabin was sitting high on the uphill side of the path looking as silent and as natural as the rotted stumps I'd been walking over. It was a very cabin-like cabin, built of medium-sized logs, with a peaked roof, tin smokestack in the middle, and old saw-blades nailed across the windows with their teeth pointed up, to discourage bears and other unwelcome visitors. The door was fastened with a rusty tongue and hasp and an old padlock that broke when I blew hard at it. Inside it was dark. I saw a woodstove with a rusty pipe slanting to the roof, a plain table with curling oilcloth, a bed with a damp-looking mattress on top, with dark stains and holes from which a froth of fuzz over-flowed. Along the wall were shelves with cans with darkened familiar labels indicating beans, vegetables, and soup. A broken bag of something white that the mice had discovered and dragged off leaned against a row of books, and there was a japanned canister that still smelled strongly of tea.

Since I was planning to stay the night, I reconnoitred light fixtures and a greasy-topped jerrycan of coal oil. I could see where candles had been mounted in dead sardine cans, but the mice had eaten them. There were signs that Dick had tried to keep the wildlife at bay: pieces of tin were nailed over holes in the floor. The place smelled musty and sour, like it hid a nasty secret.

I stashed my pack on the bed and smoked a cigarette in the single wooden chair. Not feeling up to dealing with the mysteries of Dick's stove, I ate a cold feast out of my pack: hard-boiled eggs, sardines, a handful of bread, and an orange. I even sampled Cissy's cake. While doing this, I had the leisure to cast my eye around the single room in more detail. It was roughly chinked with cement, decorated with a few crude oil paintings on slabs of wood, brothers to the ones I'd seen. There were other pictures too: a British bulldog standing firm on a Union Jack, torn from a Sunday colour supplement and going brown; a picture of four young men in uniform, two of them sprouting first moustaches. A washed-out cloth poppy was pinned to the frame, a leftover from some forgotten Remembrance Day. Above the door, stuck up with a yellowed Scotch tape, was the top of an American newspaper: *The Evening Star*, written in old Gothic type. He had a collection of cardboard beer mats from places like *The Elephant Public House, St. Nicholas Street, Worthing* and *The Midland Hotel, Peter Street, Chichester*. On one wall, between two pairs of deer antlers, a stringless guitar hung from a leather strap. On top of the table I was sitting at, I found a Spanish rope lighter, in the drawer a yellowed ivory-handled knife with rust spots on the blade along with matching single fork and spoon, all liberally sprinkled with mouse turds. In general, the cabin contained nothing of obvious value. I guess that was the saw-off in the north: you didn't fill your place with burglar-tempting stuff and left it protected by a simple lock. Outsiders, except in emergencies, played the game and respected private property.

I glanced over Berners's dusty library: *Klondike Fever*, by Pierre Berton, *North of the Opeongo*, by Philip Armstrong Scott, *Tombstone*, by Walter Noble Burns, and *Free Gold: The Story of Canadian Mining*, by Arnold Hoffman.

Holding up one end of the bed I found some Leacock, Dickens, and Sinclair Lewis. Further underneath and much nibbled, was *A Pocket Guide to the Lake District*, dated 1938. My first big discovery was a sheaf of letters, held together with a greasy piece of binder twine, from French and French, a law firm in Bancroft, Ontario, about some mining leases in the east half of Lot No. 12 in the 14th concession of Anglesea Township, County of Hastings, Province of Ontario. The letters traced a story beginning with the original claim (October 1959) and, moving through the fine print of date and hour of staking, date of recording, number of licence, I came to the name of the lessee, Richard Berners. It looked like he had done most of the manual work, including drilling, that was listed. In 1964, a new name appears: Wayne Trask, who gained a fifteen per cent interest in the project. A year later, he got another fifteen per cent. A year after that, Trask picked up another thirty per cent in two easy stages placed six months apart. French and French didn't tell me what they were mining, but I found a clipping from *The Globe and Mail* about an abandoned ruby mine in the same county and in a neighbouring township. So, that's what it was all about — rubies. But what did mining in Hastings in the 1960s have to do with what was going on now? I asked that question again when I found a cask of black powder and a dozen drill bits tied together with wire. A bottle marked nitric acid sat on the shelf next to an unmarked one that plainly contained mercury. They looked about as innocent as a pair of brass knuckles at a wedding. Mining is illegal inside the park. No known minerals of commercial value are to be found here. That's why it's a park. Find gold and the borders would bend fast enough.

And thinking back to the mid-sixties, who could our miners have been? Berners, of course, and Trask. They'd have still been in their prime. But there were other possibilities as well. Albert McCord didn't sound like the type, but he knew the bush. George would have been in his twenties, and so would my chess partner at the Woodward place. Patten came back to Canada during the Vietnam War. I couldn't actually picture him using black powder, but I couldn't remove him from my list of suspects.

Berners was beginning to irk me. Here he was six months into glory and one of the cutest characters I'd run into in years. He merited close study. And I was enjoying getting to know him by sniffing around his stuff. Unfortunately, there wasn't much more to go through. There were expected things like the rusty traps hanging on nails, the collection of axes, the beaten up 25-35 Winchester with a broken stock, and there were unexpected things like a copy of *Great Expectations* in the wood box beside the stove with the cover ripped off and half the pages torn out. Also among the accumulated fur-balls of the wood box I found newspapers with dates much more recent than six months ago. One was less than two weeks old. It had a section torn out of the front page. I made a note of the date of the *Globe* and the edition.

I found another cache of mouse-nibbled books. The one on top was *Celebrated Criminal Cases*, edited by C. L. Doran. That was my line of country. I flipped through it, looking at the faces I'd seen in other books, the drab dregs of criminality, lives at the ends of their tethers: John George Haigh, Constance Kent, Henry Jacoby, Heath and Hume, Mancini and Manuel, Madeleine Smith, Evelyn Dick, and Charley Peace. A classified index at the back divided them up into categories: Mass Murderers, Murder by Poisoning, Murder by Stabbing, Murder by Strangulation, Gang Murders, Sex Murders, Train and Trunk Murders. Ah, the English especially love their murderers. But why did Berners carry them around with him? I lost my grip on the mousey pages and when I picked it up again it fell open at a case that Berners had read more than once. The pages were dirty with fingermarks. I skimmed the history.

TAIT, Adelaide
Twenty-one-year-old doctor's daughter, who in 1926 was tried in Cornwall, Ontario, for the murder of her lover, twenty-eight-year-old printer, Georges Ravoux.

The story told of how the daughter of a respected doctor fell in love with, wrote a ton of letters to, and eventually poisoned a young man who had a fine moustache and few prospects. The crunch came when the boy threatened to show the letters to the girl's father. He claimed that they were already married in the eyes of God, and he hoped to be able to win over Adelaide's father, who, the letters claimed, was set against the match. It was a pathetic story. As soon as the young man returned to his lodgings after drinking hot milk with Adelaide, he began to feel the pains which in a few hours put him on a dissecting table. A fifth of an ounce of arsenic was found in his stomach, and Adelaide went on trial for her life at the assizes in Cornwall on January 30th, 1926. The account ended up with the following:

> *Because of contradictions in the toxicology evidence, and a witness's statement that Ravoux was a known arsenic eater, the jury brought in a verdict of "Not Guilty" and the defendant was freed.*
>
> *It was said at the time that it was her beauty that saved her from the gallows. Little is known of her later life. Soon after the trial, she left Canada. It is believed that she went to live in Great Britain.*

In the margin, Berners or somebody had written in pencil: *Algonquin Park, Ontario, Canada.*

My head needed clearing. I was dizzy with new information that I didn't know how to evaluate. I thought I'd better take a walk. It was never too far from the cabin, and the path is usually well marked. From inside the cabin I brought the big flashlight and one of the axes as well. I wasn't afraid of the dark. I didn't need to prove my bravery to anybody. I found the path and worked my way up to it for about two hundred yards. From the black wall of the bush, I heard the crack of a snapping branch. Then, farther off, a twice-repeated four-note cry of a night bird. It was echoed about a quarter of a mile away. Crickets were singing like loose change in my pocket. The path went on and up.

There's something monumental about an outhouse. It is unmistakable. I've heard that there have been octagonal outhouses; I've heard that there is a book devoted to outhouses down through the pages of history. Where on earth is there a building whose function is so perfectly suited to its form? The door opened outward. It was a one-holer. Just right for a hermit. The brown, unpainted two-by-fours that made up the doorframe on the inside were held up by spiderwebs. An ancient Eaton's catalogue for the fall of 1956 afforded the only distraction. My light was powerful, and its beam pushed the darkness back wherever I shone it, the shadows moving out of the way like cockroaches running for cover.

I thought about old Dick again. All right: he was mining illegally here in the park. But where? Probably not far from here. I promised myself a good look-round in the morning. The old coot must have been laughing at everybody. He was sitting on a gold mine; if not literally gold, it amounted to the same thing. Okay, he mined the stuff: what did he do with it then? A new avenue to look down, when all I was being paid to look down was the view from my boat to the Woodward place. Something to check out on a long winter evening. Something else made a whooping noise and darted into and out of my flashlight beam with the rustling of wings that sounded like the expert shuffling cards.

From where I was, I could see, through the doorway, another of Berners's odd pleasures. He'd built a rock garden to one side of the path. It was a built-up mound of rock and earth with tangles of roses grown wild. By moving the light, I could almost change my perspective, by forcing the shadows to move in ways that further described their relationship to the rocks behind. It was the first attempt at taming the natural beauty of the park I'd seen since leaving Joan Harbison's half-drowned beds of petunias. Why up here, I wondered. Why not by the cabin? I was beginning to get a funny feeling behind my knees. I couldn't define it at first, and then things started adding up. The rock garden was in the wrong place, there was something phoney about it. I left the outhouse to take a closer look. It wasn't made of plastic; the flowers were real, and so were the dirt and the rocks. I looked at a few of these rocks—not your average everyday rounded stone from a creek bed or from the lake. No, these were rough, irregular, sharp fragments of hard stone, light-coloured on some faces, blackened on others. Blackened? Why blackened? I thought of the black powder in the house. Damn it! It came to me at last; this was the slag-heap of Berners's mine!

Using the axe, I began rearranging the landscaping. There were plenty of blackened rocks. Under one section, near the tapering off of the slope, I found a sheet of plywood covered with earth. I shifted it and found a tidy compressor and a drum of fuel nestling underneath. Hoses from the compressor went underground in the direction of the one-holer. I put the flashlight down so that I could follow where the tubes led with both hands. I could feel the old pump beating as I was clearly on the brink of a breakthrough. I heard a stick crack behind me, but I was too far gone to pay any attention. I should have taken a firm grip on that axe and turned around quick. But I didn't, and in another second it didn't matter. The last thing I noticed was that the light had shifted. It was coming from above me. Then the light was coming from in front of me and below me and inside of me. Light exploded. Then a dark hole opened up in the light, got bigger, and swallowed me whole. I didn't feel the pain; I just heard it chirp behind my ear, and then I didn't hear anything for a couple of years.

Chapter Fifteen

My next sensations were twisted and distorted: colours at the edge of blackness, garish slashes of red and yellow like comic book illustrations, words like "Wow" and "Bang" inked in cartoon print, with letters shaded to show thickness, as though they were each carved out of stone. My cheek was resting on something gritty. I felt dirt in my mouth. Now the pain in my head was real. Somewhere I could hear the hollow thump-thump-thump of oars. No daylight penetrated my eyelids, but I kept them shut anyway. Water was lapping under my cheek. I could smell tar and rope.

When the sound of the thumping stopped, I felt a hand on my ankle. A rope was being passed around one leg. I was too far gone to figure out which one. Before I could take in the meaning—the possible purpose of taking a semi-conscious man for a boat-ride—I'd been lifted by smelly arms and dumped over the gunwales into the lake.

The chill of the water took away the headache, as the weighted rope pulled me down. Automatically, I began treading water with my hands. A new pain in my ears told me it wasn't doing any good. That pain moved all the others off stage and jumped me from behind. There was a knife somewhere. I remembered it like remembering a birthday present from long ago. I had difficulty getting my hand into the wet pocket, but it was there. My eyes were open now, but they might as well have been closed for all the good they were to me. In my mind I could see the red penknife with its little white cross on it. I tried to open the blade with my teeth. I nearly dropped it. But I got it open. My first attempt at cutting the rope sent a spike of pain up my leg. I tried again, reaching for the rope at the weighted end. I could feel the pressure on my eyes now; my ears were screaming. Suddenly, the pull of the rope was gone, and I began to kick my way to the surface. My lungs were exploding inside me; my chest was yelling bloody murder.

I shot up out of the water, but without much splashing. The loudest noise was the one I made sucking in the friendly air. I'm sure that all the trees on the shore tipped in my direction. When I'd caught my breath, I listened. I could hear the thump-thump-thump of the oarlocks getting farther away. I couldn't see the boat, and then I could. The rowing stopped and a beam of light sliced in my direction. I ducked under the surface again, until I saw the beam move away. When I came up, I'd swum about ten yards away from the spot I'd been in. The stern of the boat was about fifty feet away from me. The noise of the oars started again. The figure rowing was obscure. I kept treading water as I watched the boat get smaller. I closed the knife and put it back in my pocket before I lost it. The shore was a dark band between the comparative brightness of the water and the sky. There was no moon, and the stars had business on the other side of the clouds. The oars were echoing now, as the boat approached shore. I couldn't make out what shore. From where I was floating, the lake looked round, and all the shores far off.

I started breast-stroking just to the right of where the boat sounds were coming from. The shore seemed miles away, but I tried not to panic, and the miles melted into something closer to reality. Swimming with your clothes on is a strange sensation. You feel the drag of the extra weight, but there is more to it than that. The clothing hits you in new ways and when you don't expect it, a bit like being jostled in a crowd. I thought of getting rid of my shoes, but then I remembered how far I was from another pair. After the first shock of the water had subsided, it felt almost warm, as though it had been sucking up the heat of the day for me to use now. I couldn't hear the boat any more. I paused and rested on my back for a minute, letting the sky drift in a circle overhead. I couldn't hear a thing. I continued on my back, kicking out like a frog in loafers. Soon I saw a light. It looked to be coming from the cabin. I started off again aiming at a spot off to the right of the light. As I swam, my head began playing tricks with me: I got into rhyming games with words like *right* and *light*. My arms and feet were getting tired. I tried to talk sense to myself. I tried to stay calm. Soon I came under the shadow of the shore. The water was chillier, as though fed by underground springs. My head was light, and my stroke became weaker, more *pro forma*. I kept up the act for another few minutes. The water looked dark and murky. I tried to feel for the bottom with my feet and on the third try, like Noah and the raven (or was it a dove?) I found my footing. Cotton-headed and loose-limbed, I struggled ashore. The rocks were round and slimy, but I could see bushes and trees and beyond them I knew there were birds and bears and all manner of creeping things. Then, for the second time that day, the lights went out.

Chapter Sixteen

This time I heard flies. There were the little ones with a busy, somewhat shrill buzz, and the fat insistent whine of big flies with blue bodies. I felt the sun on the back of my neck and a pain in my foot. My head hurt top and bottom. From the air, I guess I must have looked like a casualty in a partisan landing operation. My head could move. It was on a boulder with a smear of blood on top. My blood. My extremities were still half in Little Crummock Lake, my right leg stretched tightly out behind me. I tried to pull it. It wouldn't budge. Broken, damn it, I thought. Just what I needed.

The rest of me seemed fit enough. I wasn't counting the noises and pains in my head; they were old news, except for the ones from the front. I tried the broken leg again, after rolling over. As I pulled, a line of splashing rope came out of the water at a tangent. The rope! I edged my way back to the water on my rump and tugged. The end of the rope was lodged between boulders. I tugged again and it came free. I played with the knot around the ankle while pins and needles attacked with a vengeance. I finally got it off and tried to stand up. My left leg was fine, ready for anything, but the other was wearing a beehive where my foot should have been.

I managed to crawl back from the shore and found a hiding place just behind the front rank of trees. All you had to do to disappear in the north was to stand two steps back from the shore. And there I sat, rubbing my foot, and trying to collect my wits. I had been followed from the lodge or I had been surprised by whomever had been working the mine since Berners's death. I drew up a list of candidates. Judging from the lump at the back of my skull I was looking for a right-handed batter who knew how to hit just short of crack-

ing my head open. I cursed myself for walking into that sort
of trouble. I should always stop, look, and listen before I step
out into traffic, even up here. I stripped off some of my
clothes and tried to dry them off on a flat rock. My shoes were
beyond hope, but that's the way they'd been since I stepped
out of the Olds into his mess.

Half an hour later my right leg was beginning to feel
normal again. When I got up, it didn't buckle and send me
nose-first into the peppermint leaves of the forest. I tried on
my semi-dry clothes. They were stiff with the natural starch
of lake water with a lot of sweat mixed into the mineral
content. I kept to the shoreline, or as close as I could to it
without giving myself away. The cabin lay around the curve
of the bay, and I could see it when I was still half a mile off. I
watched it from under some shady ferns for ten minutes
without seeing anything. Nothing was stirring. I moved in
closer. I felt like a character in a cowboy picture sneaking up
on the cabin. It looked like a cabin in a movie, the sort of
place the rustlers hide out in until they hear word that the
coast is clear. I tried not to snap any twigs underfoot and was
getting a good C average in soundless woodland pursuit. I
should talk to the professors up at Secord University in
Grantham about giving a course in SWP. I'd have to do better
than passing though, first.

As I moved from one cover to the next, I found myself in a
particularly good spot. The trouble was, it was too good. The
ferns had been bent down, and the cedar sheltering the place
had recently had a low-lying branch pulled off so that the
cabin could be observed all the better. In the dead leaves and
pine needles I found a wad of gum wrapped in a familiar
wrapper. Another wad, not wrapped well enough this time,
stuck on my shoe. Someone had spent half an hour or more
watching the cabin from this shelter. I pocketed the well-
wrapped wad and moved out.

I came at the cabin from an angle favouring the lakefront.
The windows missed me from that direction. I came up

under one of the saw-blade-guarded windows, found something to stand on, and carefully lifted my nose above the cracked panes. The place was empty. I felt my breathing begin normally again.

The rusty padlock was back on the front door. I took it off. Inside, I found my pack all over the floor. I rescued some food, a couple of hard-boiled eggs and a can of sardines, and put together a rough feast on the empty table. I nearly gagged trying to eat the eggs faster than I could swallow. I drank half of the remaining water from the canteen. It was a gesture in the right direction, but it didn't help much. A bar of soap that had fallen from the pack was beckoning to me. What I really needed was a bath. I took off my clothes and ran down to the lake with the soap. This I lost quickly before the shock of the cold water reached my marrow and numbed it. By the time I'd finished, I had scrubbed some of the dirt and sweat off the last of the great hikers, and the soap was now gritty with sand. I took a swim out a hundred yards, marked down to about $79.95, and then came back to the oozy black shore. Half of me thought that this was stupid and unnecessary in light of what had happened last night. The other half kept explaining that whoever had hit me and dumped me in the lake hadn't stayed around to watch me float home with the tide. It was a question of well-reasoned argument working away at an illogical truth that will never quite shut up and be quiet.

I was trying to get my mind off the threat of walking into trouble when I walked straight into it. It was standing at the corner of the cabin near one of the windows, looking like a man in a moth-eaten bear costume, matted with dung and dead insects and twigs that had got stuck in the dry wiry fur. A bloody bear, b'dad, as my friend Frank Bushmill would have said. Frank was the Irish chiropodist across from my office. I don't know why I thought of him at that moment; better him than me, I guess. The bear looked at me and I looked back at it. I didn't even have a towel to flick at it. I thought of the Winchester inside. I thought of the selection of axes. Where was the one I took to the outhouse last night? The bear didn't move. We glared at one another. I thought of the open cabin door. It could have smelled the food. I was glad I hadn't surprised it tossing my things. I think I started shivering. I wondered whether I'd have felt braver in a bathing suit. We both held our ground and our breath. I was wondering whether to growl at it, when it blinked. I'd won! It began to sniff and shuffle off sideways, as though it had other business all the time. It didn't turn and run. It didn't back away. There was no route. It subsided slowly, that's all, a shifting of ground, and finally it lumbered off into the woods like a traveller who realized at last that he was waiting at the wrong airport.

That did it. I was beginning to get the idea at last that I wasn't appreciated around old Dick's place. I wanted to be on my way. I went back into the cabin and put my stuff together. When I went past the stove, I got a shock: it was warm. Under the stove lid, I could see grey ashes with a few firefly sparks in them. Why a fire in this heat? I stirred the ashes around and uncovered underneath a potato that had been put on to bake.

Somehow that didn't increase my desire to stick around. I didn't put in a call to the front desk. This morning I felt like travelling faster than most bellhops bend for a dropped dollar bill. But I wanted to have a final look at the outhouse. In the daylight it shouldn't be too frightening. I ignored the pain in the back of my head as I climbed the path to where I'd been so rudely interrupted.

The ground it was sitting on was solid rock under a few inches of topsoil. So, the hole underneath had to have been blasted. There had to be some way of moving the shack, but I couldn't see any. I walked around it a few times, keeping my peripheral vision on the edge of the clearing. Today I was frightened of both man and beast. On the third circuit, I noticed signs that the back end had had contact with the ground: a few pine needles were stuck into the weathered boards on that side, and it looked dirtier. So, I closed the door and pushed from the front. It tipped. I felt like a country boy on Hallowe'en. It was hinged in some way on the back wall. Over it went, as easily as opening a trap door. And there it was, Berners's mine.

I took a last look around, then placed a nervous foot on the top rung of the ladder leading down into the mine. I'd brought the flashlight, so I could see very quickly that as a mine it didn't add up to much. I came to the bottom before I expected to and stood on the uneven floor. From the hole at the top, which aligned with the floor of the outhouse, the shaft ran twenty feet then tapered until it was little better than a groundhog burrow. I hunched my shoulders as I walked, but I still scraped myself on the sides as well as on the overhanging rock. I found a pneumatic drill, lying idle and still attached to the buried hoses leading outside. A wooden frame, a box on rockers with a screen bottom, blocked my way, and I nearly tipped one of the pails of dirty-looking water that stood nearby. Against the wall were shovels and hammers. The shaft came to an abrupt end after a few feet. It didn't satisfy most of the juvenile longing I had felt about secret tunnels and buried treasure. I felt a little like I had as a kid crawling under the Coleman's veranda. When I had got to the far end, I could hear the electric meter ticking. This place was like that, only I wasn't twelve and the ticking I heard was the sound of my own heart. I looked around again, shrugged, and worked my way back towards the light trying to keep my head from dislodging low-hanging ore samples. I moved at a hunkering trot along Berners's single gallery. Once up the ladder, I returned the outhouse to its more usual purpose.

From where I was sitting, I could see his landscaped slag heap with its powder-darkened rocks and flowers. I could also make out the top of the axe I'd been carrying for protection on my last trip to the mine. My head throbbed on cue to remind me of what that adventure had led to. The axe handle seemed to be low in the slag heap as I came nearer. Then I remembered the excavation with the fuel drum and compressor inside. Memory was rewarded with a sight of the corner of the plywood sheet with its overburden of rock and earth that hid the grave-like trench. The plywood had been shifted so that it was only half covering the hole. The axe handle stood up preventing the sheet from moving any farther. I grabbed two edges, collected some slivers, and pulled. I could see in the dark recess a mass of work clothes—brown trousers stuffed into yellow workboots. The untied laces of the boots were in a tangle. I began to feel funny at the back of my knees. There was a flash of dirty undershirt under a faded green flannel workshirt. A mass of dark hair grew out of the shirt. There was a patch of dark red that belonged to the wound in George McCord's head where the axe had gone in.

Chapter Seventeen

Looking back on it now, I think I was suddenly seized with a desire to seek a more densely populated area, like the Granada Theatre on James Street in Grantham during a Saturday matinée. It was time to get moving. Death was catching. I owed George a debt to get moving for both of us. Poor George wasn't going any place except to the cemetery in Hatchway when the law had done with him. His future was all mapped out.

He was lying on his stomach with one arm trapped under him and the other twisted back behind like it had been used as a handle to ease him into the pit. His head was face down, so I didn't have to deal with that familiar gloomy face. I knew I should go through his pockets, but I wasn't sure the hard-boiled eggs would stay firmly rooted in my belly if I did. So I did it before I had time to reflect completely on the subject. He rolled over easily, with his eyes and mouth open. The axe handle waved a warning as I tried his pockets quickly. Apart from the normal things you expect to find in a man's pockets, in the front pocket of his shirt I caught up with the piece torn from the front page of *The Globe and Mail*. I looked at it there and then. It made a welcome change from George's oatmeal face looking up at me with the question "Why me?" written all over it.

It was a large picture with a caption under it. I recognized the prime minister at once and the caption identified the other figures as Rosalyn Pike, the Minister of Health and Welfare, and her husband, senior civil servant Desmond Brewer. The three were standing outside the east block of the parliament buildings smiling at a reporter's inability to get a simple answer to his complex question. The arresting thing about the picture for the likes of George and me wasn't the array of tulips already in bloom behind the prime minister, or the round of political smiles, it was the presence in the photograph of fellow Petawawa guest Des Westmorland as Desmond Brewer, the civil servant and husband of the cabinet minister. It came as a shock, but considering the one I had just had, I thought I could deal with it. I considered taking the clipping back with me, but a twinge of conscience made me put it back where I'd found it. I rolled George back on his stomach so he would give the cops the same fright he gave me. I wasn't being paid to do Harry Glover's chores for him. I was getting angry, which helped the being afraid. I could feel the dry itch in my throat and I knew what that led to, so I beat it back to the cabin and got my stuff. I didn't tidy up or even set the padlock straight. I hit the trail.

I went over the first path at a trot, or so it seemed. I could feel my breathing becoming wheezy as I dodged the roots and rocks in the way. The sun was still high, and I could feel it leaning on my back between the pack and the aluminum frame. I didn't waste any time at the edge of the lake when I got there, but headed straight over the portage. It ran downhill all the way. I'd developed a stitch in my right side, but I kept up the pace as well as I could. The image of my boat, waiting for me at the end of the trail, kept me at it, one foot after the other. All I could see as I made my way along the blurred green tunnel were my feet as I placed them—one, two, one, two—between the roots, beside the stones, just short of the depression, this side of the muck, in the stupid muck and, sometimes, bending the ankle, sending me flying into the bushes because I'd skidded. At last I could see the clearing that led to the big lake. It wasn't as secretive as the other. Soon I could see the sun glinting on the hull of my tin fish, pulled up out of the river. I raced the last few hundred yards. And then I stopped short. The hull of the aluminum boat had been ventilated by nearly half a dozen chops from an axe. My yachting days were over.

If I sat down and wept it wasn't because I was beside the waters of Babylon. The waters I was up had another name, one that even Dalt Rimmer hadn't thought of. I thought absurdly of a Mickey Mouse cartoon in which he'd chopped a second hole in his boat when the water was flooding in through the first. The second was to let it run out again. I had three holes to let the water in and only two to let it out again.

I threw my pack down and tried to think what to do next. I had to get past the swearing part, past the part where I was telling myself how smart I'd been to leave my fishing spot opposite the Woodward place, how clever to have left the paved streets of Grantham, if it came to that. Oh, I was smart all right. And I'd run out of cigarettes to boot.

I turned the boat over when I stopped shaking. The mortal wounds to the hull all puckered inward. I wondered whether I could do further damage with a rock, found one, and beat the ragged pucker with it for a few minutes. It made me feel better, for a start. Then I put another stone underneath the hole I was working on. Gradually, I was able to get the two parts back together again, at least so that I couldn't see through them any more. I bashed away at the other four holes and got them all to the same state. They were in no way waterproof, but at least they didn't look like they'd sink me in ten seconds. Now it would take about thirty. In ten seconds, at least I'd be in shallow water. My playing about insured my drowning in water over my head.

What was the next step? I needed a bleeding pine tree. The place was a home away from home for bleeding pines. I found one and tried to get it to drip on my knife blade. It did, but not much. I worked away at the wound in the tree, making it bigger, and tried to hurry the drops which looked to be a third slower than molasses in January. I got another tree started. By the time I'd added a bladeful of goo to the boat, I could go back to another tree and find a couple of drops. I felt like Robinson Crusoe building his boat. At least I could carry mine to the water. *That's* where my trouble would start. After an hour—call it an hour, who knows how long it really was?—I had a patched boat. I flipped it and tried it in the river with no weight in it. I'd mended it ouside and inside, so I wasn't surprised that the water didn't start appearing right away. The problems would start when I added my weight to the hull. That would test my patches. I brought out the motor and attached it. Still no water to speak of. I left the pack where it fell and climbed in. One of the mends began to gush. I put a finger on it, like I was a little Dutch boy and my sister was standing at my back yelling, "You're only making it bigger!"

I started the motor. I figured I could get as far as the river mouth before I was in deep trouble. Deep, ha! I know how to pick words sometimes. I headed out into the channel and nothing more went wrong. The hole under my palm throbbed a bit with the vibration of the motor. I moved slowly around the curves of the river. A bloody big whooping crane or something took off in an explosion of blue-grey feathers, nearly giving me heart failure. I felt like an African explorer looking to the riverbank to see whether the logs slid into the water to become crocodiles. Nothing moved. Not far from the place where Big Bird had leapt into the air, I saw the still form of a deer, dead in the water, and not at all Disney-like. I was beginning to dislike what I'd been discovering in the north woods.

I got to the mouth of the river, spat in the water for luck, and revved the motor up a notch. I may have been feeling brave, but I kept my tiller arm moving with the shoreline. I was moving at no great speed about a hundred feet off the nearest landing spot. Another of the wounds opened, first just a trickle of sculpted water, then it rose like a fountain, until my other hand stoppered it. I tried to move the pine resin around to fix it again, but it was useless for sticking once it got wet. I had to steer, so I took my hand away and to hell with it.

I was making slow progress. I'd done for the bend at the

end of Big Crummock and put paid to the sandbar at the shank of the long run home. I grinned at the first sight of the second island. It was like a talisman, pointing up to the sky. It got bigger as I got closer. My palm was getting weary holding out the lake, and the heel of my foot was keeping the other leak from sinking me. I was clearing the island when another of the holes blossomed a fountain. In shifting to put my other heel over it, I put the right heel through the mend, and water started coming into the boat wholesale and retail combined. I revved the motor up full and lifted the prow sufficiently so that I wasn't filling up from the forward hole, but the holes near me were making up for that.

I was just coming abreast of the Woodward place when the motor cut out. I looked behind me and saw the reason: it was mostly underwater. I was in fact sinking. Three-quarters of the way home and I was sinking. My plan to stay near the shore was a good one. Unfortunately, I'd abandoned it when I first saw the island. I was like a racehorse sniffing his stall. And now I was up to the gunwales in Big Crummock Lake. The flotation tanks at the ends of the boat only served to make me more ridiculous than I would have been without them. I couldn't go anywhere; I could only wallow. I remembered the rules my camp counsellor told us: one man scuppers the group and nobody leaves the foundering boat, not even the rats. So I wallowed.

I didn't hear the other motor start. I only became aware of the noise when it got close. I was so far down in my troubles and the water that I didn't even look up to see who was off to the rescue. I heard the motor move into a lower gear, felt a hand on the gunwale, and looked up into the face of my bearded rescuer, Norbert E. Patten.

"You!" We both said it at once. Patten added: "Delivered from the deep." I was glad to see him, even with a dirty bandage on his right hand. "Have you got a painter?" he yelled over the sound of his idling motor. His boat was the aluminum twin of mine, but the motor was bigger; it could have torn all my patches off with one mighty jerk. I flipped him the limp, dripping rope. "I'll make it fast," he said, putting the rope around a cleat on the transom. "You'd better come over the side, Benny."

"Where do I stand on salvage?" I asked lamely. "It's not my boat." He didn't seem to think I was being funny, keeping my head and all that, so I shrugged and climbed aboard his craft. He lent me a steadying hand, and I found myself tripping over cans of bait and landing nets. As soon as I'd picked myself up, I could see that he had his act in gear and we were heading towards his familiar dock.

"Who sprung you from the hospital?" I asked.

"I checked myself out after a couple of hours. There wasn't anything they could do that you hadn't already done. Luckily the thing wasn't poisoned, Benny. Just the same I'm in your debt again, fella."

"You've evened the score now." I was beginning to feel strange: cold and sweaty at the same time. Not poisoned? Damn it.

"What happened to you anyway?" he asked after tying up both boats to his dock. "That thing's not seaworthy." An unconscious humorist was my rescuer. He didn't show it playing chess.

Suddenly, I began to come apart at the seams. Shivering started it, then the feeling that my gut was trying to climb past my tonsils. He saw that I was soaking, threw me a rough wool sweater, and motioned me up to the house. I followed leaving wet marks from my feet all the way up to the front door. Pausing there, because I didn't want to warp his floors, I waited until he grabbed my arm and hauled me into the cabin.

Twenty minutes later, I was in dry clothes—Patten's, I think—and trying to get my jaw to stop snapping like a new elastic. Except for the girl, Lorca, Patten was alone in the place. She had appeared wearing a bathrobe fresh from a swim, had looked at the shivering wreck that was dripping everywhere, brought a towel that still smelled sweetly of shampoo, and began pulling off my wet clothes. She made no more than a stab at this. Since this wasn't really a matter of life and death, the proprieties might be observed. She tried to get circulation moving in my blueish feet. My skin was grey with dirt and exposure. My fingers and toes had water-logged furrows running between dead-looking white puckered flesh. My fingers were filthy under the shock, with grave-digger's fingernails. I saw a face in a mirror but couldn't focus on it. With a turban made from an undershirt, it looked like Gunga Din's.

Lorca'd made coffee and brought a blanket to wrap around me. Patten stood by like he was directing a play or movie. "Fix a fire, Lorca. How you feeling now, fella?" I nearly chipped a tooth smiling my assurances that I was on the mend. Lorca put birch logs together, crumpled a two-day-old copy of all the news that's fit to print and started a fire in front of the couch I was sitting on. Patten finally settled down at the other end and watched me like I was a burning fuse. When he thought I was calmed down enough to talk, he started with the questions.

"What happened out there?" I shook my head as though I'd just arrived on the scene myself.

"Boat leaks," I offered, sipping the coffee and feeling light in the head.

"Leaks? Hell, it was full of holes. What were you trying to prove, fella?" He leaned forward like a referee waiting for a foul. "I have to know what's going on on this lake, fella. I don't believe in chance."

"Somebody chopped holes in the hull up on the north side of the lake," I said. "Not my idea of clean sport, exactly. I bent it back into shape again and used pine gum to seal it."

"So," said Lorca, "that explains the disinfectant smell."

"Saw somebody do it in a movie once," I said. My shivers

had turned my speech into clipped British public-schoolboy understatements. Lorca took my empty mug from me and retreated to the kitchen.

"That took fast thinking. Any idea who did it?"

"No, but I guess it probably has something to do with you."

"Yes," Patten said through his teeth. "I wanted to get around to that, fella. It didn't hit me until I was being processed at the hospital that you've known who I was right from the start. What's your game, Benny? I know you're on my side, but who are you working for? Did Van send you? P.J.? What's your story, Benny?"

"That's not my secret, Mr. Patten. Sorry." I stirred uncomfortably under the blanket. It must have made quite a show — half drowned rat, half drowned Sinbad.

"Not your secret? What kind of talk is that? Don't forget who I am, Benny. I could have you blown away in a minute. I won't have secrets. Get that straight. There's no secret you can hide from me." He was getting red in the face and those lidless eyes were bulging in their dark hollows. If there'd been a crack of thunder right then, I would have got up and run. There was that crazy look on his face you see on television. He looked like he was possessed.

"I'm sorry, Mr. Patten, but it's not my secret to tell." It wasn't any better, but I hoped he would accept it the second time around.

"We've got to have a serious little talk, fella," he said making each word a poison-pen letter.

"Fine," I said, "fine. Always glad to talk."

"They've tried to get me twice, and now they're shooting at you. They know you come here. That's it."

"You can't lump these things." He was calming down now, letting his right hand pull the fingers of his left, one finger at a time. "All we know is that three things have happened. For all I know there are three guys out there with grudges. And we can't forget Aeneas, the Indian guide. He's part of this, too. He didn't die of old age. I don't have any answers, I'm just trying to ask better questions."

"Well, there are bloody well answers about you I'd like to hear. I've been lied to, taken advantage of. Security's out the window."

"That's the only safe way to look at security. Relax. You're getting the shakes from me."

"Cooperman, I'm staying on top of this. There can only be one man in control, you understand? I'm the Lord's anointed, not you. Remember that." I told him I would.

Noises from the kitchen sounded like they were coming to a head. In a moment Lorca brought me a cup of warm soup—vegetable from a can, the way my mother makes it. It tasted good and I said so. My clothes had been hung up on the backs of chairs in front of the fireplace. Patten sat in the full glare of the fire, the flames reflected in his lenses. He looked into the fire which was curling the bark and taking hold of the hardwood logs. Lorca seated herself on the step to the left of the fireplace with a pillow at her back and started brushing her damp hair so that it too shone in the flames. She moved like she knew I'd been calling her Body Beautiful at the beginning of my stay in the park. "There's more coffee on the stove," she said.

"Thanks," said Patten without looking up. After a while he went on as though he'd been interrupted in the middle of a lengthy self-justification. "You know, Benny, I always knew I had enemies. The forces of darkness have always been turned against me. And I looked around and I was friendless, and daggers grew behind every smile. Lord, I was prepared. He prepared me, but fella, I wasn't ready for the enemies within, the enemies of my bosom. Van Woodward was the best friend a man can have. I've known him since I was a teenager. I met him right here in this cabin. He showed me that there was a great world out there, and that I could get out and shake the dust of this place off me. And now, now . . . I don't know about him any more. I don't trust him. I don't know who I trust."

He looked like he'd just got news of an overdraught and a tax audit in the same mail. I excused myself and went on a bathroom hunt. When I found it, it looked just like a city bathroom. Up here in the park, that ordinariness must have cost a fortune. I took the opportunity of having a locked door between me and the others to ransack the drug cabinet. I saw signs of expensive items for sensitive skins, sleepless nights, contraception, and nervous stomachs. Lorca was devoted to odd shampoos and hair conditioners. I sniffed three of these before I found her supply of bourbon. Smart not to leave it in her room. Out in public was as good as in a vault. The label alone would keep a mere man well away. I bowed to her cleverness before rejoining the party in front of the fire. I was still shivering and could feel the welcome heat of the fire.

"Don't misunderstand me, Lorca," Patten was saying, "My idea of hell is a half-filled stadium. Hey, that's good! Write it down."

"It's not original."

"It will be. Write it down. Ah, feeling better? I am."

"That soup went down well. Thanks." The thanks was directed at Lorca. She short-changed me with her responding smile.

"Sure, any time. By the way," she said, getting up, "I took these things from your pockets." She handed me my wallet and some keys. As she put the wallet in my hand, she gave me the whisper of a smile. I found a place in my borrowed trousers for the wallet and keys. So, the game was up as far as she was concerned. How long would it take before she mentioned it casually to Patten?

"How would you like a roll in the hay, Mr. Cooperman? For medicinal purposes of course." She was looking at Patten. "I saw it in a movie."

"Just coffee, thanks." She went back to brushing her hair.

Patten's eyes moved from the fire and settled for a moment on Lorca before coming to me. They looked pained, even persecuted.

"Lorca's rebellion sometimes takes strange turns," he explained. "She's really very immature, fella. I wouldn't take her seriously. I never have."

"Norrie, you're a bastard you know? There isn't anything to do up here but screw, and you won't even talk to me. You didn't tell me it was going to be like this."

"You may do as you please, Lorca. I wish you wouldn't whine in public. I told you we would be here for some time. You came because you wanted to and because of certain favours—"

"You don't have to go into that. It's just that I get so lonesome without anybody to talk to. No telephone, nothing. I just want to know how long it's going to be, that's all. Pardon me for living."

"Would you count Lorca as an average sinner, Mr. Cooperman?"

"I'm not the only sinner, am I, Mr. Cooperman?" She was going to make her big play now. I wondered how fast I could run in my condition. "You must tell us all about your real-life experiences selling ladies' ready-to-wear. I'll bet it's more exciting than we thought."

"You should use a little hair conditioner before brushing your hair. It gives it more body. It's amazing what a belt of conditioner can do. It can sometimes turn you right around so you see things differently." It was my best shot. After that I had nothing but blanks. Her hand stopped mid-stroke and stayed that way while a smile slowly warmed her face. Then she continued brushing her hair until it gleamed with life.

A car drove up outside. Lorca jumped up and took a fast look out the window, while Patten gripped his knee.

"It's them," she said, shaking her hair from her face.

"And about time." Spence came into the house along with Wilf. They each set down cardboard boxes of groceries on the kitchen counter. When they saw me camped out in front of the fire with my clothes drying they looked at Lorca, who slipped them reassurance and me a conspiratorial smirk.

"Wilf," Patten said, "you remember Ben Cooperman from over at the lodge. I brought him forth from the waters, you might say. Somebody hacked up his boat." Wilf bobbed his impressive bald head impatiently. There was something on his mind. He tried to catch Patten's eye.

"We saw somebody as we were driving through the lodge."

"Benny," he paid no attention, "Wilf'll see that you get home safely. Spence, see to his boat, will you?" Wilf nodded in the same abstracted manner, like I wasn't the most important celebrity of his day. Spence, too, was trying to find a way into my host's face. I excused myself and headed again for the bathroom, where I moved a yellow terrycloth robe away from the door to make way for my ear. I couldn't catch all of it, but I heard a little.

"We both saw her. . . . It's her all right. . . . What could she want now? She was just walking across the road as we came through the lodge from Hatchway. . . . She didn't see us."

"Damn it!" said Patten at intervals, drowning out more interesting news. "She must know I'm here. It can't be an accident. She knows the lodge from years ago. Damn it! She wants me dead!"

They were looking back in my direction as I rejoined the group. The only extra information came from Lorca who called whoever it was they were talking about "a revengeful bitch."

"Well, we should pack you off back to the lodge before you catch cold," said Patten without much warmth. Lorca brought my clothes wrapped in a sopping towel, and my shoes in a plastic shopping bag marked "Onions." "Keep the things you've got on. I've got other stuff, fella. I'll send somebody over with your boat later on." I tried to show that I was grateful, and that I would return the clothes as soon as I'd turned around. Both Patten and Lorca walked out to the Mercedes with me. I got into the front seat, since that was the door Wilf was holding open. He slammed the door shut, so I opened the window.

"We'll have to have another game before I go back," I said.

"Any time, fella. So long!" He waved, and the car backed up, turned around, and carried me off through the trees.

Chapter Eighteen

The OPP detachment at Whitney was manned by a red-headed constable with pink eyelids and freckles. He didn't come close to filling the swivel chair he was sitting in. I wondered if there was such a thing as a summer-relief policeman while he took the information about George McCord and made a few calls. Soon I got to do my song and dance all over again for my old friend Harry Glover. I mentioned the body, the mine, and my bump on the head. Details that were still unattached to recent events I kept to myself. No sense confusing either one of us. The main thing I didn't tell him was that I'd walk back to the cabin with him. He didn't press me, but he let me draw him a map.

"I suppose you've told everybody about it?" Glover looked his question at me like I was on the carpet.

"I came right here. Nobody knows about it except the Indians and you." That was a line from the Camp Northern Pine hymn. It didn't mean anything to Glover.

"Well, let's try to keep it that way. Better tell the old lady, but apart from that leave the police work to the OPP."

"Suits me."

"We can get a plane in there easy from Smoke Lake," he said, and the freckled kid went back to the telephone. Glover didn't waste any further time with me after I told him I was returning to the lodge. He didn't like me any better than he had at our first meeting, but this time he didn't pick away at me. For some reason I think he trusted me, which was a leg up for one of us. We left the office at the same time. He watched me settle behind the wheel of my car and didn't move back to business until he'd seen me take the road back to the park.

The beavers had been at work again at the culvert as I came back towards the lodge. But two beavers can't plug a hole the way a body can. I splashed through without reducing speed. I was driving with the devil-may-care abandon of a drunk or a fool who doesn't know what time to go to bed. Bed: that was the name of the game from now on. Just then I could have fallen asleep on Dick Berners's stained and torn mattress without thinking the tumbling stuffing was anything other than friendly.

Joan was waiting for me when I finished parking the car. I hadn't even brought back a bag of milk. I remembered with horror that if I got hungry I had some fillets of lake trout in the cabin.

"You went through so fast before, I couldn't catch you. When you didn't come back, I was beginning to get worried. Are you all right, Benny?" I wasn't purposely falling asleep in my shoes, but I was close to it.

"Joan, a lot of things have been happening. I don't know where to start. I've just come back from telling Harry Glover that I found George McCord's body back in there. I'm sorry to tell you, but it looks like he was killed. It was no accident. Glover is flying into the lake to take charge, but I guess we should tell Maggie. Are you feeling strong?"

"George dead? I can't believe it. First Aeneas, now George. Benny, what's happening?"

"Honest, I wish I could tell you. I wish I knew." Joan was pushing her glasses farther up with a finger on the nose-piece.

"I still can't believe it," she said, shaking her head.

"I'd better get over there while I can still walk. Can you find Cissy? It'll be better if there are other women around."

"They're all down on the dock. Maggie went swimming. It was quite a sight. What happened?"

We started walking down to the dock. For the first time in hours, since the sun bore into my back at the break of dawn, I was conscious that there was weather going on outside. I'd been feeling wet and cold so long then, I felt like that was the

normal condition of man. This one anyway. I could see Cissy
standing on the edge of the dock addressing something large
and white in the water alongside it. Most of the regulars were
there, although I was too sleepy to count noses. There were
several greetings, sour grins, and faint-hearted waves from
the deck chairs. Maggie was walking out of the lake towards
me, blocking out the sun and dripping. I couldn't do it, not
then. I felt like I was facing the bear again. It was a dirty
trick to say anything when she didn't even have a towel to
protect herself with. So, I waited until she had dried off and
slipped into a purple bathrobe. She looked like two wrestlers
standing in the ring talking to the referee. I moved closer.
Cissy placed a skinny arm on my shoulder. There was no
chat. I guess my face was spilling the beans. I couldn't help
that. I told Maggie to sit down. I didn't ask her, I told her,
and she took it from me. The heat had gone out of the sun
again as she looked up at me, her eyes puffy, her chins
stretched, her face going white.

"Maggie, it's George," I said. "He's dead. I'm sorry." Pause.
"I found him up at Dick Berners's cabin." I thought maybe
she'd take it well, so I didn't pad it or stretch it out. I said
dead not *passed away* or any of the other cushions I couldn't
seem to think of. Maybe I thought if the words hurt her, she'd
somehow take the news and the shock better.

"Not George! Not George!" The words seemed to snake out
of her in a rising whimper that became a cry. Cissy moved in
at the right time. "NOT GEORGE! Ohhhh!" I couldn't see
her face any more. That was as it should be. What happened
now was private. The women shielded her, supported her.
She didn't say anything more, just issued great sobs and
unrecognizable half-syllables. Joan was on one side and Cissy
on the other, with Delia Alexander holding close to the huge
purple shape, a shape which was now gently rocking back
and forth as though she was cradling something. I stood back
like an extra holding a spear in some moth-eaten revival of
Julius Caesar. There's an extra in *Macbeth* who comes in at

every performance and says "The Queen, my Lord, is dead."
I always wondered whether after the first few weeks of the
run if he wasn't tempted to alter the line to: "The Queen, my
Lord, is better."

At the first telling of the news, Lloyd had walked off quickly
to get his car. By the time the gaggle surrounding Maggie
had got her to her feet, the car was waiting in the sodden
grass as close to the dock as possible. They moved towards
the car, a cooing and a whimpering filling the afternoon air.
They tucked her in; Cissy and Joan got in with her. Delia
climbed in beside Lloyd, and off they went. I told Desmond
that Harry Glover knew all the details I did, and excused
myself before I fell on my face again.

I wanted a bath badly, but I doubt whether I could have
coped with knobs and plugs let alone the pump and pails and
the propane stove. I pulled the curtains together where I
could find any and addressed myself to sleep. I didn't seal the
envelope. I didn't add a return address.

Chapter Nineteen

When I awoke, it was dark. I closed my eyes again. This time I was trying to row my way out of the way of a huge freighter, which kept coming at me from all directions through a fog. When it was clear that there was no escape, whichever side I was sleeping on, I threw my legs out of bed and followed them. I looked at my watch at the side of the bed, where I'd left it behind as I sloughed all my city clothes nearly a week ago. Eleven thirty-three. But the Delco was still pounding away, and the electric lights were burning in the Annex. Maybe Glover was grilling everybody. Maybe somebody from CIB had taken over. Maybe it was like the hotdog roast I missed.

I was too turned around to go back to sleep, so I pulled on some clean clothes, added a sweater because I felt a chill, and walked over towards the Annex. It was like the last time I was there, and the time before that. Lloyd Pearcy was at the old record player trying to get the words of "Lindy Lou" straight. Directly under one of the bearskins, Des Westmorland and Delia were sitting and not talking. David Kipp was sitting at the card table playing solitaire, but it didn't look like he knew what cards he was holding. Maggie, of course, was not there. Her seat was about twice as empty as any other place in the room.

All the faces were uniformly long. It was hard to understand that this was all for George. George, whom nobody had a good word for. George, the dim; George, the noisy; George, the nosy; Gloomy George; George, the dead, the late, the deceased, the dear departed of Maggie, the un-dear departed of the rest of us. Maybe the long looks were for Maggie. Maybe, not feeling the loss themselves, they were trying to come at it through the back door. They all liked Maggie. That sounded about right so I didn't worry about it any more. I drew myself a cup of coffee, added milk and three teaspoonfuls of sugar. I usually have two, but I was practically in mourning.

David Kipp drifted up to me. "I hope you can tell me what this is all about. I can't get anybody to open up. You were there; what happened?"

"I got hit on the head. After a while I woke up. Somebody got to George while I was out. George isn't going to wake up. Somewhere between me and George the attacker lost his amateur standing."

"This is turning out to be one lousy holiday. Cooped up here, kept in the dark. It's like television."

"What do you hate most, the plot or the cast?"

"Oh, what's the use talking to you? You wouldn't understand this, but I came up here to look at birds not sit around waiting for policemen to ask me idiotic questions."

"Such as where did you go when the lights went out on the night of Friday, July sixth?" Kipp's lip actually quivered. Like he'd learned to do it from practising before a mirror. I suddenly felt like I'd hit him with a brick in a pillow fight. He backed away from me and bumped into the coffee urn. "Hey, be careful!"

I grabbed the urn and pushed him out of the way. "This isn't your night, is it?"

"Goddamn you, Cooperman. Why don't you bugger off?" Kipp's last words were bitten off with a whispering rasp, which made him all the easier to dislike. He gave me one more dirty look then went back to his cards. I moved over to Lloyd Pearcy. He was twirling a small gizmo with emery-paper attached to a wheel.

"I'm sharpening the needles," he explained. "None of your Victor Red Seal needles. These are cut thorns from out back," and he held the thing up for me to see, although I didn't doubt him. "You ruffled David Kipp's feathers," he said with a tilt of his eyebrow. "And him so full of news about seeing both a great blue heron and a dead deer in the water all in one morning. Is that any way to treat a summer naturalist, Benny?" I smiled. He took the needle he'd been working on out, held it up to the light, and fitted it back into the tone arm. He didn't look up when he said: "I hear you've been knocked about."

"Not as bad as some."

"Cissy's over with Maggie now. She's been there ever since Harry Glover flew in here. Neither one of us much cared for George, you know. He was a mean-spirited man. Stunted. No joy or bounce in him. But, Maggie, now . . ." I bobbed my head to show that I understood, when his words died on the vine. Joan came up to us wearing a proprietary, grim face. All these deaths wouldn't do the lodge any good. If somebody wanted the Harbisons to fail, there are few better ways of doing it than killing off a guide and the next able-bodied man down the road. Joan slipped me a tight little smile with no lingering in it and turned to Lloyd.

"Have you seen Cissy?"

"Not since she went back after supper. Said she'd try to give her something to sleep. She said she's never seen a body broke up like Maggie is. Seems a shame to waste it on George." Joan raised a mocking, rather teacherly, eyebrow, and Lloyd pretended to bite his tongue for penance. Then she looked a question at me.

"Harry Glover said he'd be back tomorrow, or as soon as a medical report comes in. But I think they'll send bigger fish than Harry, don't you? I mean, don't they have to?" I shrugged, and that was as close to an opinion with weight as they were going to get until Glover himself got back.

"I wish Mike was here," Joan said. "The city's a thousand miles away when something like this happens. He left just before you came back. Damn it all to hell."

"Nobody liked George," I thought out loud. "Couldn't he

get along with anybody?" I glanced first at Joan and then back to Lloyd.

"Joan, here, seemed to manage him without too much fuss."

"Oh, he had his good points, I guess. Most of the time he was like a half-tame bear. And not a bright bear at that. He was always lifting things . . ."

"Yeah," said Lloyd, "he was light fingered. Used to pocket things like my best lures when I wasn't looking."

"He was always denouncing my friends to me, saying nasty things about the Rimmers. Dalt was at the top of George's hate list. He didn't like either Aeneas or Hector, although both of them were harmless."

"Aeneas once warned him to stop poaching or he'd report him."

"Oh, he was in trouble with everybody. He crowded the guests, like a store clerk who asks you what you want before you've closed the door behind you. I've always blamed some of the empty cabins on George. After today, I'll be able to blame them all on him. And poor Aeneas."

"Did George ever bother the people staying over at the Woodward place?"

"No more than he did anybody else. He didn't get along with the senator. No, I guess George was a real democrat: he was terrible to everybody alike."

The new couple, whose name I never mastered, got up and said goodnight to everybody in a subdued way. As they went out, Cissy Pearcy came in, looking haggard and a little unsteady on her feet. She came over to where we were standing.

"How's Maggie?" Joan asked for all of us.

"She's sleeping now. I gave her some pills. I just held her like a baby, rocking her back and forth, until she fell asleep. Lloyd, do you still have that bottle of rye in the cabin? I think I could use a small drink. I think I'm going into shock." Lloyd went out the door as though Cissy'd had the best idea advanced so far that evening. He was back in less than two minutes. It was a new bottle, still in its slim liquor-store bag. Joan found some plastic glasses and Lloyd poured a drink for the four of us. Nobody else seemed to mind.

I sipped at my glass without swallowing anything but a burning sensation. I wasn't very good with booze. Usually it just sent me to sleep. Lloyd sipped at his, too, but Cissy was pouring herself a second drink before any of us had finished the first.

"She got morbid first, then maudlin. Sloppy sentimental, I mean. She was talking about her ruined life, how nobody ever understood her, how she'd thrown herself away, first for one man and then for one after another." She banged the glass against the bottle when she poured out her third straight shot. "She told me about how her father was the only man who ever cared about her, about how George had always taken and taken and never said thank you. How he wouldn't grow up." I worked away at my drink, wishing I could dilute it with some water from the well. But drinking it neat was the unspoken fashion, so I sipped it between my teeth. It lit up a chilly spot under my liver and the glow spread and worked its way out to my fingers.

"Then, she's not just broken up about George?" I asked.

"Go on with you," she said, making a pass at my arm with her glass. "She doesn't know what she's saying. She always was one for the romantic posture."

"She loved that George of hers. Watched him like a hawk," said Lloyd.

"Duffwack!" said Cissy, at the bottle again.

"That's not cooking sherry, Cissy. You'll make yourself sick."

"Lies, lies, lies."

"Maggie always did have a sense of the dramatic," Joan said, looking at her glass. "She never gave George much chance to say anything in here."

"Stuff!" said Cissy.

"Is this a private party, or may anyone join?" That was Des Westmorland, as he chose to be called up there, with his girlfriend at his elbow. "If you're running short, I have another bottle in my cabin."

"This isn't a dead soldier yet," said Cissy, pouring cold coffee from one half-empty cup into another. "Here's one," and she passed bottle and cup to Delia Alexander. Joan found another plastic glass for Des and we were all back in business.

From the doorway, we must have looked peculiar. There was no reason for us to huddle so closely together. Des and Delia nodded thanks but offered no more than mute company for a few minutes.

"Don't give *him* any," Cissy said, pointing over at David Kipp, who had just looked up from the couch. "I don't like the low hang of his arms. I don't like his hairy knuckles."

"Cissy!"

"It's the drink."

"My glass is empty! Lloyd, I saw you. I'm a grown woman. I don't need to be coddled. Hold the bottle still!" Lloyd's attempt to remove the contagion failed and Cissy was nose-deep in her glass again. A brand-new Cissy for me. "That George was a son of a bitch," she said. "Whoever killed him did everybody a favour."

"Really?" said Des, showing bright teeth. "In what way?"

"Well, you must know all about that," she said, her face suddenly thrust close to his. "A man who ruins a child's camera just to show off." Des's teeth disappeared under his moustache, and he worried his mouth to the shape of a drain before answering.

"Mrs. Pearcy, I'm sorry about the camera, as though it's any of your affair, and I paid the boy so he'll be able to buy another."

"Desmond, let's go for a walk." Delia took Westmorland's arm, but he shook her off.

"And I wasn't showing off."

"No, you just didn't like having your picture taken with

Miss Alexander, did you? Did you think the boy was going to send it to the papers?"

"Please, Des. Let's go."

"No, I want to hear this. I guess you think that fools and drunkards are licenced. Well, let me tell you— "

"Bullshit!" said Cissy. After that, I took a real swallow of rye. Delia had Des's arm again, and this time she was not to be shaken loose. Westmorland tried his smile again, but it didn't fool anybody; his eyes were as cold as a leg of New Zealand lamb.

"And why, pray, would the papers be interested in such photographs?"

"Come on, Des!"

"No. I want to hear more. You were saying, Mrs. Pearcy?"

"Oh, belt up. Think nobody reads the weekend papers? I may live in Sudbury, but I do keep my eyes open."

She took another glance at Joan, then lifted her glass. It was more the need for a gesture than anything else. The glass was empty.

"Well, people shouldn't go around ruining the cameras of children. I could run for parliament on a slogan like that, couldn't I, Joan?"

Joan took in a welcome breath of relief and nodded. The scene was sliced through and each of us was left holding a scrap of the painted backdrop in our hands. When he was quite sure that he had nothing further to fear from Cissy, Des led Delia through a chorus of icy good nights out of the lodge and into the night.

It was Cissy herself who broke the silence that had settled around us and seeped into all the cracks between the logs of the wall.

"Damn it! He has the other bottle. When will I learn to keep my big fat mouth shut?"

"You made him very cross," said Joan.

"Why shouldn't I? If he wants to play games. He knows that I know. I just didn't want to spoil things for Joan."

"Oh, great!" said Joan. "Now's the time to think of that."

"Cissy, I'm taking you home," said Lloyd. Cissy looked at the empty bottle and nodded at the inevitable.

"Me and my big mouth. I sometimes think I'm a little juvenile delinquent, you know that? If I were you I wouldn't put up with me."

"Upsy-daisy," said Lloyd. "There hasn't been a night like this in Algonquin Park since the night the mill burned down." We each grabbed an arm, while Joan began to clean up the signs of the party. Cissy moved her feet between Lloyd and me as though she were using them for walking as we went down the two steps and across to their cabin. When we got to the steps leading to their porch, I lifted her nearly dead weight and caught a worried look on Lloyd's face as he reached for the screen door.

"Up and over; up and over. That's the way to do it," said Cissy. Inside, we stretched her on her bed. She didn't budge, but gave a sort of groan when I pulled away an arm that had been trapped under her back. Lloyd turned off the light and closed the door. He tilted his head in the direction of a chair in the kitchen, and I relaxed into it. Lloyd found two beers in the refrigerator.

"Cissy," Lloyd said, "hasn't had a skinful for a couple of years now. I almost forgot what she was like. Sort of comes out of herself."

"Lloyd, how well do you remember that fire at the mill?"

"Like I said, it was a night to remember. Fifteen years ago if it's a day. Cissy and me were camped about half a mile away. As soon as we saw it, we came as fast as we could."

"It must have been going full tilt by then?"

"Like a bat outa hell. There was no saving her. Not even if we'd had a hose and pump."

"Where was Trask when you got there?"

"Sleeping it off over on the motel porch."

"And Maggie?"

"Safe in the arms of Jesus!" came a voice from the bedroom.

"Maggie was watching the fire. We passed George in his boat as we came up to the old dock and we watched it together," said Lloyd.

"What about the hotel guests?"

"The place was empty by the time we got there. Wayne couldn't keep guests, even in high summer. No sign of anybody when we got there anyway."

"Eyewash," said Cissy.

"Any sign of Dick Berners?" Lloyd's face moved around the room, stopping on the blue coffee pot on the stove.

"Old Dick? No. He didn't show up for a couple of days. No, he and Wayne didn't do much talking in those days. He wasn't sociable."

"Wingdoodle!" from the bedroom.

"Dick was all scarred on his face; burns he got in the war. He stayed by himself. He didn't show his dirty face around here that night."

"Duffwack!" came a cry from the bedroom, followed by a loud snort. We listened for a moment, but there was nothing further to report. Soon a steady snore could be heard. I finished my beer, Lloyd walked me to the screen door, and I retreated to my own cabin to do some snoring of my own.

Chapter Twenty

In the days I'd been at Petawawa Lodge, I'd only taken advantage of the swimming facilities a couple of times. First thing on Monday morning, first thing for me anyway — others had been up and about for hours — I rolled out of bed, played games with the china ewer and basin, the nearest thing to running water in my cabin, and changed from pajamas directly into my swimming trunks. The day was going to be another seamless day of blue cloudless skies and heat that hits you between the shoulder blades. I folded a towel on the end of the dock and dove into Big Crummock Lake. I came up half-way to the wooden raft tingling. From the raft, I inspected the mushy, mollusk-strewn bottom a few times then returned to the dock, where I spread out the towel and stretched out along the sun-warmed planks. I could feel the itch of water evaporating before I had fairly caught my breath. From where I was lying, I could see past the second island well up to the far end of the lake. The Rimmers' point was glinting above the waterline, with the cruiser, looking smaller than a fingernail, anchored at the end of its dock. The Woodward place was invisible behind a near headland.

Nearer at hand were the things the lodge guests had left behind them. In the nearby deckchair, a pair of sunglasses and a paperback book lying face down waiting for Aline Barbour. Lloyd's grey-blue fishing-tackle box was resting under the shade of a chair, with bright narrow stripes of light crossing it six times. Chris Kipp's water-logged camera sat at the corner of the arm of one chair, another kid's sand-pail and shovel not far away.

From where I was lying, sizzling, drinking up the sun, and

to hell with Ray Thornton, I could see an ant's-eye view of the scene of Wayne Trask's sudden departure from this life. I could reach out and drip water on the very corner of the board that had stunned him. The water darkened the wood and spread down and out along the wood grain, much like blood. The sun quickly dried up the evidence, so I dripped again, speading out the stain with my fingers, moving pools of water to cover as wide an area as possible, and watching the sun working closely behind me, drying up any pool left too shallow. I was quickly dozing off. I hadn't felt so relaxed in days.

Under my chin, an ant, a real one, not the ant I was imagining a moment before, walked along the board in front of me. It tried to find a way to continue its progress by walking over the gap between boards, but each time was turned back because the gap was too great. Soon it discovered that the dock was built by resting and nailing these boards across heavy wooden rails. I couldn't see the beams, but I could see where the nails went into them. The ant, once he found the rail to my left, made his way out to the end of the dock, walking from board to beam, then up to the next board again, and so on. Near my chin, the boards were nailed in with two nails into each beam. The work of the economical Dalt Rimmer, according to Lloyd Pearcy. Out at the end of the dock, far beyond where the ant had progressed so far, the nailing was erratic with some nails bent over and mangled, four or five nails being used in each spot. I turned the other cheek. On the right side, the same pattern was there—neat nailing by Rimmer, and beginning at the end of the dock, drunken nailing. Then I noticed something new. Between these two types, or styles, of carpentry was a third. Lloyd hadn't mentioned that the dock had had three builders, only two. I got up on my hands and knees to look closer. Yes, between Trask's work and Rimmer's, three boards had been nailed to the beams with four neat nails at each point of contact. There were no crescent-shaped dints in the wood, such as those you could still see left over from Trask's hammering.

It wasn't a trick of the sun. It wasn't some dream enjoyed after I'd dozed off on the warm boards. I checked the details. Trask and the second carpenter used the same nails. Dalt Rimmer used another sort. Rimmer and the second carpenter appeared to have gone about their tasks cold sober. Trask's work looked like a textbook example of how not to build a dock. For a long time I felt like I was playing a game of observation, a game in no way attached to reality. Then it hit me: if the board with the cleat attached was the one that killed Trask, as Lloyd had pointed out to me, then at the time it hit him, it had not yet been nailed to the dock. It was the first of the boards put in place by the second carpenter. In fact, the second carpenter could have been Trask's murderer, hitting him from behind with the board, dumping the unconscious body into the water, then calmly nailing it in place so that it testified to the fact that Trask hit the board, and not the other way around. For insurance, two more boards were nailed into place before the second carpenter took his leave of the scene of the crime.

We were dealing with a very cool customer here. Not a hit-and-miss act of violence, but a well-thought-out crime that could up to now be described as perfect. But the ant and I were now on the trail, and with luck one of us would run him to ground.

Aline Barbour came up behind me wearing that pink bikini with black edging. "Beat you to the raft," she said, and running to the edge of the dock, plunged, a tan blur, into the water. I knew that I'd run a poor second, but I jumped in and followed her. By the time I got there, she was holding onto the raft with one hand, having already caught her breath. It took me a minute to corral mine, and then I hoisted myself aboard the float.

"I've been hearing about your adventures," she said, pulling herself half out of the water and resting her arms on the canvas matting so that her bust rested on the edge of the raft.

"Who's been talking out of school?"

"I heard about how you nearly got killed going back of beyond somewhere."

"Oh, that, well, the serious fisherman has to be ready for anything. Have you been taking midnight canoe rides lately?"

"Every night. I love the lake when it's quiet." She pulled the rest of her body out of the water and lay alongside me on the canvas top of the raft. She took her white bathing cap off, and let her hair loose, like it was alive and demanding its freedom. Again, I found it hard not to concentrate on the tanned body. I watched the water drip from her forehead and off the tip of her nose and disappear in the crevice of the pink bikini top. Her toes were painted the colour of dried blood, her shoulders were smooth and luminous, with depth to them, like velvet.

"I hear that you were rescued by the man at the Woodward place. He's quite a man of mystery. What's he like?"

"We both know the answer to that, Miss Barbour."

"What can you mean by that?"

"Only that you have been watching that spot as often as you can. I think that we might get farther if we begin to trust one another."

"You aren't very tactful, are you?"

"It's a waste of time when he's getting ready to move out."

"When? How do you know?" She was on her elbows, looking over me with sudden interest. She saw the trap she'd fallen into and relaxed. "Well, it doesn't hurt to share information," she said at length. We were now lying side by side with our knees up under the sun: hers, smooth and brown; mine white with curly black hair. We looked like examples of two species, not just different sexes of the same species.

"He bought a couple of boxes of groceries yesterday. I'm not guessing he'll move before the middle of the week."

"That's not based just on groceries?"

"No. He's waiting for something, and he won't leave until he gets his hands on it."

"On what?" she asked, and I said nothing. She lifted herself on one elbow and looked down at me. "You're a funny man," she said.

"Why am I a funny man?"

"Because you keep everything so tightly controlled it's like you'd taken an oath or something. Are you always so serious?" She gave me the full extent of her smile. It was hard to remember that I was working.

"Where do you know Patten from?" I asked when I could get my mind back on the case.

"I'm just one of the people he swindled. Just one of the millions he's trying to run out on." Her cheeks began to glow with this, and her eyes were dark and serious. "We were all so young and impressionable. He seemed to offer us a new beginning, a new hope." The blush had moved to her neck and beyond the frontier where it is normally possible to follow these rosy index fingers of feeling.

"Are you one of the group taking him, or trying to take him, to court?"

"You're thinking of Elmo Nash, T.C. Sagarin, and the others. All they're trying to get is money. I want more than money. I want to see him crawl."

"That sounds like more than your wounded youth talking. His church is on the brink. You don't talk like any of the little people he hurt."

"People like David Kipp, you mean?" I tried to take that gift without showing any surprise.

"Sure, people like him. You want those fingernails pressed into him deeper than you've got them into your palm right now." She looked down at her hand and released the pressure. "What's your plot?"

"What's yours? I know who you're working for, and why you're doing it. I could have you pulled off the case like *that* if I wanted to." Suntan oil prevented an audible snap.

"But you don't want to?"

"Not yet, anyway. In the meantime, we can both wait for him to make his move."

"I see," I said, wheels running in circles inside my head. She shifted so that I was getting, not only the curve of her torso, but now also the curve of her hips. She was physically persuasive, and I was only human. We didn't change for about a minute, and then Chris and Roger Kipp shouted and climbed up on the raft, splashing cold water on both of us. That killed it. Or I thought it had. We rolled off into the water and swam back to shore. I grabbed my stuff on the dock and took my gooseflesh back towards my cabin to change.

David Kipp was just coming out of the screen door of my place when I got there. "Did you find what you were looking for?" He gave me that quivering lip again and leaned back against the wood of the cabin for moral support. I stood in his path and tried to look as though I might hit him if I had to. I was sucking in my gut to look less like a ninety-seven-pound weakling.

"Get out of my way, Cooperman. You're not the law up here."

'That's right. But there's lots of law around now that I need it."

"Now wait a minute. Don't get sore. Your door was open . . ."

". . . and you just stopped by to prevent my belongings from blowing into the lake. Listen Kipp, I could bounce one off you and then get down on my knees and apologize for the blunder." I thought of Cissy's description of his long ape-like arms and hairy knuckles. I had to avoid a bear-hug or wrestling around in the remains of Joan's petunias. "Did you uncover my black belt under my shirts? Kipp, you bother me. You're bugging Mrs. Harbison and that bothers me. Stay away, she doesn't like it. And as for the business up at the other end of the lake . . ."

"What are you talking about? I haven't been over the

sandbar in the whole week I've been here."

"You were up the river leading from Little Crummock. Don't play games with me. You were seen, Kipp." The lip told me that he didn't guess I was bluffing. "Besides, you gave it away yourself when you boasted about seeing the heron and dead deer. We both know where you saw them, don't we?" Kipp was leaning away from me and making me feel like a bully in the schoolyard. I tried not to look at either of his big hands. If he made fists of them, I'd had it. I thought I'd better keep the banter sassy. "You saw more than wildlife up there, didn't you, Kipp? You know that George McCord didn't die of old age yesterday morning. I think we'd better find Corporal Glover and first you tell him what you know, and then I'll tell him what I know. We can flip a coin if you don't think that's fair. I'll talk first if you want."

"Look, I'm not saying anything to Glover I don't have to. I hope you don't misunderstand my being here. I'm not sore at you. I just want to know what's going on, that's all. And as for what I did to Patten's boat, let him take me to court. I just lost my head when I recognized him under those whiskers. That bastard owes me, and I've probably had more satisfaction than most people are going to get." Another gift landing in my lap.

"Where were you when Patten went by?"

"Back in the marsh getting pictures. I caught him in my telephoto lens. I was sure he didn't see me. Or did you mean somebody else?"

"Keep talking. How long did you give him before you followed?"

"Ten minutes. No more. He left the boat at the clearing by the portage. I'm glad I did it to him, Cooperman. You can't take that away from me." I looked at Kipp and relaxed a notch. What the hell, I thought, let him keep that much.

"Kipp, what put Patten on your hit list? Aren't you one of the gang taking him to court? What did he do to you that makes you chop holes in boats among other things?"

"What do you care? You're here protecting him. I know that. I've seen you fishing together and playing chess on his dock. What do you care about the people he's hurt?"

"Did he hurt you?"

"No, not me. It's the boys' mother. She's all used up since she joined the Ultimate Church. Those TV evanglists are all a bunch of crooks, but Patten's the worst of the lot. She can't keep an idea in her head for two seconds any more. She won't settle. She sits and watches TV all the time without seeing anything. Patten destroyed her belief in God, in religion, and in her family. There's nobody at home inside my wife, Cooperman, and she used to be the dearest, most—"

"Okay, I get the idea. I'm sorry for your trouble, but remember there are laws in this country just like you have at home. I want you to stay out of my way from now on, Kipp. You hear?"

"I hear. Now you listen: somehow I'm going to get even with Patten."

"Kipp," I said with my face close to his, "you know in seven days time you could be dead a week." His lip started quaking again and those hairy hands with the hairy knuckles and service-club rings came up to guard his mid-section. "Now beat it," I said and he did that. As he ran off in the direction of his cabin, I heard the line I'd just used on him again in my head. Only this time I heard it in the voice of the TV actor who'd said it originally. He may have had it first, but my reading got results.

Chapter Twenty-one

I had shed my trunks and was walking around in a towel sarong, when I heard the screen door slap shut. It was Aline. "I didn't think we'd finished our conversation," she said, parking her towel, bathing cap, sunglasses, and suntan oil on the kitchen table. She was in a light-blue terrycloth beach robe. I felt ill-prepared to throw myself into the role of host, since I was only a tuck away from total candour. She sat in one of the arrowback chairs, her robe falling open just enough so that I forgot that I'd already seen the pink bikini, and how she made it live up to its promises.

"Sorry I can't offer you a drink," I said. "I'm completely out of booze." I hadn't bothered to bring any, but she didn't have to know all my secrets.

"I could make coffee," she suggested, and I agreed, thinking that it would give me a minute to put some pants on. She swished the kettle to see that it was nearly half full, then lit the gas as though to the manner born. It came on with a wump. She found my instant, and spooned out two heaping teaspoonfuls into two cups. For some reason, I just watched her do it, like it was a trick or something I'd never been able to master. I settled down on the couch, where she joined me waiting for signs of awakening from the kettle. "You were saying that you thought Patten was waiting for something, Mr. Cooperman."

"Call me Benny." I didn't answer her question. I was thinking about the perfect dark arches of her eyebrows, one of which slowly lifted as I forgot the question.

"Did you mean his passport?"

"Hmmmm? Yes, well, I knew he had to get one, and that it would take a while. You've seen that he has picked it up, have you?"

"One of his boys collected a large envelope from the box he has at the post office in Hatchway. But I don't know in what name. That was this morning."

"It won't take long to find out," I suggested.

"But I'm not sure you were talking about the passport."

"Sure I was. That and the announcement of the Supreme Court on the church's status. That's the red light or the green light as far as his future in the States is concerned. They expect the decision around Friday. With two murder investigations going on, he's not going to stay in the park a minute longer than necessary."

Once again the terrycloth was letting me have free glimpses of Aline's tanned self under the blue robe. I guess it was the robe's approximation of a dress that found the tickling place. Not counting Maggie, I hadn't seen a woman in a dress in over a week. I hadn't realized how hooked I was on them. It must be all the fresh air and exercise in the park. It summoned up the blood as Frank Bushmill used to say. Aline was looking at my towel. She leaned close and kissed me, breaking away only long enough to whisper something in my ear.

"I finally understand what Mae West meant when she said, 'Is that a pistol in your pocket, or are you just glad to see me?' " She was all over me like a tent and showed no sign of taking the kettle off the stove.

"Hey, wait a minute! What's going on?" I said between the kisses, without putting everything I had into the reading of the line. I held on to the terrycloth until it came away, and then there was nothing but tanned arms and legs and the pink bikini with black piping. I hung on to some of that, and lost, somewhere along the line, the tuck in my towel.

The kettle was nearly boiling dry when I turned it off. Aline was asleep on the couch. The two cups stood side by side on the pine table. One of the cats was staring in the screen door and giving me a look I didn't think I'd ever get from a furry creature. I slipped into my wet trunks and went into the water off the end of the dock for another short swim. When I came out, I saw Joan wrestling with a big Johnson outboard motor which she'd attached to a mounted two-by-four between twin birches. She had the top off and was exploring the inner depths with her nose nearly touching the carburetor.

"Mike said the weather in Toronto's terrible. I talked with him on the phone in town. He said it was like a Turkish bath in the Black Hole of Calcutta. Maybe we'll get some business on the weekend." She didn't look me in the eye but went on smiling at the cylinder. "I'm the last of the optimists." She wiped her hands on an oily rag and straightened up. "That'll do until I get the part I need. That's one thing we don't have to order from the city. There's a good marine-supply store in Hatchway." I was wondering why she made me a gift of her thinking out loud.

"I never did thank you for getting me ready for that excursion of mine. The sardines were right up my street. The bear didn't fancy them."

"Bear? God, Benny, we didn't spare you anything, did we?"

"You've held the poison ivy off. Let's accept the poison ivy as read. Any opposed?"

"Something else that doesn't let up is coming back in a while and wants to talk to you."

"Harry Glover of the Mounted?"

"Show no disrespect. The OPP are very powerful in the park." She still wasn't looking at me. I finished drying off with the damp towel and went back to the cabin. Aline was awake and bundled securely inside her terrycloth robe. There was instant coffee on the table.

"Glover's coming back to ask a few more questions."

"He's not very original, is he?"

"There are questions I'd like to ask you myself."

"I'm thirty-five, married but with an independent income. I like fast cars, chilled Chablis, and the clothes of the fifties. I'm a Libra, I have a low boiling point, love to scrap, but prefer making up. I'm a pushover for men with curly knees, only it's not easy in town to separate the unshorn lambs from the shorn . . ."

"And you've known Patten for a very long time."

"I thought we were talking about me? Here I am, opening myself up in an uncharacteristic way, and you have to bring up my *bête noire*. Benny, you have no couth."

"How'd he win his *bête noire* status?"

"Oh, you are so boring. You should hear yourself. Boring! I want to hear you tell me about you. Who are you when you're at home?"

"It's a long sad story, and I'll tell it to you sometime. We'll go out for a canoe ride or sit in front of the fire in the Annex when I'm sure you aren't just trying to change the subject. We are talking about Patten. When did you meet him?"

"Now you really are boring. I don't care to answer questions. And you know you can't make me. So why don't we change the subject? Where'd you buy this instant? It must be twenty years old." She was being touchy but trying her best not to seem touchy. She might not want an ally in whatever she was doing, but she couldn't afford to turn my offer of friendship around altogether. I didn't have a hold on her, I had no right to cross-examine her, and I couldn't even storm out of the room and slam the door. It was my cabin. Besides, she'd already told me several things; I shouldn't get greedy in my old age.

Ten minutes after Aline returned to her cabin, Glover's car pulled into the clearing covered with a fine powdering of yellow dust. I watched him slowly climb out of the front seat, decide to leave his cap where it was lying on the seat beside him, and head in my direction. I walked away from the door and had climbed into my clothes before I heard Glover's rattle at the screen door.

"Have you got a boat?" he asked as he pretended not to see the two cups on the table.

"There's a rowboat I was using. The boat with the outboard met with an accident." He didn't sound interested.

"Okay, take me rowing. I'll tell you where." We went down to the dock. I untied the bow line and Glover got in heavily. "Head off to the right," he said from the stern, and I figured out that that meant my left as I sat facing him and the shore. Rowing is a peculiar art. It is arranged so that you get the best possible work out of your muscles but at the cost of having your back turned towards the direction you want to go. I skirted the raft and already the lodge clearing was beginning to close up to resemble a brief break in the forested shoreline. "That's right," Glover said. "Keep heading in this direction."

"Will you give me a hint about where we're going, or do you want to wait until we're in the middle, in case we're overheard?"

"You're pretty good with the cheap shots, Mr. Cooperman. May I remind you this is a murder investigation? We can do without your big-city sarcasm."

"Cut it out, Glover. That stuff doesn't rile me. Save it for the old ladies who wouldn't think of spitting in your eye." I thought I'd have a try at bearding the bully in him. It couldn't make matters worse.

"Now, look here, Mr. Cooperman. There's been two murders, and I was the first police officer on the scene both times. That means I'm working close to the inspector. I've got the feeling that you're not helping out as much as you could." It was working. I could tell when he began to explain himself. He must have forgotten the golden rule of aggression: never apologize, never explain. Or is it the other way around?

We were coming down to the bottom of the lake where the far shore, with a few brief changes of direction, moves closer and closer to the shore I was familiar with. I kept looking over my shoulder to see if I was headed correctly, but frankly I got better headings from Glover's expression. When I was moving too far from his destination, I could see his lips tightening in displeasure, so I leaned on the other oar until his jaw relaxed. "Has the body count mounted overnight? Have you got the medical reports you were waiting for?"

"Yeah, I've got all that. Couple of days ago. Didn't change much: we knew that Aeneas hadn't been dead more than twenty-four hours when you found him. And George, we got to him when he was six to eight hours dead. We flew him right to Huntsville. Besides the time of death, we didn't find out anything you couldn't tell by looking. Aeneas had his head concussed, but it didn't kill him. He drowned. George, well, I don't have to tell you about George. Was that an axe from the cabin?"

"It was the one I'd taken with me for protection against being surprised by a bear. In fact I did run into one."

"Bear, eh? They don't usually range this far south so early in the season. I guess it's because the flies were bad this spring." He looked at me with a blankish look that could mean anything. He moved his head to the right and I strained my neck trying to see what he was pointing to. There were reeds in this part of the lake, but through them I could see a wooden dock standing about a foot above the water line. I pointed the boat in that direction and soon I could hear the gentle caress of the reeds on the boat's underbelly. Now I could hear shore sounds: birds squawking at one another, chipmunks chattering, and the buzz of insects on a hot afternoon. A policeman in his short-sleeved blue shirt came down steps cut in the clay bank and waited for us on the dock. He caught the end of the boat which threatened for a moment to shift the dock inland by a few feet. He tied the painter to a ring and Glover introduced him as Sergeant Ted Valentine, who had been taking pictures of the site of Aeneas's camp. So, I knew where I was.

The part of the landscape the OPP was interested in had been surrounded by string with pieces of masking tape hanging down and blowing in the wind. Seeing pieces of scenery isolated like that, washed the colour out of the rest of the setting. The trees and bushes within the barrier looked like trees and bushes in a museum diorama or on a stage. They were both realer than real and not quite real, all at the same time. The principal island of string surrounded Aeneas's tent and campfire. It was a small pup tent, slit open and laid back like the corpse of its owner in the dissecting room in Huntsville's hospital. The orange plastic underside looked nearly new. The sleeping bag in it was spotted and stained with much distinguished service indoors and out. While I was looking around outside the marked areas, Glover and Valentine conferred silently.

Aeneas had pitched his tent on flat ground where a cabin had once stood. It commanded a view that went from the southernmost part of the lake to the top, where the lake twisted in its crook. The two islands looked small and were made into afterthoughts or details on the lake. The lodge was hidden, so was Patten's place. I could see the point of land with the Rimmers' house standing on it. The surface of the lake was calm but unreflecting, like the matte finish on a photograph. The four corners of Aeneas's camp were marked by piles of fieldstone which had been the supports for the cabin's main sill beams. The piles looked like monuments you see in pictures of the Arctic tundra. Glover came back and looked with me, sympathetically.

"The Pearcys had a cabin here once. I remember it from when I was a kid. My brother and me used to keep a boat just over there." He pointed through a stand of trees to where the shoreline must have been. "You see, the road's just below here, less than an eighth of a mile. Come over here." I followed him inland for about fifty yards. I wasn't thinking metric today. Neither one of us was. That's metric for you; it hits you every so often and then goes away. We were standing at the edge of a flooded piece of ground. I could see that it was usually dry from the trees and bushes that were awash and the grass swept in the direction of the flow.

"There's a brook comes down that hill," he said. "But instead of emptying into the lake here, it runs down in the other direction, crosses the road, and joins the Dennison Creek, which feeds into the Rock Lake."

"But on the map it's called something else."

"How'd you know?"

"I'm a great reader." We both looked around. I found a well-worn path that led from the campsite to the road.

"Is that path dry all the way?" I asked Sergeant Valentine who was hunkering nearby and examining a wad of chewing gum disposed of in its wrapper. I knew the brand. I'd seen it around.

"Oh, no. It runs into the water just beyond the trees ahead. It used to be wide enough to bring a car in, but now there's only one narrow path open, when it's open."

"Did you find what hit Aeneas?" Glover shook his head and rubbed his nose with a run of knuckles.

"Well, what have you got then? What do you make of it all?" Glover motioned me down the slope away from the campsite and the sergeant. I hoped that he was in a mood to trot out all his treasures. At least he didn't lean over and push my face in as we sat on some flat rocks above the shore. He took out a cigarette, lit it with a wooden match, which he then broke between his fingers and threw into the bush. I took out my Player's and borrowed a match, just to show I wasn't rejecting him altogether, just his brand of cigarettes.

"I got suspects coming out my ass," Glover said. "Every cabin is full of suspicious people. It's like in a movie. Maybe they all did it. I saw that in a movie once."

"Besides the people at the lodge, have you talked to anybody else at the lake?"

"Sure. I saw the Rimmers and a fellow named Edgar who's staying in Senator Woodward's place. And I talked to Maggie McCord, naturally."

"Anything interesting develop?"

"I told you. I got suspects coming out my ass."

"All you need is one live one. Let's go over the list," I said, trying to be helpful. Glover was focusing on a spot out in the lake where a loon might poke his black head out of the water. He took a thoughtful drag on his cigarette.

"I can't do that," he said.

"Okay, let's not go over your list. The fish are biting out there," I said, getting up and brushing off the dirt from my trousers. "Give you a lift back?" He got up, went to speak to Valentine for a minute, then returned to the boat. He got into the stern and I did the honours of casting off. Valentine watched us from the high ground like we were the last human beings he was likely to see for some time. "You still haven't found a murder weapon at the site?"

"No," Glover mumbled. "We're looking for something that could give a serious, long but narrow impression to the back of Aeneas's head. He wasn't battered with a rough piece of firewood."

"Not a piece of pipe? That would be easy to drop or throw into the lake."

"They've covered the area with divers and metal detectors. Nothing. Besides, the bump he got was even narrower than you could get from a pipe that was heavy enough to do serious damage." I was rowing out into the middle of the lake, taking the long way back to the lodge. I thought about the murder weapon while the oars gave my muscles something to think about.

"I'd like to help, if I could," I said.

"We're doing fine. Everything's on schedule. So don't get your shirt in an uproar for me, eh? Don't get high blood pressure on my account. The sergeant's getting things in shipshape order." I could hear the echo of my oars from the first island. We didn't talk for a minute. "I can't get advice from you, Cooperman. We don't pay for it. The OPP don't deal with hustlers. You're not the law up here, I am."

"Uh-huh." Glover and I listened to the water and the sound of my oars.

"There are rules about seeking outside help."

"Uh-huh." There was a squeak in the oar lock punctuating the silence.

"If anybody ever found out . . ."

"Uh-huh." Another silence.

"It wouldn't hurt just to talk, I guess, would it? After all, I'm supposed to gather information from all possible sources. But we're not doing business together. You got that? I'm not buying anything. That clear?"

"Uh-huh. Okay, who are your suspicious characters? Let's deal with them. I mean the ones whose stories don't check out."

"That fellow Westmorland's at the top of my list. He asks too many questions and answers too few. It's like talking to the chief inspector. He's nervous enough to be holding something back."

"George McCord was trying to gouge money out of Westmorland. If you want the reason, take another look at that clipping you found in George's breast pocket."

"I don't see . . ."

"Westmorland's a big shot in Ottawa. So is his wife. The lady on the other end of his amorous glances in the last motel unit isn't his wife. George was dumb, but he was smart enough to see where he could make some extra change."

"Blackmail, eh?"

"Add that to the other things that made George everybody's least favourite character up here. You've got the photograph and you can check up on his car plates."

"So Westmorland followed George into the bush and killed him to stop him spoiling things for him in Ottawa. Except we only have a clipping that says so."

"For what it's worth, I saw Westmorland throw George out the back door of his cottage unit on Saturday."

"Good, so we've got the clipping, a motive, and a witness." I told Glover about the elaborate way in which Des avoided being caught on the Kipp boy's film. I didn't want to throw

Des to the wolves, but I figured that if he was innocent of murder they wouldn't come down on him for the extra-mural hanky-panky.

We were sitting about a quarter mile off the Rimmers' point. Their cruiser was tied to the dock and I could hear the distant high-pitched whine of a circular saw. Across the lake I could see the boat from the Woodward place was cutting doughnuts in the water not far from their cove. I didn't think it was Patten, but I couldn't be sure that cabin fever hadn't spread from Lorca to other members of the household.

"At the end of the first day up here," Glover said, "I'd figured the first killing was a hate killing; you know, like somebody didn't like Indians. But McCord was the prime suspect. He never did have a good word for either Aeneas or Hec. Then George gets himself killed just to spoil my plot."

"I'd heard that George was hard on Indians. Was it really as pronounced as that? Would he have, say, picked a fight with Aeneas in town?"

"Naw, that wasn't George's style at all. George would have waited for him where he parked his truck and pounded him there. He didn't want any witnesses. He comes from canny stock, you know. That mother of his got him out of more trouble than you got minnows in a bait pail."

"What sort?"

"Oh, illegal stuff: theft under two hundred dollars, poaching, trapping in the park, hunting without a permit, or out of season, other things contrary to statute or the Provincial Park Act."

"I heard that you grew out of wild days too."

"That's right, I grew out of them. Hell, I'm not perfect. I got a girl in trouble when I was in grade ten, but I made it right. I married her. I'm supporting her and four kids. It's a real world out there and I'm real seven days a week. Some days I think I'll bust if I don't get a promotion. I sometimes think I'm in a dead end, that the clockwork of my life is running down. My wheels are spinning but they ain't even touching the ground. Damn it. It makes me so mad! Who told you about that? Never mind. I don't want to know. I suppose you heard that there was bad blood between me and Aeneas?"

"Yes, I did. Was there?"

"There was on his side. I tried to warn him off a woman once. She'd been keeping a whole clinic busy trying to keep up with her exploits. Aeneas thought I was telling him not to fool around with her because he was Indian. I was trying to do him a good turn without citing chapter and verse about the woman. That'll teach me to ration good turns." He grinned, which deepened the dark lines on either side of his nose.

From out in the middle of the lake I could hear pieces of distant conversations without knowing from which direction they came. Far away I could hear a lumber truck crunching over a corduroy road deep in the bush. I heard a plop close at hand, and when I looked, concentric circles were opening out from the direction of the noise. "Trout," Glover said. I took his word for it, and charted a new course back to the lodge. It only took me about ten minutes without asking any more questions.

Chapter Twenty-two

I didn't want to drive all the way into Hatchway just to phone Ray Thornton, but that's what I was being paid for, so I did it. The Band-aids on my hands covering the blisters felt awkward on the steering wheel. I listened to news of the outside world sprinkled with static on the car radio. Hearing the names of heads of state in the newscasts made me feel like I'd been away in the woods for eight months not eight days. I parked the car in Onions' nearly deserted lot and dialled Thornton's office in Grantham.

"Yes, I'm still alive, but no thanks to you. Somebody up here's trying to kill me, Ray. I should get danger pay."

"You're expendable. What about our friend? Is he still in one piece?"

"Sure. At least he was when I saw him yesterday. The bastard saved my life, Ray. He pulled me out of a sinking boat."

"You're always dramatizing, Benny. Why can't you have a day like everybody else? You get up, you go to work, you come home, and you go to bed: what's wrong with that?"

"I can't make a living that way. Tell me, did you get that information I asked you about?" Ray then went over the car ownerships with me. After I'd cleared that up I tried to get him to open up about Aline Barbour. He wouldn't budge.

"Look, Benny, maybe I should drive up and talk to you. It's about my client. Let me think about it overnight." I'd asked him about Aline, and he started talking about his client. I supposed that it added up, but right then I couldn't see it.

I bought some hamburger buns and a package of Shopsy's corned beef at Onions' and then hit the homeward trail. I tried baking potatoes in the big stove but I couldn't get it going. The cats weren't interested in my leftovers either.

I didn't go into the Annex that evening. I intended to but I fell asleep waiting for it to get dark. It was after eleven when I heard the power go off. The sound of the dying generator brought me out of a dream in which Patten and his friends were chasing me over the Little Crummock portage with me in full pack and carrying a canoe. Whenever they started gaining on me, Aline appeared in her terrycloth robe and made them run up a different path for a minute. Then they were hot on my trail all over again. I got up, went outside, listened to the crickets for a few minutes, and then tried to go back to sleep again. This time the dream involved a rattlesnake that wiggled its way out of a burlap bag in the bow of the canoe I was paddling far from shore. It had the face of a massasauga rattler I'd seen stuffed once, but this one wasn't crooked or dusty. It was well aware of where my bare feet were placed flat-footed on the ribs of the boat. When I sat up in a sweat, the rattle continued. But the snake wasn't at the foot of my bed. It was the screen door, and somebody was scratching fingernails over the wire.

My wristwatch, parked on the night table, blinked 12:46 at me in ruby numerals. "Who is it?" I shouted at the screen.

"It's me," came a woman's voice. "Lorca Shahn."

"Who?"

"You know—Lorca, Norrie's friend." I heard the door open and close just as I slipped out of bed and put warm feet on a cool floor.

"You have strange visiting hours," I said as I reached for my pants. I hadn't brought a bathrobe with me. I lit a candle on the night table and pulled the bed together to hide the snakes and the chase through the woods. The candle sculpted Lorca's cheekbones dramatically. She leaned against the doorpost. "What's this all about?"

"You don't have a drink by any chance, do you?" she said as she pulled a chair around from the kitchen table.

"Sorry, I'm all out. How would you like a lake trout fillet instead? I may have some shampoo or hair conditioner."

"Skip it. I hope you're not mad at me for going through your wallet? I didn't tell anybody."

"That's nice to know. What's eating you at this time of night?" Lorca was wearing tight jeans, a white T-shirt, and a green plaid shirt over it with the sleeves half-rolled.

"Nobody knows I'm here, if you're worried."

"What's happened up at the Woodward place?"

"Norrie's getting ready to leave."

"That's not exactly news."

"He wants me to go with him and I don't want to go."

"Where's he planning to go?"

"He has some sort of idea to live on a boat for a while. I'd hate that. I don't want to waste years of my life on a God-damn boat, never seeing people, never getting ashore because the cops are waiting with subpoenas and warrants. I hate that stuff."

"But you don't know yet whether he has to do that kind of a flit. The Supreme Court may rule in his favour."

"Okay, if that happens I'm happy. I don't mind living in San Clemente or Vegas. I mean, I know all those people. But I don't want to become Mrs. Arthur Shipley for the rest of my life. I'm too young to be buried alive running around the Mediterranean Sea. I mean, I can't even talk to the people. Who would I talk to? I don't know Greek or Italian or Spanish. I don't even know any French, except for the names of perfumes."

"You've got troubles all right. So Shipley's the name on Norrie's new passport? It didn't take him as long as I thought."

"He got the birth certificate almost by return mail. That helped."

"The Canadian passport is one of the most esteemed the world over. All sorts of people go to great lengths to get one. Tell me, Lorca, what if Patten just goes back to the States?"

"I'll go with him. I mean, I love Norrie. He's been real

sweet to me. Don't get me wrong. I like going to the big rallies and seeing Norrie out there and helping so many thousands. I mean, he is truly a great man. But if he's going to go off and live on a boat and get the news on the radio forget it. He doesn't need me. I'd rather just get a job somewhere. I was a receptionist once, I can do it again."

"That's the spirit."

"You're making fun of me, Mr. Cooperman." She was resting her chin on the palm of her hand with the elbow supported by one faded blue knee. I pulled out a cigarette and lighted it in the candle flame. I tried to look serious.

"What does the name Aline Barbour mean to you?" I couldn't miss the reaction the name had on her—a slight tightening of her mouth, a small change in her posture.

"I don't think I know the name. Is she one of the guests at the lodge? I haven't had a chance to . . ."

"I thought you wanted help? If I'm going to help you I need to know you're being straight with me. I know you know what I want to know."

"Just because I don't want to run away with Norrie and live on his boat doesn't mean that I'm going to turn State's evidence, or whatever they call it up here. Norrie trusts me."

"Okay, so trust him back. Just tell him you'd prefer to live in San Clemente and hear from him regularly by mail. I'm sure he'll understand."

"You're making this hard on me, Mr. Cooperman. I don't like telling tales out of school."

"Don't say another word. I'm on your side. Mum's the word." She got up from where she was sitting and began walking around the darkened cabin. I could see her silhouetted in the doorway, and later hear a match strike. The flare of her match caught a white mask-like face for a second. She threw her shadow around the room like a sail in a heavy gale as she shook out the match, then the dark returned, darker than ever.

"There's a ride back to Toronto with me, when I'm finished up here," I said to the red end of a suspended cigarette. "And I'll be finished the moment Norrie leaves. Now why don't you tell me about that revengeful bitch."

"You were listening? You bastard! I have nothing but contempt for you."

"The offer stands. I've been called worse. I used to be in the divorce business. Murder's clean by comparison. Less personal, somehow. Aline's up here for a reason. She's not just diving for clams and working on her tan. If she's planning a big surprise for Patten, the more people that know about it, the less chance it has of succeeding. I'm going to put the kettle on. Will you stay and have a cup of tea?" I couldn't see her face, but I saw that she was drawing thoughtfully on the cigarette, and I heard her release the breath. I brought the candle in from the bedroom and set it down on the pine table. When I wobbled the kettle, I could feel it had enough water left. I lit the gas burner and set about finding mugs and teabags. I didn't look at Lorca; I kept my head aimed at the kitchen counter. It was a ploy to make her talk. If it worked I'd know more about Aline; if it didn't it would be a long time before the kettle boiled.

"Aline used to know Norrie a long time ago. Before I came along. I never met her, but I heard from the boys. She was with him maybe five years. But that was ten years ago. I've been with Norrie nearly three years, on and off. We split up one time when he was getting a little too ecumenical with his relationships. I put a stop to that. I moved to Washington and let Van show me around."

"Who's this Van I've been hearing about?" I asked innocently.

"Van? That's Senator Gideon Van Rensselaer Woodward. From Vermont. It's his cabin we're staying at. He doesn't come up any more, not since he lost his son."

"Did Patten meet the senator up here in the park?"

"Sure. He practically adopted him. He was the same age as Gideon Jr., but he was much more at home in the woods. He taught young Gideon all about fishing and trapping and things like that. That's how the senator got to take such a fancy to Norrie."

"So later on, Patten followed Woodward to Washington."

"That's where everything started. That's where Norrie saw the blinding light."

"How long after the kid, Junior, died?"

"He was a teenager — seventeen, eighteen, something like that."

"Same age Patten went to Washington. Interesting."

"The senator thinks the world of Norrie. Norrie helped Van get on his feet again after his kid's death. So what if he helped Norrie when he began his ministry?"

"So what, indeed. Tell me, Lorca, about Aeneas DuFond."

"Who? I never heard of him."

"He's lying dead in the morgue at Huntsville. He's the Indian who was murdered."

"That's right. I remember. He came to see Norrie."

"And he gave something to him and asked him to do a favour. What was it he gave Norrie and what was the favour?"

"It was a lump of gold. I mean it looked like gold. He came to see Norrie the day it rained last week. Was that Thursday? He came in his canoe about an hour before it got dark."

"Why did he give it to Norrie?"

"Because he wanted Norrie to have it assayed to see if it was real."

"And was it?"

"Ask him yourself. How should I know? He gave it to Ozzie Prothroe to look after. Ozzie'll be back tomorrow." I got the teabag out of the first cup and into the second. I added a squirt of condensed milk from a small can with gummy-looking holes punched in the lid. We sat down with the candle between us. Her eyes were very blue, her hair was very dyed. In the candlelight it looked black, but by day it looked like antique furniture, a little darker than chestnuts. I was looking away, conscious that I'd been staring, when a new source of light entered the room. A moving yellow circle bobbed on the dark screen door, like a drunken full moon. I heard a voice in something like a stage whisper.

"Benny? Can I come in?" It was Aline Barbour. When the door slapped shut, I found that I'd stood up without thinking. It wasn't because I was confusing Aline with the Queen Mother. There were natural laws affecting the behaviour of men in the company of one woman when another comes into the room. It isn't a question of form; it's more basic than that. "Oh, I'm sorry, I thought you were—Oh, it's you! Well, isn't this cosy. He give you the evening off?"

Lorca recognized the manner if not the face at once. But even that wasn't long in coming. She took in the jeans, turtleneck, and denim jacket as well as the fresh makeup Aline was wearing. Lorca didn't move, none of us did, until Lorca's hand went to her face.

"Turn off that Goddamned light," she said. Aline didn't flick off her light at once. She lowered the beam to the table first. I was still finding my tongue. I felt like Archie in the comics telling Veronica and Betty that he could explain everything. But neither of them was looking at me. I could have done a handstand on the table and it wouldn't have sliced through the daggers running between them.

"Sit down and have some tea," I said when I could manage to put words together. Aline didn't budge.

"With her? With Norrie's incumbent? Don't make me laugh!"

"We've been having a talk," I said, reaching.

"Is that what you call it now? I'm sorry I intruded."

"Shut up, Aline, and sit down. Do yourself some good."

"And interrupt this charming spectacle? Certainly not. I'll bet the maid doesn't get a night out more than once every two weeks." Her eyes were black with anger, and I knew that it didn't have anything to do with me or this afternoon. Norrie Patten was the third person in the room, not me.

"So this is Aline Barbour?" Lorca asked, scanning the

figure facing the end of the table, whose face was thrown into high relief by the stub of a candle. "I'd heard that you were good-looking, but now I can see you're fading away. Norrie likes them young, like me. I guess you know that."

"You'll never trick him into a run-of-the-play contract. He doesn't work that way. You're all washed up. The only thing is, you don't know it yet."

"You Goddamned bitch," she said flatly, even dully, as she lifted her raised cup in her hand and flung it in Aline's face. The cup bounced off her raised elbow, but the tea reached her face. She screamed. It must have been shock. It couldn't have been that hot.

"Get the hell out of here, both of you!" I heard myself shouting, and then heard the hills across the lake yell at them too. "Get out of here, Aline. Just turn around and get out!" I threw her a damp towel from the back of a chair. She turned and went without saying anything. But I could hear her sobbing as she made her way across the field with the aid of her flashlight.

"Well you've picked yourself a good enemy," I said. "Norrie'll love you for this. What's to prevent her from going off to get the cops? There's a reason for all the secrecy, remember?"

"Oh, Benny! What am I going to do? Norrie can't find out. He can't! And that woman! She's got to be stopped! We've got to do something!"

" 'We'?"

"Well, yes. You and me. We have to stop her."

"Look, Lorca. I'd do a lot to please a lady, but I'm not going to try to get between Aline Barbour and Norbert E. Patten without knowing a lot more about them than I do now. A man'd have to be crazy to get involved. Now, I'm all for watching what happens, but I won't be pushed into the ring with them, not for all the gold in the local gold mine."

"But I don't know anything! I've told you all I know."

"Where did they know each other?"

"I told you I don't know! Why won't you believe me?"

"There has to be something you remember. Some scrap. Something unconnected with anything else. A fragment, a name, anything."

"There is a name. I'm not sure where it fits. I heard Norrie say it once, almost to himself. John Malbeck. It's somehow tied up with Aline Barbour. Don't ask me how."

"Good. Now we're getting somewhere. Try to remember anything else. Get back to the cottage now. I'll think of a reason to drop in tomorrow. Something short of having another shipwreck. Does that make sense?" Malbeck? The name was lurking somewhere.

"Yes. Sure. But please don't forget what I said. I don't want to get trapped into an extended cruise. You understand?"

"You have my sympathy, Lorca. You really do. If worse comes to worse you can always bury your passport, can't you?"

"Benny, I never thought of that. You're right. There is a bright side. I could be a stateless person."

Chapter Twenty-three

Joan Harbison was still cool when I saw her in the morning. She talked to me about the fine weather and about the fact that an OPP bigwig from Toronto had been asking her questions and pacing off the distances from the culvert to Aeneas's campsite. She knew he must be a big shot because Harry Glover left his cap on and his shirt buttoned. From the dock, where I went to take a fast swim, I couldn't see a cop car in the parking lot, only the regulars frying in the early sun. I could almost smell the rubber sizzling.

"Joan, how well do you know David Kipp?" Joan lost a beat as she stirred the contents of a can marked "Williamsburg White."

"Oh, not so very well. He spends most of his time watching birds. He's never without his binoculars. He's from New England. He looks after his kids. What else? He brought me this whiter-than-white paint."

"Then he's been up here before?"

"According to Cissy, he and his wife used to be regulars. But she's been unwell for some years now. Mental, she said, but I didn't go into it. I'd never seen him before this summer. The paint was a goodwill gesture to the struggling new owner. Cissy said that they used to be very fussy about their food. She said that Michelle once made a fuss about Onions' not stocking a brand of yoghurt she liked. Can you beat it?" She still wouldn't look me in the eye. She had a strip of paint on her cheek. Apart from that, she was making a good beginning at the deck chair she was painting. "Why do you ask?" she said not looking up.

"I just had a run in with him. He seems to take himself very seriously."

"Oh, he's a fanatic! I like to see lots of people around me when he comes into the Annex."

I watched her making long strokes with her paint brush along the slats of the chair. I liked the calm it seemed to write on her face as she dipped the brush into the can and carefully removed the excess from both sides of the brush before continuing. I thought a moment about Tom Sawyer white-washing his Aunt Polly's fence, then I went for my swim.

I made it to the raft in about fifty lazy strokes, then hauled myself, walrus-like, out of the water, and flopped on the belly-warming canvas. From this happy position I saw David Kipp come out his door to retrieve some towels and bathing suits from the line. Everything on the shore looked hazy and moved at half-speed. I rolled back into the water again and kicked my way down to the mollusk-strewn bottom. I swam a few metres observing the shadow of the raft. A chain attached to one corner of the raft arced down to a millstone or other heavy weight half-sunk in the fine marl and sand. I swam closer and got a surprise. The anchor was a circular flat stone with an equilateral triangle cut into the nearly buried face of the stone. I rubbed away the fine mud that covered part of it and found myself looking into a rough relief etching of a goat with monstrous horns. My lungs were beginning to crack, so I forced my way up through the warmer water at the surface, breathing in a mouthful that was mostly air.

When I stopped coughing, I went down for another look. There was no mistake: the stone anchor was the altar stone I'd seen in Dick Berners's crude painting in Aeneas's room in Hatchway. I kicked my way up once more, thinking that the stone was about four metres below the surface. Something was making me feel good. Maybe it was thinking metric so early in the day.

Half an hour later, I was sitting in the Annex with Harry Glover. His shirt was wet under the arms, unbuttoned. There was no sign of his cap, so I knew his superior officer was probably on his way back to Toronto. He didn't smile when I came in and found a place to sit down. We both knew this wasn't a social call. How is it that some cops can do their jobs and remain human at the same time? Glover looked worried, tired, and cross, like he'd just had a bad half-hour with his boss and he was going to see if something good could be salvaged by passing on some of the heat to me.

"Ain't it nice to get paid for taking it easy when the weather is as good as this? Why I hear it's a real sizzler in Toronto today."

"You keep putting me in Toronto, Harry. It's Grantham, remember. We get the breeze off Lake Ontario and the spray off Niagara Falls." I gave him a glance that I hoped he'd take as wondering whether he was going simple on me.

"That tip about Mr. Westmorland paid off. I had me a long heart-to-heart with the head of Security in Ottawa. It's Desmond Brewer all right. No mistake about that. And George McCord knew all about it and was trying to make hay while the sun shines. He didn't get far. But it doesn't look like Brewer killed him just to shut him up."

"It's nice to be sure. How do you know?"

"Well, I mean, an Ottawa type like that? A bureaucrat? Hell, he'd get lost in the bush ten minutes after leaving the lodge. He's a tenderfoot if I ever saw one."

"Think again, Harry. This tenderfoot goes white-water canoeing when things get dull at the Treasury Board. Maybe he used to be a mountain climber like the former prime minister. Don't write off all the Ottawa mandarins as cream puffs. I'm not saying he did it, but right now we don't know."

"Shit. Nobody ever lets me off easy. I always have to walk the long way round. Say, Benny, the fingerprint man from Toronto told me the craziest thing this morning. He says he saw your prints on the axe that killed George. Isn't that a howl, now?"

"Sure, that's why I'm sending you after Des Brewer. Just to get you off my track. You know, Harry, I always carry an axe in my ungloved hand. Very careless of me. Where'd you get my prints for comparison, by the way?"

"We lifted a plate you'd just washed up. That's not positive ID, but it can be firmed up if we get more interested. You sure are house-proud about that cabin of yours. Bet you don't see any dust in your place in Grantham."

"If you're still playing games with me, I can see you must have been making a lot of headway with the three murders."

"We are carrying on a textbook investigation up here. We got pictures, sketches; we got . . . What do you mean *three* murders? I can only count up to two. Where'd you go to school? You count with me: Aeneas Dufond, one, and George McCord, two. Ain't that right?"

"You didn't give a place to Wayne Trask. Trask was murdered, Harry. His death wasn't an accident, whatever you said about it in your report. Sorry."

"That's ancient history. Why drag that up? I'm not saying I'm buying it. What's the sense in bringing it in now?" I shrugged. I didn't have the whole answer, only parts. So I tried to explain that to him.

"Trask's death is tangled up in other things that are still going on around here. He's connected to that mine I found for one thing. He's as important to the unravelling of this case, Harry, as any of the things we've found out so far."

"Well, I'll be."

"Who was up here at that time, Harry? Who'd you talk to?"

"Damn it man, you don't want much for nothing, do you?" He was resting his chin on his hand and making shaving motions over his right cheek with his thumb. "Come to think of it, there were a lot of the same people: Maggie and George, the Rimmers from over on the point, the Pearcys . . ."

"What about Kipp?"

"Remember, we're talking about early spring. There was still snow in patches on the ground when they brought him out. This was only a couple of months after old Dick died."

"Three months, I heard."

"Yeah, well, make something of that if you can. The Pearcys weren't staying at the lodge. They come up to see the Rimmers that time. The park made them get off their own land, because the policy then was that there were to be no more private camps. But there were always exceptions to the rule. When they changed the policy, Lloyd had pulled the cabin down and sold everything."

"Did that make him bitter?"

"Well, Lloyd still works for the goverment up in Sudbury, don't he? I guess he knows about governments. City, province, country: they're all the same. One end's making rules and the other end's trying to get them changed."

"Did you ask any questions about Trask's wife, the one that disappeared?"

"Sure. I talked to Flora on the phone myself, down in St. Mary's or St. Thomas or someplace. It was natural to get suspicious when she disappeared like that. I thought we'd end up dragging the lake for her. But no, I found her mother's name and number and Flora answered the phone herself. I phoned her again when Wayne died. She even got a little weepy on the phone but didn't come up to the funeral."

"That was when the Harbisons bought the lodge?"

"Yes, I guess it was. Flora'd been cut out of Trask's will. At least that's what he kept telling everybody. But he didn't ever bother to get a lawyer to make the change. Yes, Flora sold the place, and these new people picked it up real reasonable. Old Wayne'd let it go to wrack and ruin. He got some city crazies up here with loud music. You wouldn't believe the strange goings-on. The only fishermen that ever came up then were were those mostly interested in fishing the stopper out of a bottle." He was pulling at his earlobes now and trying to whistle a double note between his teeth, while looking up at the beams of the ceiling. "Chestnut," he said, hoisting a thumb in the direction of the beams. "Discourages spiders."

"I'll make a note," I said.

"You still haven't told me why you think Trask was murdered."

"That's right, I haven't. Because I don't know who did it. When I do, I'll make sure you're the first to hear. If that's fine with you."

"Help yourself." He made another broad gesture, sailing his hand, palm upward, half-way across the room.

"Thanks, I'll do that. But first, I've got to return some dry clothes to Norrie Edgar, the man who rescued me from a watery grave."

"Nobody does things right the first time any more."

"Somebody's tried to tamper with Edgar's longevity, too. Have you thought that he might be mixed up in this whole mess?"

"Thanks, Benny. I'll put six men on it." He laughed. Maybe it was a good feeling for a moment talking like a big-city cop.

"Will you still be here when I get back?"

"Maybe. Maybe not. If I'm not, you know how to reach me." I shook my head and made my way out of the Annex into the bright light of day.

Chapter Twenty-four

"Well, look who's here! It's the fisherman delivered from the flood! Good to see you, Benny. How are you, fella?" Patten placed a round white stone over the pile of paper he was writing on and left the table under the cedars to shake my hand. "Come up to the house." He was no longer wearing a bandage. That made me feel a little foolish.

"I brought back the clothes you lent me."

" '. . . And David returned to bless his household.' Not at all necessary. I told you to keep them. Remember Proverbs: '. . . and the borrower is servant to the lender.' Now we are back on an equal footing, Benny. He led the way up the rustic steps to the back door of the cabin. Once Patten knew your name, he made sure he used it on you early in every conversation. It was a how-to-win-friends-and-influence-people sort of trick. But he had what my Grantham friend, Frank Bushmill, called a heavy hand with the vocative. Thinking about it, I realized that Patten had built up most of his empire on a first-name basis. His was a multi-million-dollar business and all run by Bills and Charleys and Petes and Joes.

He was wearing a blue velvet sweatshirt over white chino slacks. His sunglasses and beard obliterated the familiar television face. He led me into the big sitting room of the cottage with its huge fieldstone fireplace. "You remember Lorca, Benny? I'm sure Lorca remembers you. Lorca has such a good memory for some things."

Lorca was sitting in a wicker chair with her back to the unlit fire. She raised her head more at Norrie's comment than as a welcome to me. She was playing it cool. Her polite smile's exaggeration was a measure of our special knowledge.

She had a photograph album open across her knees. Nothing like spending a sunny morning looking at pictures. I put my bundle of clothes down and immediately felt less like a pedlar. Patten put his arm on a chair across from Lorca, and I took it.

"Lorca here's just found the senator's picture album, Benny. Wonderful thing about cottages is that they're as close to time machines as we'll likely see this side of paradise. This place has its period written all over it from the kitchen table-ware to the reading that's been left behind. Lorca," he said, in a voice like a drawn wire, "we have a guest." Lorca slapped the heavy halves of the album together and got up at once. She looked to be beyond rebellion.

"Would you like some fruit juice, Mr. Cooperman? Or some coffee? It wouldn't be any trouble."

"Juice'll be fine," I said. I couldn't see that there had been much conversation between these two recently. Norrie and Lorca viewed each other with suspicion and contempt. Lorca was there because there was no escape, as far as Patten could see, and because of "certain favours" which bound them together. She returned from the kitchen and handed me a chilled glass of what tasted like prune juice.

"Happy days!" I said and caught Lorca in a subversive smile. I sipped in silence for a few minutes. Then I thought of a possible line of attack. "I spent the morning talking to the policeman from Whitney. Has he been up here bothering you?"

"Yes. About that Indian guide and the son of the fat woman down the road. Yes, that was too bad. I was sorry I couldn't help him."

"The Indian guide was Aeneas DuFond, the fat woman's son was George McCord. Stop playing games with me, Mr. Patten. I'm only half as dumb as I look. You knew both of them, but you told the cops you knew nothing about either one of them."

"That's easy. I just can't afford to get involved."

"Whether you like it or not, you're involved. Aeneas's death could have had something to do with his visit here the other day."

Patten dug in his pocket for a cheroot. He bit the end off and spat the tobacco where the winter mice would find it. His thumb spun the wheel of his Spanish lighter and he blew on the end of the orange rope until it glowed. I fished out a smoke myself and let him light it for me.

"Poor bastards," said Lorca.

"They rest with the Lord, Lorca. Mind your mouth."

"George McCord had been working an illegal mine up in the bush. It looks as though Aeneas found a sample from the mine and George found out about it."

"We keep to ourselves up here, Benny. Isn't that right, Lorca?" Patten made it sound luxurious, even depraved.

"I hadn't noticed. I've been getting ready to watch the leaves change colour."

"Before he was killed, Aeneas brought you a sample from the mine. He wanted it assayed."

"Do you sleep with your ear against the front door, Benny, or what? I don't like to feel spied on and betrayed." Patten was beginning to look ugly. His brows began to crowd together the way they did on television when he was about to make his prime-time pitch of the week. "We never did clear up the little matter of why you've been hanging around here, have we, fella?"

"He saved your life, Norrie," Lorca said with the big album of photographs open again across her knees.

"That, my dear Lorca, could have been a device to win my trust. Oh, it's been done before. Greedy people trying to stop God's work."

"I told you before, it's not my secret. I don't care who you think I am or what you think I'm doing. I found out who chopped holes in my boat. Maybe you think that has nothing to do with you. Well, it does. Maybe it has something to do with George McCord's or Aeneas's death. I don't know yet, but I'm going to find out, and I'm not going to be put off by your worries about being spied on or betrayed." I let that sink in for a minute and watched the lines around Patten's mouth deepen. Even Lorca began looking like a mother cat standing off the brutish hound to protect her kittens. Little Belgium in an old poster. The album had slipped out of her lap and landed at her sandalled feet. She reminded me of the wife or girlfriend who turns to stare angrily at you when you honk at her old man for not paying attention to the bright green of the newly changed traffic light.

"Benny, you can't talk to Norrie like that. He's got nothing to do with these murders. Can you imagine him taking an axe and killing someone with it? It's crazy. People don't do such things."

"Lorca, shut up and clear out of here. Benny and I have to talk." Patten hadn't bothered to look at Lorca as he said this.

"But, Norrie . . ."

"Just clear out, damn it!" She cleared out, giving Patten a wounded look that he didn't even see. "Okay, fella, it's time to have that talk we've been promising ourselves. I want to know you. I will not have mine enemy triumph over me." Patten moistened his lips with a tongue that darted from right to left like a pink mouse. I took a breath and wondered what I was going to say next.

"Let's go back to that mine."

"Dead end, Benny. What the hell use have I got for a penny-ante gold mine? Do you know approximately what the net worth of the Ultimate Church is today? Can you see me scraping up ore like some filthy sourdough in the movies?"

"I agree. Nowadays a small-time gold mine is outside your interest. But that's only since you made it in the big time. What about those summers years ago? You had a cousin, or was it an uncle, in the bush, a prospector named Berners. A gold mine, however small, could make a big difference to a trapper like old Dick." I waited for some response. I waited again.

"You're doing the talking. I have nothing to say on that score."

"All right, let's start someplace else. What about Aline Barbour?" Whoever said that names can never hurt you missed my glimpse of Patten when I caught him with that missile. He winced like I'd put too much vinegar on his french fries. "I know you know her. I know she was very important to you at one time. And I can guess that she isn't tepid about you. She's been watching this house, Norrie. She's up to no good."

Here Lorca burst into the room again looking daggers at me and spitting bullets. "Watch out for him, Norrie. I'll bet they're in this together. I saw them both. He may deny it, but I saw them plotting . . ." Norrie recovered quickly from the shock of the interruption and slapped Lorca across the face. Her tan drained away, at least the blood under it did, leaving a grey, angry face.

"Norrie, don't ever do that to me! You hear? Not ever again. I owe you plenty, but I'm not putting up with being slapped around. You don't touch me again!"

"I'll pitch you, woman, out of my house and bolt the door! Get out and leave us!" He grabbed Lorca by the arm and helped propel her out of the room. He didn't look to see where she landed or even if she landed.

"Cooperman, what is your game? Are you a friend of Aline? What does she want with me? Let the dead bury the dead. She pursues me like an unclean spirit. I uplifted her once. I sent away the scarlet-coloured beast. What does she want of me?"

"There's a name that pulls you together—John Malbeck."

"Oh, God! He meant nothing to Aline. She may have thought she loved him, but it was deception. Malbeck didn't love her. But I looked after her. I kept her for five years. She was closer to me than that blasphemous child in there." He sank down into one of the big rustic chairs facing the fireplace and looked into the black hole in front of him as though it were bright with flames and heat.

"You've been set on me, Cooperman. I'm ringed about with spies. I regret nothing in my treatment of Aline Barbour. We shared bad times and good. Malbeck's death had nothing to do with me. He was weak, he wanted sensation. He was too old to hold her."

"Tell me about it. Maybe I can understand."

"You? You'd better just close the door behind you and never come back. Goodbye, Cooperman. Get out." He said the words, but he didn't pack enough meat into them. They hit me like balloons the morning after a party, half deflated and slipped from their place of honour. I held my ground and waited.

"I don't suppose you've ever heard of the ritual known as the Golden Dawn? It doesn't matter. It was practised by such people as Aleister Crowley, the man who called himself 'The Beast 666.' Malbeck was a Canadian disciple. Before Crowley died he had acquired a large North American following. For a short while there was a Thanet-worshipping cult in Ibiza with Canadians involved. Like all cults, this group splintered and fragmented. It drew its strength from Crowley but later disavowed any connection with him. It was called *Ordo Templi Orientis*. They lifted that from Crowley. They practiced ritual magic of a baldly sexual kind. The leader, or chief magician, was a tax auditor for the federal government living in Toronto. He was the leader until things got out of hand."

"John Malbeck?"

"Yes. He killed himself after his mistress, a partner in the ritual, turned her affections towards the third member of the ritual team. They acted out ritually the impregnation of the Scarlet Woman, Revelation XVII. It had to do with the Mother of Harlots, the woman arrayed in purple and scarlet and decked with gold and precious stones and pearls, having a golden cup in her hand full of abominations and filthiness of her fornications. The purpose of the rite was to spawn the Evil One himself on the body of the Bitch of Babylon. The rituals were long and elaborate: incantations, talisman-waving, with music. The full rite took four days. And in the centre of the altar was the beautiful raven-haired beauty called Aline Barbour. At first glance she saw only her man, but then she looked again and saw a young man without experience, without guile or deceitfulness. She looked and she saw me." He looked into the ghosts of the fireplace for a long time. Then he turned and added:

"The ritual was written up in the occult journal called *Agape*. I'm sorry, but I no longer have a copy. Of course the location was never disclosed. After Malbeck's strange suicide, the life went out of the Canadian group for several years. I left the country. I cleansed myself. I washed myself in the stream of repentance. I changed my life. I never saw any of those people again."

"You say 'strange suicide'? I'll bite; how did he do it?"

"Malbeck had no starch. He said I'd cheated him. *Cheated* him. Do you think he could have built what I've built? He was a little man in every way; not one mark of originality or calling. I despise the man."

"And his death?"

"In a rented room, Malbeck designed, built, tested, and operated a home-made guillotine. The police in Toronto have it in their Black Museum." Now I knew where I'd heard Malbeck's name before. It was from Delia Alexander in the Annex the night Aeneas was found.

"Nice people."

"Some of them, Benny, some of them. It's not all feeling bumps on the head, table-rattling, and ectoplasm. As mythology it's every bit as respectable as Zeus and Hermes, or such modern-day figments as Democracy, Liberty, and the Free World."

"Why did you tell the police that you didn't know DuFond or McCord when you knew them both?"

"Cooperman, I have nothing to do with this place. It may be part of me and who I am, but I am not entangled in any life or death in Algonquin Park."

"Deaths sometimes entangle us when it's least convenient. You knew Aeneas from when you were a boy. And you saw him the day he died. McCord brought you lake trout. You saw him several times."

"So what? I can't afford to be recognized. I played no part in their deaths."

"Neither of us can judge that until all the facts are in. That gold sample Aeneas gave you could be the key to the whole thing. You've no right to keep that to yourself."

"You're a very persistent fellow, Cooperman. Yes, he came here. The day of the thunderstorm, just before dark. We talked about old times for a while: the senator, his late son, Gideon, and about what had happened to various people I used to know on the lake. He showed me the sample and asked me to have it assayed. I was touched that he remembered my early interest in minerals, and that the senator saw me following in his footsteps into geology. One of my associates, Ozzie Prothroe, took it in to have it checked. It's the real thing, all right. Nothing phoney about it. I mean there isn't any other metal worked into it, so it's pure gold. The impurities all have to do with crude refining, that's all."

"You took your geology seriously."

"Yes, things could have been very different. This mine is somewhere in the park. 'The land of Havilah where there is gold.' Genesis II."

"I found letters about a ruby mine up at Dick Berners's cabin. That put me off the scent for a while."

"That would be over in Hastings County. I knew that he and—what was his name?—Trask, Wayne Trask, used to work a site there. But Trask took it over from Berners until it was mostly his. And then the market for native rubies disappeared, even for industrial uses."

"When I found the mine up on Little Crummock, I thought it would be rubies too."

"If you find kittens in the doghouse are they puppies?"

"What?"

"Tell me, Benny, was there a stove in this cabin? Did you look inside? Tell me what you saw?" I described the potato I found in the ashes. "Perfect! That's perfect! If you'd taken the trouble to remove the potato you would have seen that the miner had been using it as a crucible."

"What?"

"You cut a potato in half, make a hollow in one half, fill the hole with concentrate, after giving it a bath under water with nitric acid to get rid of the iron. Then you tie the potato together with wire. Oh, I forgot to mention, you mix mercury into the concentrate. My God, I'm amazed how all of this is coming back!"

"You're doing fine."

"Pop it into the stove. When you open it up after an hour or so, you might be lucky enough to find a quarter of a thimbleful of pure gold. But remember always that the trial of faith is more precious than gold."

"I'll bear that in mind. How would he get rid of it up here? I never heard that Berners made regular trips to the big city."

"Gold is priced above rubies. That's not the Bible, that's simple business. Gems carry their story with them. Any expert can tell where you got a ruby or any other stone. But gold is untraceable. He wouldn't have had to take it to Toronto. Any dentist would give him a fair price for all he could refine. That potato trick is an old sourdough technique. Still good. But don't eat the potato. Oh, no. Not unless you want to die from mercury poisoning."

"You've been a big help."

"Ha! You amaze me, Mr. Cooperman. Here I am, the leader of a church with adherents numbered in the millions. Millions that are constantly asking questions about their immortal souls. We deal with countless letters every day at each of our centres. And now you come along and ask me, not about salvation, but for information you could get from any first-year student of geology."

"I guess that is amazing."

"The most amazing thing of all is that I enjoyed remembering. It's as though you opened up an old mineshaft that had been shut up twenty-five years ago. Amazing. Now, Benny, you must go."

"Sure. Thanks for everything."

"I'd rather not see that policeman again until the end of the week. If that could be arranged I know the church would be very generous in its thanks."

"Have you ever met anyone who couldn't be bought, Mr. Patten?" Norrie Patten tugged at his beard and thought a moment. Then he shook his head.

"No, Mr. Cooperman. It surprises me as well. But I never have."

Chapter Twenty-five

The Mercedes came back into the clearing. It turned around so that the nose pointed the way of escape. As Wilf and Spence got out of the car, the Buick arrived and parked blocking the Mercedes. My old friend Surf's Up slammed the door and joined the others as Ozzie Prothroe climbed out of the Buick's back seat. I watched this from the front room. Patten had gone into Lorca's room, having given me full permission to let myself out and not come back. The arrival of the two cars made me decide to stick around.

"Well," said Wilf, who was the first over the threshold, "it's the fisherman! Did your boat sink on you again?"

"No. I just came to visit the wreck. Not that I distrust you boys, but the law on salvage is very clear."

"What would we want with a boat full of holes? Come on." Surf's Up and Ozzie came in and did the same double-take that Wilf had already demonstrated when they saw me. They looked at Wilf for direction and he shrugged to show that he took no responsibility.

"Where's Mr. Edgar?" Prothroe asked.

"Your boss, Mr. Patten, is talking to Lorca in her room. She isn't feeling well."

"Nothing a taste of Fifth Avenue wouldn't fix, I'll bet," said Wilf to Spence with a leer. I flopped down in the wicker chair near the fireplace like a member of the family and picked up the fallen photograph album. When Patten came into the room, he didn't appear to see me.

"Well?" he asked Ozzie. "Did you speak to him?" Ozzie beamed at Patten. He looked like he had already planned how he was going to act out this moment.

"I had a good line and talked to Van for ten minutes. Norrie, we're in the clear. Van says that he has excellent information that the court will rule in our favour!"

"But does he *know*, Ozzie? I've got to be certain."

"Well, Norrie, there's no telling for sure until the court meets and you know that security's tight about Supreme Court rulings. But Van says he has it on the best authority. He didn't say how it broke down, but the majority sees things your way. You won, Norrie, you beat the system!"

"Congratulations, boss," said Wilf and Spence in turn. Surf's Up grinned. Norrie had called him Ethan, but I liked Surf's Up better.

"Let's not jump wrong on this, Ozzie. How did Van sound on the phone? Was he nervous, happy, what?" He looked into Ozzie like he was trying to read the omens written on his innards. "Did he say that we should come back right away? Come on, Ozzie, for the love of Christ, spill it. You're my eyes and ears out there. I want a full report." Ozzie blinked and wiped his sweating head with a crumpled handkerchief. He started again and reported fully on the telephone call omitting nothing but the dial tone and the graffiti in the phone booth. I couldn't detect any new helping of information but Patten seemed to like it better. And he was the guy paying the shot after all. The news in fact made Patten almost swell with joy. He clapped Ozzie on the back and sang out for Lorca to come in to hear the good news. She came into the room, rubbing red eyes. She had changed out of her shorts into slim white slacks made of sailcloth. She'd changed the crumpled white shirt for a blue and white T-shirt. Her eyes ran over the contents of the room without showing surprise or pleasure. Patten broke the news.

"You mean it? We're going home? Oh, Norrie, you're wonderful! Isn't that great! When can we go? I can start packing now. It won't take me ten minutes."

"Now hold on. Possess your soul in patience." Norrie then broke the bubble he'd blown himself for her by adding conditions to her parole.

" 'Confirmation,' what do you mean? Are we leaving or

not? Norrie, stop torturing me! If we don't leave today, can we go in the morning? Just say when." Norrie didn't like this role: he had exalted her; now he was dragging her back to earth. He tried, rather awkwardly, to take her in his arms. It was as though he'd never done it before; her parts and his didn't blend, they just seemed to get in the way of one another like pieces of a jigsaw puzzle that should fit but don't.

"Lorca, we should know by Friday. That's just three days."

"We're no better off than we were! You said we had to wait until Friday last week. So, nothing's different."

"Woman, try to understand. We are going home on Friday, or as soon as Van can tell us it's official. If I return now, I might get into a lot of trouble. Trust me on this. You've learned to trust me. Trust me again." Lorca looked beaten.

"Yes, Norrie." She sat down like the starch had gone out of her.

"Now," Patten said to Surf's Up, "what do you say to some lunch? I'm starved if nobody else is." Spence disappeared into the kitchen, where noises began making suggestions to my saliva glands and digestive juices. The boys settled variously. Wilf went out to attend to the boats. Surf's Up spread himself over the patio. Lorca picked up the picture album staining her white slacks with the perished binding. Ozzie had paperwork to do. He emptied out a briefcase on the rattan table and began sifting through things. I recognized the familiar blue of Canadian passports and the yellow of International Certificates of Vaccination. There was a measurable lull which left Patten suspended between the pages of an act.

Then Aline was in the room with a gun in her hand. I didn't see her come in. I don't think anyone else did either. It was like she'd dropped through the roof in a puff of smoke. The bright red of her pullover and the familiar blue of her faded jeans did nothing to domesticate the gun in her hand. It was a .32 by the look of it—a revolver. In the textbook a .32 is said to lack the stopping power of the larger calibres.

But in Aline's hand it looked bigger than a .45 and the newer guns that can blow you away with a whisper.

"Aline! What the hell do you mean by this?"

"Say your prayers, Norrie. I'm not fooling!"

"Woman, be reasonable!"

"You're going to see John Malbeck, Norrie. The past is catching up. I'll bet you forgot all about poor John." Patten was fingering the back of a wicker chair. It offered no protection at all. And I was sitting right behind him. I dropped to the floor and moved to the outside wall. The others remained frozen.

"Malbeck was unstable. His death didn't have anything to do with me. We were in Chicago. There was nothing we could do."

"You took me and you took all his money. You ruined him."

"I took money from the company, not from John. If you'll only let me . . ."

"John had over seventeen thousand invested. What did you put in? Less than a thousand. But you took it all. Do you wonder he killed himself?" Lorca had moved in my direction too. To neither of us did Patten look like he could stop all of the bullets. Aline went on, waving the gun as she made her arguments. "He trusted you. He was the first. How many millions have you betrayed since John? Answer me! I'm not talking about myself. I was young, but I made my own choice. I'm not an object you took under your arm, thief. But you owed John better than that. We both did."

Wilf was looking through the screen door listening. He didn't dare move except while Aline was talking. Once he was inside the door he would be only three steps from Aline. To me it looked like miles.

"Pray, Norrie! Put your hands together! 'Our Father . . .' " Wilf was inside the door. He hadn't made a sound, but something startled Aline. She looked over her shoulder, caught his shadow in the corner of her eye, then put her left hand on her right and fired, as Wilf hit her on the back of the neck with his linked hands. She went down slowly into the explosion that nearly blew out the windows. The noise was just starting to fade into its own echo, when Patten crumbled face forward. Lorca's fingers were digging into my arm. Wilf was hitting Aline again. Ozzie sat on the floor. I didn't see him fall. He crawled over to Patten who didn't move. I saw Wilf lift his arms and strike Aline again. That was when I found I could still move. I crossed the room and pulled Wilf away from the girl on the floor. I remember seeing the surprise and anger in his eyes as he gave me with both hands what he'd been preparing for her. That was a new kind of explosion. I was riding the fluorescent tubes again. I was in a room without shadows, and a blue-rinsed light winked on and off like a faraway electric storm somewhere above Little Crummock Lake. I felt I was bouncing on the inside of all six faces of the inside of a cube before I irised out completely, like the end of a Chaplin short, with my face buried into the pine floor. And that's the way matters stood for some time.

"Here, try to drink this." The voice came from far away, but I recognized it. I didn't open my eyes because I didn't want to find out I couldn't open them. The smell in the air was familiar — the police shooting range. I felt a cold hard edge of glass pressed against my lower lip. I did what I was told. It was that damned prune juice again. But the voice was Joan's. I tried to take an inventory of my parts: I could feel toes and fingers. I had a pain on the side of my head running from above my ear to low on my jaw. When I squinted it wasn't Joan I was looking at, it was Harry Glover. He was staring down at me like the light in the dentist's office.

"You going to live?" he asked. It seemed like a good idea until I tried to nod, then I felt as though I'd been introduced to the Scottish Maiden that Maggie had been talking about. I didn't hear the head roll on the floor and began to think that maybe it was still on my shoulders. I thought of John Malbeck and his machine in a rented room.

I tried to shift my weight so that I was half sitting. That seemed to help. I looked around. The room was full of people. At the edge of my vision, a uniformed cop was talking to Lloyd Pearcy. Joan Harbison was standing next to Maggie McCord, who was sitting in Lorca's wicker chair. I couldn't see Patten or the other residents anywhere.

"What's going on?" I asked in Glover's direction. He leaned in closer: "Aline Barbour burst in and started blasting away with a .32."

"I stayed awake for that part. I mean, what happened next?"

"She didn't kill anybody, but she nicked Patten pretty bad. He's on his way to the hospital in Huntsville. They've got heart-lung machines there. Miss Barbour went to pieces after we got here and she's under guard. I never saw the like of her face when I got here: the woman's crazy as a loon." Harry might not know a lot about crazies, but he knew more about loons than most.

"When did all this happen. I mean how long have I been like this?"

"That Lorca woman says she ran right over to the lodge. That would have taken ten minutes. I was talking with Joan in the clearing near the gas pumps, and so it didn't take more than another couple of minutes to get my car here. Patten was down behind that chair. Take my word for it; don't turn around. I've had everybody that was here taken back to the Annex. You were keeping things from me, Benny. You knew it was Patten all along. Sly as a ferret you are. See where it gets you."

"I'm going to try to get up," I said. Nobody seemed to think much of the idea, and, after the first try, neither did I. I'd been lying on the couch. The wooden top plank of the back was shattered by a bullet within a football field of where my head had been. There was a blood stain on the rag carpet. I looked at Glover, who looked off at a piece of fly-paper dangling from a Coleman lantern. The second try got me on my feet, and the third was a complete success.

"Benny, what do you know about Aline Barbour?"

"Won't it keep? My brain rattles when I talk. I think I've got it all straight now, but it has to settle."

"All right, everybody. The show's over. He's going to be right as rain tomorrow. Thanks for your help, Mrs. Harbison. Thanks everybody." Maggie leaned over and pressed my hand. It was the first time I'd seen her since George's death. She looked more like her true age than before. Joan sent a pained smile over Maggie's shoulder. The others waved or called out something reassuring. The uniformed men were making chalk marks on the floor and measuring off distances with a metal tape.

"Can I give you a lift?" Lloyd Pearcy asked. After getting a confirming nod from Glover, I walked out into the afternoon sun, a little wobbly, like Disney's Bambi when he stood up for the first time. Lloyd didn't say anything but opened the door of his Ford and I got in.

"Just settle back and don't worry," Lloyd said, starting the motor. The front seat felt like a sauna even with the windows open. I tried to close my eyes, but things began turning upside down. Once things begin turning, I might as well cancel all immediate plans. I kept my eyes off the road, away from the forest parting around us. The sky proved the right target. I kept my eyes there.

"Lloyd, do you remember me asking you about the fire at the mill?"

"The night Cissy took a snootful? That was quite a night."

"Sunday. Seems like a month ago. You told me that Dick Berners wasn't around."

"That's right."

"But it isn't right, Lloyd, and you know it." Lloyd kept his eyes on the road. He didn't offer anything, so I went back at him. "I respect your motives, Lloyd, but Dick's dead and right now the truth is more important. You think he set that fire, don't you?"

"I don't rightly know what I think about that. I know I don't have to say anything. So I don't intend to, if it's all the same."

"If it was all the same I'd agree with you. But people have been killed, Lloyd. Maybe the murderer isn't finished yet. In books—I don't know about true life—but in books it's secrets that account for half the bodies on the library floor. Secrets are a one-way ticket to the mortuary. Best way to escape the curse of a secret is to give it to somebody else. You said Dick hadn't showed his dirty face around the lodge at the time of the fire, right?"

"Uh-huh. I said that."

"And?"

"Well, I guess it's a few degrees off the dead centre of the truth."

"You did see him?"

"I seen him in the bushes sneaking off to his canoe. He was black with smoke and ashes. I mean, even more than usual. And for Dick that's saying something."

"Did it ever occur to you that Dick might have pulled Trask out of the fire?" Lloyd swallowed and I saw his neck in profile as his Adam's apple rose and fell.

"No, it never did. Hell, Trask couldn't have made it on his own that night." We'd come into the clearing. Lloyd rounded the gas pumps and pulled up to my place. "So you think it was Dick? Well, now that's a poser. Maybe gettin' burned in the war made Dick do a crazy thing like rescuing Wayne Trask. It kinda makes sense."

"What about the guests at the mill?"

"I don't know. Wayne never mentioned them. They just took off. But I can't say whether it was before or after the fire started. Hell, Benny, that was a long time ago."

Two minutes later, I was in my cabin, where everything was looking strange and half-forgotten, including my face in the mirror.

Chapter Twenty-six

It was that evening in the Annex that I tried out some of the ideas I'd been having about the case. All of the usuals were there with the addition of Harry Glover and his two constables. Lloyd was sharpening thorns for the Victrola, which was playing his favourite, "Mah Lindy Lou." There was a fire burning, and a card game was in progress, involving Maggie, Cissy, David Kipp, and Joan. Young Roger was looking on without too much interest. A few heads turned when I came in. I looked like a stranger with Joan's Band-aids on my cheek and my jaw swollen to whale-like proportions.

I took a place by the fire. Chris Kipp handed me a stick with a marshmallow on the end of it. I put it in the fire until it caught. When it was properly ablaze, I pulled it out and turned it so that the fire heated the interior until it was smooth and liquid. Then I blew out the flame, and ate it with a private grin. The only problem was that I could feel eyes on my back. I turned and saw that not a card had been played since I sat down. What did they want? My face was too sore to make a speech. Were they angry at me for fooling them? So, what if I wasn't in ladies' ready-to-wear? I could have been. My father was. I could be yet. You never know. They were looking at me whenever they thought I wasn't looking at them. Even Harry Glover, who should have known better. Des Westmorland, also known as Des Brewer, and Delia were watching me like a pair of cats at a mousehole. Delia was wearing a pink sweater and a denim skirt. I could see that Des was very fond of her. In fact the two of them looked more devoted than newlyweds. Where did that leave his cabinet-minister wife I wondered. Was there a divinity that smoothed over the rough-hewn ends of highly placed public officials? If there was, then I wouldn't be reading about it in the paper.

Outside, I could hear a far-off commotion as a car came out of the woods and settled into the black muck of the parking lot. A minute later, looking like he'd been up all night, Ray Thornton, my client, and a stranger walked into the Annex. Joan got up and, after a word or two, passed them along to where I was staring into the fire.

"Now we'll get some plain sense. Benny, this is Bert Addison, Aline Barbour's husband, and my principal in this business. He asked me to get you to determine whether it was Patten staying on the lake and then to keep an eye on his movements." We exchanged nods, and how-do-you-dos, but no smiles or handshakes. Both their faces were grey and grim. Ray picked up the story: "We've left Rob Kobayashi, one of my juniors, in Huntsville to monitor things there. Patten seems to be out of danger, and that's a relief. We should get a bail hearing before Friday, earlier I hope." Addison looked around the room as though he'd just had a blindfold removed in a fresh-man initiation. What was he doing there, he seemed to be asking with his raised eyebrows.

I gave them an account of Aline's attack on the Woodward place, adding Harry Glover's additional information. Addison still looked like a perplexed businessman. I could imagine him looking at himself in the shaving mirror and saying: "Does he look like a fellow whose wife goes around shooting people?" Addison had a face that didn't like the five o'clock shadow on his chin. He appeared out of place in this rustic setting. His casual clothes were stiff and unbending. I tried to say something.

"Mr. Addison, Patten was mixed up in diabolism fifteen years ago. This was before he got mixed up in the Ultimate Church. You know, strange rites and ceremonies. His part-ners were an older man and his girlfriend. The girlfriend was your wife."

"I didn't know about that," he said rather testily, with even teeth showing under a reddish moustache. "But I knew in general that she'd lived a raffish, Bohemian life. That didn't matter to me. She put all that behind her." He didn't look as though he was doing any of this easily, and I got the feeling that this wasn't the beginning of a rich, new acquaintance. I could imagine Addison looking right through me if we met again sometime.

"From what I've learned, these rites that they performed had a peculiar object in mind."

"What object was that?" Addison asked, hoping, I think, that I wouldn't answer.

"I don't pretend to know the ins and outs of it." I thought that would make him happy.

"Please try to be clear, Mr. Cooperman." Now he was asking for it.

"These rites were highly charged things, I understand. They were trying to bring about the birth of a purely evil being, maybe even the devil himself."

"Do we have to hear the details, Benny?" asked Ray.

"I'll shut up altogether if you like. It hurts to talk."

"Let him get on with it, Ray."

"Well, use your judgement, Benny. Don't take all night."

"Needless to say they didn't engender the evil one. She didn't even get pregnant. More important, Aline transferred her affections from the older man to the younger. That was Patten. She went off with him and stayed for about five years. She was in on the beginnings of his religious reawakening. They started this whole movement together. She felt that she was just as much at the centre of it as he was. Meanwhile, the man she'd left killed himself in a bizarre manner, passing on seeds of guilt to Aline. More seeds were planted when Patten discarded Aline from both his personal life and the life at the core of his new church. Today we saw the fruit of those seeds. Today's attack wasn't a random meeting, Mr. Addison. Maybe you can tell us something about that?" Addison nodded.

"Yes, she left home on Thursday morning on a holiday. I didn't know she was here. I thought she was in Muskoka with friends. She called every day or so and asked for your latest news. I didn't imagine she was watching Patten's every move herself."

"Ray, when you first brought me into this, you told me that you'd located Patten on this lake. You said 'a little bird' had told you. Who was the little bird and where did he get his information?"

"I'd better answer that, Ray," said Addison, worrying his moustache with a nervous thumb. "P.J. Tredway is an associate of both Norbert Patten and Senator Van Woodward. I got to know him through some investments I had made in the church. It was through the senator that I met Aline. Tredway, I'm afraid, has been playing a cautious game. He wants to save himself if the cult founders but isn't ready to make a break with it *unless* it founders. Is that what you call a waiting game?"

"So Tredway is sweating out the Supreme Court decision along with everyone else. I can see now why Patten was sure that the senator had shopped him, sold him out."

"Is that the whole story, Benny? Is that it?" Thornton was restless. I felt like he didn't trust me to serve the dinner without getting my tie in the gravy boat.

"Mr. Addison, your wife tried to hurt Patten a few days ago. I wasn't sure it was Aline. She didn't do any harm to Patten. Not like today. She fixed Patten's boat so it blew up."

"Have a heart, Benny!" Thornton was getting cross, but Addison was looking at me calmly enough.

"Where'd she learn about motors, Mr. Addison?"

"She looks after her sports cars herself. Tunes them, that sort of thing. Tell me, Mr. Cooperman, what sort of woman does these things?" He looked like he was about to break in two. I thought hard about what to tell him and hadn't organized my thoughts very well when I started talking.

"I'm just a peeper, Mr. Addison. I know a lot about divorce work. Your question takes me out of my territory. You need to talk to somebody who knows these kinds of things, somebody like my cousin Simon Heller. He's a shrink, I mean a psychiatrist, in Toronto. For what it's worth I'd say a person who does these things does them because of serious injury to her sense of herself. I don't think a person like that is a danger to the public at large. But, like I say, I'm out of my depth talking about that kind of stuff."

"Thank you just the same. I hope you're right." I smiled, and Ray and Addison smiled, as though the smiles would float the hope higher.

"Will you be coming back to Grantham now, Benny?" Ray asked.

"Sure. Just as soon as I can get clear of the other investigation that's going on up here." Then I told them about the three deaths and how I happened to be involved in two of them. Ray told me to take it easy and to come into his office as soon as I got back in town. They had a cup of coffee with me, met Joan and the Pearcys, before they started the long drive back to Huntsville.

Then the unexpected happened. It was Mike Harbison standing in the doorway. I counted the days on my fingers but couldn't make it come out better than Wednesday, which Cissy, when I leaned over, corrected to Tuesday. He stood there for a minute. Joan hadn't noticed anything since she'd picked up a smoky globe from a lantern and started giving it a polish. Harbison went to the coffee urn, drew two cups, added sugar and stuff, then took them over to Joan. She looked up at him with a smudge of soot on her forehead, and her face lit up like she was the lantern. It was a smile that included all her features. She nearly upset the lantern when she pulled him over her for a hug and kiss. I caught myself smiling to myself, then looked around to see if anybody else had noticed. I could have guessed that it would be Maggie. Old Maggie hadn't missed the grand reunion or my observation of it.

For somebody who didn't like talking, I'd not been exactly silent that evening in the Annex. I had another cup of coffee, watched Mike and Joan sneak out the back door and saw Kipp bundle his two off to the cabin. By the time the fire was reduced to a fine grey ash, the company was reduced to the nub of regulars. Maggie was bidding a no-trump hand, Des and Delia were reading, and Paul Robeson was belting out "Mah Lindy Lou" as Lloyd turned the crank on the Victrola.

I'll lay right down and die, and die . . .

"I'll be heading back to Whitney for the night now, Benny," Harry Glover said, placing his dirty cup near the urn. "Good night everybody. I'll be back in the morning. I think we're beginning to get somewhere on this thing." He went out, and everybody breathed a detectable sigh of relief when the two uniformed men followed him through the double screen door.

"I pass," said Cissy, giggling at the loud noise she seemed to be making in the otherwise silent room. Even the fire had stopped snapping its fingers. Lloyd's record began to run down. I glanced in the direction and saw an empty place where Lloyd had been. I hadn't heard him go out, but he wasn't there. While I was wondering where he'd gone, leaving his pet spinning on the turntable, I could hear voices coming towards the door.

"Well," Dalt Rimmer was saying, "it will have to wait until morning. Glover said he'd be here, so here I came. Good evening everybody!" Dalt was wearing a rust-coloured corduroy jacket, whose boxy shape whittled another two inches from his stature. "I just wanted to tell him my lad saw Aeneas run his pick-up truck up the old lumber trail behind my place last Thursday. The road's not on any of the maps, and I have them all." Peg, who'd gone right over to Maggie when she came in to press her shoulder and whisper something, looked the room over while Maggie patted her hand with her thanks.

"Benny here's a private investigator from the city, Dalt. So you'd better watch what you say."

"Hoots! I don't care whether he's the attorney general himself. They're all a bunch of Nosy Parkers."

"When was that on Thursday, Mr. Rimmer?" I tried to put a kilo of authority into my voice and hoped.

"He went up just before the storm hit and came back about an hour and a half or two hours later. The lad only told me this evening."

"Yes, you were away from the lake on Thursday. Is the boy sure it was Aeneas in the truck?"

"I only know what he told me. I said what I know, man, what else I say is no help to anybody."

"Where does that road go?" Rimmer looked on me as though I couldn't tell the difference between Toronto and Timmins.

"You know the one I mean, Lloyd; it takes you in to Buck Lake . . . ?"

"Sure. It's called Four Corners on the map." I nearly rolled my eyes towards the spider-free beams of the ceiling. For a moment I thought Dalt Rimmer and Lloyd were going to lead me on that merry chase all over again.

"It heads north behind my place and circles around the south end of Little Crummock. It's a fair piece of road as those old trails go: deeply rutted in places, but you don't need a four-wheel drive to manage it. I'm sorry the lad didn't speak up sooner. He just remembered and asked me if it was important."

"So," I said, thinking aloud, "Aeneas overcame his fear of Little Crummock. He had an argument with Hector about it, then decided to overcome his superstition."

"He had an argument with his brother. I heard that in town," Maggie said. "I heard people talking about it in Onions' store."

"And he told me himself that the subject was Aeneas's long-standing fear of that part of the country."

"So?" said David Kipp, putting in his hand-crafted paddle.

"So, not long after he left his brother, he drove his truck up that road. He went as far as he could go on wheels towards Little Crummock. He must have gone the rest of the way on foot."

"Heading for Dick's cabin!" suggested Lloyd.

"Why would he want to go in there?" asked Maggie McCord, who had moved a chair up to where the talk was. "He wasn't seen after Thursday, the night of the big thunderstorm. Why would he pick a time like that?"

"But, you see, it was the thunder that frightened him."

"Don't be silly, Benny," Maggie said. "Aeneas wasn't frightened of anything."

"He was frightened of thunder when it wasn't preceded by lightning, Maggie. That shook him all his life. But not this time. This time he was going to pursue his fear all the way to the lake, then along to old Dick's cabin." Everybody'd given up all attempts at looking busy or being not busy. Delia Alexander dropped her knitting. Desmond sat with his mouth open. Maggie was on the edge of her chair, a dangerous place for Maggie.

"What he found when he got there exploded his superstition. What he found was a mine, with someone working it during the storm, blasting with black powder."

"Well, I'll be!" Lloyd said, with his fingers in his mouth.

"Go on, Benny, please don't stop now," said Cissy.

"He saw the mine. It was hidden by an outhouse. The workings were down below. Mining in the park is illegal, of course, and so far the miner had managed to keep the secret to himself. So he decided to kill Aeneas. It was nothing personal; just good business. Our friend the miner isn't a murderer by profession, remember. He's not naturally callous. He's not a hit-man. He probably didn't intend that the body would be discovered so fast. That put the wind up him. He didn't want Harry Glover running around asking questions. He'd been hoping for a crime that at best would be apprehended, snuck up on, come across. You know: Aeneas at first is just missing; after several weeks it becomes more serious, but still not a federal case, because Aeneas was quite a loner with only his brother to worry about his absence.

"There's another thing about our miner: he wasn't the original miner. That was old Dick Berners, who hid his mining by pretending to still be prospecting. Berners was clever. He also had a soft spot for somebody who could take over the place for him once he got sick and knew he was going to die.

"A few days after Aeneas's body was found, I went up to Dick's cabin and stumbled across the mine. That was the second interruption for the miner. He hit me, tied a weight to my leg, and dumped me into the lake. Luckily, I cut free of the weight and came up for air. When I visited the mine again, I came across the miner again. Only this time he was dead."

"Liar! Liar! Cut his tongue out!"

"Maggie!"

"George didn't do it. George wouldn't. Don't listen to him! George is dead. He didn't kill anybody."

"It doesn't matter, Maggie. Not now. He had a larcenous streak in him, George did. You admitted that much to me. He was afraid because he was found out, Maggie. It's not like he'd planned to do it from the beginning. It's not like that other time."

"What?" The voice was high, like a plucked string. "What other time?"

"I'm talking about another time, Maggie, and a time before that." Maggie McCord slumped forward off her chair, upsetting the chair as she fell, so that it came down heavily on top of her large inert figure.

Chapter Twenty-seven

It was Wednesday morning. Through the screen I could see Mike Harbison cutting the grass in front of my place. Joan was replacing the green skirting around the motel units. Mike was whistling and from time to time went over to confer about something with Joan. He never forgot to collect a kiss or hug on each of these trips. Closer to home, I was completely out of socks, and the refrigerator was as bare as a peeled grape, except for half a dozen pieces of no longer freshly-caught lake trout, a jar of mayonnaise, and an egg. I put the latter on to boil and remembered to take it off after thirty minutes or so. While it boiled, I saw Harry Glover roll up in his car. A police cruiser followed him into the spongy lot and the two familiar uniforms climbed out. Glover tilted his hat at Mike and Joan, then ambled up to my screen door. He looked in, shielding his face from the sun so he could see through to my domestic mess. I opened the door.

"I'll put some coffee on," I said, and turned the propane stove back on. Glover settled down in one of the arrowback chairs and took one of my Player's from the table. He lit up with a wooden match, which he broke between his fingers after he'd shaken it out.

"Staff Sergeant Chris Savas sends his regards," Glover said.

"Checking up on me in Grantham? Good."

"He says the only hope for Niagara Regional is to keep you private." He sounded like he enjoyed his work today. "Anything happen after I left?"

"You just missed Dalt Rimmer. His boy saw Aeneas drive up a lumber trail to Little Crummock and back on Thursday afternoon. He thought you should know about it."

"I like his attitude."

"It was on an abandoned trail just behind his place." He nodded, put his cigarette in the ashtray, and went out the door. I found the jar of instant and began peeling my egg. Glover huddled with his men for a minute then they went down to the dock. Soon I heard a motor start. Before the sound began to fade, Glover had retrieved his cigarette and was watching me again.

"You sure got lots of excitement these last few days," he said, talking through a wreath of smoke that was pulled apart by the sun coming in the open door. And I remembered that it was just under a week ago that I made tea for Joan and we'd watched the rain batter the Rimmers' cruiser and flatten the petunias together. From outside, I could hear Joan laughing. That was better.

"Patten's conscious and complaining, I hear," Glover said, grinning wickedly and putting his feet up on another chair. "He's giving them a devil of a time at the hospital; threatens to buy the place just so he can fire the whole staff. Brave words from a man with a hole in his lung and a shattered shoulder blade."

"What about Aline?"

"She got bail and is free to go back to the city."

"And you don't like that?"

"I didn't say I didn't."

"All the same . . . ?"

"All the same they wouldn't have let her out if she'd been working in the poultry-packing house on a vacuum gun."

"Special treatment for middle-class crime, eh?"

"Now you'll make me out a socialist. I should keep my mouth shut, Cooperman, when you're around." He watched me for a minute mashing the egg and then mixing mayonnaise into it. "We weren't able to keep the lid on Patten. Newspapers are on to us."

"Uh-huh." There was a curling piece of stale bread that I moved the mixture to. Glover watched like I was walking a tightrope.

"Why aren't you fielding the journalists?"

"Getting my picture taken and my name in the paper?" He stared at the lighted end of his cigarette for a second. "I guess I don't care as much about that as I thought I did."

"Can I see Patten?"

"Why? You're not one for gloating either."

"If I can, I'll tell you on the road."

"I can't leave here!" He got up and finished making the coffee I'd neglected.

"You're all finished here. Take my word for it."

"Damn it, Benny, I just got here. Let me drink my coffee." He drank and I wolfed my stale sandwich. I washed it down with a swallow of coffee and wiped spilled mayonnaise and egg off my fingers on a towel.

Ten minutes later, Harry Glover's police car was purring along at an even fifty miles an hour in the direction of Huntsville. He didn't break the speed limit, but he knew how not to lose time because of it.

"Okay, you were saying?"

"Yeah, I'm just trying to find a good place to start. Give me a minute." Harry left me alone while pink granite outcroppings danced from one side of the road to the other. Sometimes the road went through the rock like we were Moses and it was a petrified Red Sea, with huge cleft waves on either side. "Well, no matter where it takes you, you have to start with Maggie McCord. You know she has a hard time telling the truth?"

"Yes, there's some cock and bull about coming from Scotland. She doesn't mean anything by it. I mean it doesn't fool anybody over twelve."

"Well, there's been more pretending than most of us guessed. First of all, her name. She was born Adelaide Tait in Cornwall, Ontario. Does that ring a bell?"

"Can't say it does. Sound's like the name of an actress."

"I found a book up in Dick's cabin that told all about her. Adelaide Tait was accused of killing her lover back in the twenties. She got off, but the case has remained one of the best-known criminal cases on record. The book says she got off because of her looks, which in those days were nothing less than spectacular."

"But if they found her innocent, I don't see— "

"You don't see the nasty old figure of Wayne Trask running across this information. I know Dick Berners knew. Remember Dick and Trask were partners in a mine over in Hastings County. We know that Berners was in the mine on his own to start with, then little by little it passed to Trask. Why? We don't know. Both Adelaide and Trask came from Cornwall, Ontario. The murder of the boyfriend was the biggest thing to hit Cornwall until the St. Lawrence Seaway. When Trask met park ranger Albert McCord's new wife, he knew who she was, and it didn't take him long to figure out how to turn it to his advantage."

"Are you talking blackmail, Benny?"

"Unless it's changed its name for business reasons. From all accounts, Trask was a greedy bastard. He tricked his pal out of sixty per cent of that mine. Even though the court had found her 'Not Guilty,' she'd chosen to come up here under a false name. She might have something to lose if the story of her past became public knowledge."

"What kind of blackmail could Maggie have paid? Do you know what a park ranger makes? Benny, you've gone too far." We'd come out of the road from the lodge in front of Onions' store in Hatchway. Glover moved the car along Highway 648, past Wilberforce, and on through Tory Hill, through the granite-rimmed road that twisted around the small lakes of the Haliburton Highlands. Summer people were growing on the shores of these lakes, and jay-walking in the main streets of Haliburton and Carnarvon. A few locals stood back in the shade, blinking as we drove by.

"Blackmail isn't just a rich man's game, Harry. The smaller the crook, the more pitiful the mark."

"Wayne Trask? When was he sober enough?"

"Where did he get the money to pay his drinking bills? He turned the lodge from a paying proposition into near liability fast enough."

"Keep going. At least it helps pass the time."

"Where were we? Maggie is living with Albert, her park ranger; Berners is prospecting for a mine to replace the one Trask beat him out of; and Trask has discovered that Maggie is willing to pay a little to keep him quiet."

"Berners was a character all right," Glover said, wiping first one then the other driving hand on his trousers. "I don't mean he was a lush like Trask. Lloyd Pearcy told me that when old Dick came up the last time he brought a bottle for him and Trask and they killed it together. Then he went into the bush to die. He weighed less than ninety pounds when we brought him out."

"Well, I have a lot of respect for him. He was a funny old cuss: telling everybody that he was still looking for a big gold strike, becoming a walking joke, then settling in as an eccentric so he could work the mine. He was patient too: he only blasted during a thunderstorm. He wasn't greedy. Maggie said the other night that he was a better man than anyone knew. That's hinting darkly without dotting all the i's."

"Smelly old coot. Looked like the devil's breakfast."

"With some people, you have to go deeper."

Kids were jumping off the one-lane bridge into the bright water as we went through Dorset. Small cars were pulling large boats up to the cottage. Other cars were packed so high on top with boats, paddles, and suitcases I was afraid they might turn turtle on Highway 35 and block traffic. Huntsville had been ringed by a circular access highway since I'd been there last. At that time there'd been no trick to going to Huntsville: the road went straight to it, then straight through it. Now you see a bunch of franchised restaurants first, and then an assortment of gas stations. When we got to the main street, it was the one I remembered. I even found a sign pointing the way to Camp Northern Pine. Glover drove straight up to the Provincial Police building. The yellow and black sign neither winked nor smiled, it just stood there looking sober. The trees of the neighbourhood always abandon a police station to the undiffused rays of the sun. I couldn't see anything growing outside. The grass looked like pretend grass at a funeral.

Inside, the place smelled of new industrial paint, and the floors were sticky in the heat. Glover talked a minute to a sergeant, who was built like a tenor, with most of his bulk sucked up into his barrel chest. The sergeant made a phone call and then came over to me with Harry.

"This is Sergeant Aubey LePage. He'll go with us to the hospital. Okay?" As if I had a choice. We got back into the car and, three minutes later, entered the hospital through the Emergency door.

Coming into a hospital with two policemen has its advantages: nobody asks you who you want to see, or whether you're aware that visitors are unwelcome until three in the afternoon. There is something about the businesslike tread, the faint rattle of handcuffs, that makes nurses rustle quickly through the door and orderlies push their trollies out of the road. I came behind them like a little cock boat in their wake. The guard sitting outside Patten's door got up, dropping his magazine as the metal legs of the chair squeaked on the terrazzo floor. The three talked for a minute, and no conversation spilled out between those large huddled backs. The door looked open. I tried it, and it opened wider. Inside, I could see an acre of blue sky between white curtains hanging on tracks around the single bed. Patten was propped up in a bed the shape of a wilted "W." An intravenous bottle was emptying through a tube into his left wrist. Another, fatter tube, came from under the same arm and disappeared into a pump-like machine on the floor. He wasn't asleep, but his eyes were closed when I slipped into the room. They came open at once.

"You son of a bitch," he hissed through his teeth, but in a

friendly manner. He didn't want to bring a guard or orderly, so he joined the plot just to see where it led. "You blew the whistle on me, fella, and I'm not going to forget it."

"Don't get yourself excited. I've got some questions, but I don't want you to rip a stitch." His eyes darkened, so I added before he yelled, "Not about you. I want to know about the fire. How did it get started? Was it part of the ritual gone wrong? Was it Malbeck? Aline? What happened?"

"Why should I tell you anything?"

"That's right. There's no reason. Only I think that something happened that night that has been on your mind since then. I'll bet on it." Patten's white hands were playing with the top of the white sheet where the hospital name was printed. He wasn't looking at his hands. He was searching the corners of the room for an answer written there. He came back at last to my face.

"Okay, fella. Something might have happened. But I don't see how it could make any difference."

"You, Aline, and Malbeck were doing some sort of incantation. Where was Trask, the owner of the lodge?"

"He had passed out in a corner hours ago. All we had to do was put a bottle of cheap rye or rum where he could get it, and he took care of the rest. He didn't care a damn what we did, as long as we kept it private and paid cash."

"So, he was asleep. The rest of you were performing the rite?"

"Yes. I can see it quite clearly now. I had felt a hand on me that night. I'd been a novice, then I'd taken Aline away from John. But he was still the priest. He called up the coloured fires of Ephron. His strength was palpable there in the octagon. But the words of the incantation had found my mouth, not his. I called by the Keys of Enoch: 'And let there be after the Calls an evocation by the Wand and let the Marrow of the Wand be preserved within the pyramid.' Aline had turned to me, seeing in me, not Malbeck, the true priest of the Evil One. Then John, white with anger, called out in the Enochian language: 'Behold the face of your God, the beginning of Comfort, whose eyes are the brightness of the heavens. . . .' Then he pointed at the window and screamed. He said he'd seen the Evil One himself through the window. He had pressed his magnificent ugliness against the glass. I'd seen nothing, and I said so. She looked frightened, and left the octagon, sinking down on a couch. John and I went outside to look at the glass where he said he'd seen the face. The window was dark with soot.

"Malbeck lost all control; he began blubbering. I had to pack both of them into his car and drive back to the city. Aline came with me. I never saw Malbeck again. They say he — "

"Yes, I know. So, the fire wasn't started while you were there. But you left your candles and lamps inside the figures on the floor."

"They could have been knocked over by Trask when he woke up, but that floor was made of massive planks. I doubt whether an upset candle would account for it."

"Well, I guess that wraps up the easy part."

"What's the hard part, fella?"

"It's hard because I don't enjoy sticking it to you. I've tried to figure it out six different ways, but this is the only way that it makes sense." I took hold of the back of the bed and didn't realize my own highly nervous state until I heard the handle of the bed-crank rattle. I moved closer to the chest-high table that straddled the bed. "You knew Dick Berners and Wayne Trask from the old days?"

"Sure. Dick Berners was my uncle. I liked him. But Trask I only knew by sight and kept my distance. I was a kid, remember, Benny. They were both of them bigger than life."

"When I first talked to you about old Dick, you didn't know that he was dead. You used the present tense. Who told you that he'd died?"

"I don't know. Somebody on the lake, I guess."

"Did you know that Trask was blackmailing Maggie McCord about her past?"

"I didn't know she had one."

"You haven't the monopoly, Mr. Patten. To put it briefly Berners saved Trask from the mill fire and forced Trask to stop pressuring the old lady. The blackmail stopped as long as Berners was alive. Berners liked Maggie enough to show her boy, George, the gold mine he was quietly working. George also knew about how Trask had twisted his mother until she paid up. Now George didn't have much imagination, but he could see that between what he learned from Berners and Trask he would never go hungry."

"Interesting, but I don't see what it has to do with me, fella."

"George dabbled in blackmail as well as petty theft. He tried to take a bite out of a couple up at the lodge, but they sent him packing."

"So? Come to the point, fella."

"I think he was putting the bite on you, too."

"You can bloody well think what you like, Benny, but, supposing he did, why couldn't I chase him away like the lodge couple did? I mean, do you imagine I haven't had to deal with extortionists before?"

"It was the Spanish lighter that gave you away. George must have picked it up on one of his visits. I saw it in Dick's cabin. George had been working the mine; you could tell by the recent newspapers and the way some of Dick's books had been torn up to start the stove. George tried to kill me, but by the time I got back to collect my things, the lighter was gone. There can't be too many of those Spanish lighters in Algonquin Park. The story ended when I saw that the lighter had been restored to its rightful owner. You were at the cabin, Mr. Patten. You killed George."

"Come off it, Benny. Do you think that the only way to deal with a blackmailer is to plant an axe in his head?"

"That's right. There must be hundreds of responses to a nasty fellow like George. That's why I find it so interesting to hear you say that George was killed by being hit with an axe on the head."

"If that was a trap, I call it pathetic, Benny."

"Nobody knew how George died. The lid was on tight. You blew it, Norrie. I wondered how Lorca knew about George. You told her. Not very smart. You thought that it would be general knowledge. All the gory details. You were wrong."

"There's not a crown prosecutor in the country who would come down on me with something as flimsy as that. You'll just get the horse laugh, Benny. It's too pathetic."

"Oh, I won't say you didn't have a motive. There was that whole satanist business. How would that sit with the elders of the Ultimate Church? How would the senator have reacted to that?"

"Cooperman, you're talking about murder."

"Yeah, when the stakes are high, it's the only logical step. I mean look at it as a game. Your options were to pay George or tell him to climb a lone pine tree. There sure are enough of them up here. His options were to keep quiet or to tell the world. Paying George doesn't give you a better hold on George than not paying, because whatever you did, George could have still told the world about the great cult leader running around in the altogether trying to impregnate a virgin with the seed of the devil. Now I can't think of too many papers that would tell George to peddle the story to the competition. So, your only real option was to stop George from saying anything permanently."

"You make it sound like I'm some kind of monster, fella. You know me better than that."

"You were just in a corner, Norrie, that's all. I mean, George was capable of pulling down everything you'd built. He guessed that it meant a good deal to you, but he underestimated how far you'd go to keep it intact." Patten stared at me and for a moment we both listened to the hum of the hospital. One of the bottles on a stand near the bed gurgled.

"Look, Norrie, I don't have any more proof than I've told you about. I'm sure it was George and not you who tried to kill me up on Little Crummock." I shifted haunches and tried to look blank. "Oh well, I don't expect the local cops will believe me about any of this, but you understand that for the record and for my conscience I have to go through the motions. Even if I get laughed at. Hell, getting peppered by Aline kind of evens the score anyway." I put out my hand towards the bed, and after a momentary wrestling down of qualms, Patten took it and gave it a harder squeeze than I would have expected from a man in his condition.

"So long, fella. Don't take getting whipped so hard. The deck was stacked against you. No witnesses, no fingerprints, and I've got a steel-edged alibi. Lorca and the boys will back me up on that. You see, I couldn't let that dim-witted yokel ruin things for me and just at a time when I needed to keep a very low profile. No hard feelings, Benny?"

"As long as it works both ways, I'm agreed."

"Hell, remember, 'He will swallow up death in victory . . .' The work of the Lord must go on."

"Oh, it will. It will."

At this point, Glover, LePage, and the guard opened the door. A nurse pushed between them. "Out!" she said. "Out!" I put the bed between us. "This patient is to have no visitors. I have my instructions."

"We're the police," LePage said quietly, in a tone that cuts through instructions.

"I don't care if you're the Pope. Dr. Sumi told me 'No visitors' and that means police, firemen, and insurance agents."

"Okay, I'm going." I made every sign that I was going quietly. At the door, I turned back to Patten. "By the way," I said, "I know whose face that was at the window. It wasn't the Evil One. In fact it was someone almost angelic. It was your Uncle Dick. So long." Patten slipped me a sneer through the triangle of the nurse's hip and akimbo arm.

Listening to our echoing footsteps as we walked towards daylight, I noticed that I'd developed an affection for Patten. Maybe it was the fact that I could wipe the floor with him on the chessboard. Maybe I'm a sucker for a face I've seen on television so often. I'm a snob at heart, I think. I wasn't forgetting Section 212 of the Criminal Code, and the fact that George McCord was a victim within the meaning of the code. But the facts were plain; I liked Patten and I never did care much for George McCord.

Sergeant LePage was leading Glover into an empty private room around the corner from Patten's. I followed along so as not to get lost. They went into the room and I followed.

". . . Nobody knew how George died. The lid was on tight. You blew it, Norrie. I wondered how Lorca knew about George. You told her. Not very smart . . ." It was my voice, sounding a little like my brother's.

"Harry, what's going on here?" Both Glover and LePage turned to me.

"Oh, yeah. I meant to tell you about this set-up while we were on the road. Only you didn't give me a chance to open my mouth. I figured you'd get him talking. Bet you really got him going, eh?"

"That's dirty pool in any league, Harry."

"Can't wait to hear the rest of it."

"It won't get you far in court, you know."

"Hey, whose side are you on all of a sudden?"

"Mr. Cooperman, don't blame Harry here. I'm afraid I put him up to it. We just got this equipment in, you know, and I was eager to try it somewhere. Harry, you'd better put your autograph on the reel, while I remember. It's hard enough getting this electronic evidence admitted." LePage poked a plastic pen at Glover, who took it and put his signature on the reel. LePage added his own.

"Well, I feel like I've been taken for a ride."

"You really got him to spill his guts, didn't you?"

"More of a slow leak. Damn it, now you know everything

about it that I know, except about Kipp."

"Kipp?" asked LePage. Glover didn't look at him.

"What about Kipp?

"He ties it all up, that's all. He saw Patten in the river between Big and Little Crummock on the morning George was killed. It bothered him so much he followed and chopped holes in his boat with an axe."

"But that was your boat."

"They looked alike. Patten must have parked his farther up the river. Kipp took the first aluminum boat he came to and ventilated it." When I'd said that, I didn't have anything more to say to either one of them. They were more interested in rewinding the tape to the beginning. The reels whirred as the dark tape collected on the left-hand capstan. They didn't even look up as I went down the corridor wondering if I would blow my profit hiring a cab to take me back into the park.

Chapter Twenty-eight

I'd just about finished packing. I hadn't brought much, and from the look of that I didn't think I could ever stand to see any of it again. It was all grist to the laundromat. When Joan came through the screen door, I'd picked out a pair of socks and decided to make Algonquin Park their final resting place. A pair of socks could do worse. By the time we were into our second cup of tea, I'd paid my bill and tucked the receipt into my wallet. I didn't much like the idea of leaving now that I didn't have to play fisherman two hundred yards off the Woodward place. Joan could read it on my face, I guess.

"Well, you could work on your tan out at the end of the dock. You could help Mike refinish the bow of pointer. You could chop wood. I've got to get a lot of wood cut before the leaves begin to fall."

"Come on, Joan. It's hardly summer. Give yourself a break." She laughed through her teeth at that.

"I told Mike I've changed my mind about my birthday present. I'd told him I wanted a new chainsaw. The old one is in terrible shape."

"Uh-huh."

"Well, I told him I wanted two new dresses instead."

"Good for you!"

"I should have guessed that you were a detective."

"Why?"

"I just should have, that's all." She gave me a look and the meaning went right past me. "I've got the cabins rented through to September 15th and the motel units are booked with hardly a break until Thanksgiving. And I thought we were going to go broke. That piece in the Toronto paper worked like a miracle. And now it'll be in all the papers. Just think: *The New York Times!* You'd think that people would stay as far as they could, from the scene of three murders but instead, they start leaving messages at Onions' for me to call. Is it that we're a bloody-minded lot, Benny?"

"It's only human."

"There's a writer coming up. Says he wants to put it all on TV."

"Get a certified cheque up front."

"I'll remember. What will you do now?"

"Oh, I've got a week's mail to get through, bills to pay, a licence to renew, rent to renegotiate, parents to placate."

"I'm glad to hear you'll keep busy. Do you get on with your parents?"

"They'll do. My Ma's a wonderful cook. It'll be good to get back to her Friday-night dinners." Joan sipped her tea thoughtfully. "It's too bad you didn't really get a chance to fish up here. I'll bet with a little practice . . ."

"Yeah, I know. I'll never get the hang of it like Lloyd. It's just as well; I'm getting so that I hate the sight of fish."

"Then," she said, "what the hell am I supposed to do with the six-pound lake trout Lloyd and Cissy asked me to give you as a parting gift?"

"Tomorrow's Friday. I can always give it to my mother for making gefilte fish."

When I had my stuff in the car, I backed it up the road to Maggie's cabin. I listened to the quiet there in the shade after I'd killed the motor, then I got out and knocked on Maggie's screen door. At first I thought that there was nobody home. Then I heard slippers flip-flopping over the bare pine boards.

"Oh, it's you. I thought you'd gone. Never thought I'd see you again in this life." She sounded tired and looked terrible. There were purple marks under her eyes, and her skin looked like it was about three sizes too large. She was wearing a flame-coloured wrapper, tied with a belt. She held the door

open for me, and I brushed by her. The place was in bad
shape. Clothes were decorating chairs and parts of the floor.
A bottle of Scotch stood upright on the coffee table. She'd
been drinking it in a water tumbler. I didn't see any sign of
water. "Forgive the mess," she said, waving a rippling arm at
the room. "I've not been well."

"You've had a rough time."

"You think so? You really think so?"

"Well . . ."

"Let me tell you, Benny. I've had it good. I've lived a long
time, and I've always floated to the top. I've been lucky and
I've been loved. There aren't many who can say both. Do you
want a drink? I'm out of tea. I mean I don't think I could
make it if I knew where Cissy hid the stuff. She's been trying
to bring me around, to get me to accept what I can't change—
How does that go? 'The strength to accept . . .' Never mind.
Albert. Albert was a good man. Everybody loved Albert, and
Albert loved me. Poor me, so stupid, willful, and so in love
with Richard I couldn't keep my hands off him."

"Richard? You mean Dick Berners?"

"Yes," she said, looking at me as though she'd already
repeated the story seven times. "Yes, that's the Richard I
mean. You should have seen him standing in Piccadilly in
his uniform. You'd have thought Boadicea herself would
climb down from her monument to claim him. Ah, he was
bonny!"

"Then the story I got was wrong?"

"You got a lot of things wrong. Wherever I moved in my
life, Richard was standing just out of reach. I messed up
enough of my life in the early years for six lifetimes, but after
I met him. . . He looked after me, when he could."

"He got Trask to stop the blackmail."

"But then he died, and it started again."

"He saw the orgy going on in the mill."

"And pulled Wayne out of the fire, burning himself, scar-
ring himself even more. He used his ugliness as a shield."

"You set the fire, didn't you, Maggie?"

"Stuff. What makes you say that? Why do you accuse me?"

"It would have got Trask off your back forever, wouldn't it?"

"It might have. But Richard was there. He wouldn't let me abandon Wayne. He didn't want his death to be blamed on me."

"And it never was."

"Of course not, silly. Richard saved him."

"I mean later, when Dick wasn't there to help."

"You think you know something, but you don't."

"I know that Trask didn't fall onto the dock he was building. I know that he was hit from behind with a piece of timber and allowed to fall into the lake to drown. I know that then the plank was nailed into place. And then another, and then another."

"Talk. That's all it is. Talk. You can't prove anything."

"Oh, I'm not out to prove anything, Maggie. You're too old, and I'm too tired. But, you see, I studied the pattern the nails in the dock made. Trask's, Dalt Rimmer's, and yours."

"You're turning all my swans to geese, young man. No wonder I never trusted you."

"So Richard Berners was loyal all those years."

"You wouldn't understand such things. But he could see. A woman of a certain kind can will people to do things for her. They ask nothing more than the opportunity to serve such a one. Richard would never speak to me because of Albert. My misfortune was in marrying a man that other men respected. I always knew it wasn't me they respected — loved, perhaps, lusted after, but never respected. But Richard was always near when I needed help. And he gave me things."

"Money?"

"Of course, money. I may be sentimental, but I'm not a fool. I needed it to pay off Trask. I needed it to get George out of scrapes."

"There were lots of scrapes, weren't there, Maggie? I mean apart from George. There was the other George: Georges Ravoux in Cornwall. He put you in a scrape, threatened to show your letters to your father. You'd been stringing Georges, hadn't you? Your father knew nothing about him. And when Georges threatened to speak to your father, you had to do something. You didn't want your father to know about your affair, and you didn't want Georges to know you'd lied in your letters about your father's opposition to the marriage."

"That was a hundred years ago. I was a frightened girl. I had to do something. I couldn't let it happen."

"You know the police think George killed Aeneas. Your George, I mean. And they've arrested Norbert Patten for killing George."

"I wish they'd hang him! If there was any justice they'd hang him."

"What about the justice of letting poor George take the rap for you? You were always getting George out of scrapes you said. The worst of the lot came when he told you that he had to do something about Aeneas, after Aeneas blundered into the mine up on Little Crummock. You managed that very well, Maggie. You had everybody fooled.

"Stuff and nonsense. You don't know what you are talking about." She sniffed and took the glass in her hand for comfort. It was empty, so it was just for company.

"You said good night to Cissy and the rest of us outside the Annex on Thursday night and walked by yourself back here to your cottage. Then you took the boat with the silent, battery-operated motor and went calling on Aeneas at the old Pearcy site Aeneas was using. There would be no reason for him to suspect foul play from you, Maggie. He trusted you. Or at least he didn't not trust you. I doubt whether he would have turned his back on George. George wouldn't have been able to hit him hard with a paddle in the back of the head, then drag him into the flooded creek that runs under the road. But now it is George's name in the police report. *Pawn takes Pawn. Pawn takes Pawn.* Their books are balanced. They aren't looking for the murderer, Maggie. They think they've got him. You've pulled George out of a lot scrapes, Maggie, but he's pulled you out of this one."

Maggie wiped her nose on the back of her hand with something like dignity. She was sitting very straight, looking almost tall. For a moment her carriage was all it had been. She didn't say anything right away.

"I'm going back to the city now."

"I supposed that." She was quiet for a moment, then she looked up at me with those piercing eyes. "I was thinking of trying to poison you with some preserves I have. But, I declined the temptation. I'm a wicked old woman, Benny; not to be trusted. And I'm a sad old woman, surrounded by the ghosts of her men. The strong ones and the weak ones. The ones I wanted, I could never have; the ones I had, I never deserved and at the same time deserved better. I've a violent temper. Oh, when I was a girl I broke hearts all across the room. It was wonderful . . ." She broke off. "You'd better be off with you, before I change my mind. Think of me sometime when you eat a bite of cake or put the last scoop of sugar in your tea. You've a fine voice, and I'd hate to still that, too."

"Goodbye, Maggie. I'm sorry."

"Tush. Remember, I'm like cream, I float to the top."

I got back in the car and circled through the familiar buildings: the cabins, the motel units, the Annex with its open-faced piano and Victrola, the slanted gas pump, the bug-zapper, and the view over the lake to the first and second island. Beyond the islands, at the Rimmers' point, the cruiser was bobbing at its dock. I was looking forward to getting back to work behind a desk.

Joan waved from the porch where she was repairing a window screen. As I completed the arc, I think I saw Lloyd Pearcy with his rods and landing net getting into his boat. I headed down the road towards Hatchway. The water at the culvert had subsided a little in the dry weather, but there were bundles of sharp-ended sticks and branches pointing out of the water, sure signs that the beavers were up to their old tricks.

Norbert Patton

Des Westmoreland
&
Delia Alexander

Wayne Trask — drunken former owner

Joan

Cissy Peary
Lloyd Peary

Maggie McCord
George